HAZARD CHASE

Alfred Pratt, the shady cockney millionaire, is all smiles when he ceremonially re-opens the real tennis court on the High Cheney estate recently bought from the young Lord Cheney. But his good humour vanishes when the theft of a valuable manuscript is quickly followed by a sudden and gruesome death in the ancient tennis court. Talbot B. Talbot, the American tennis champion, now turned amateur sleuth, becomes violently involved when he tries to unravel the mystery.

JEREMY POTTER

HAZARD CHASE

Complete and Unabridged

LINFORD
Leicester

First Linford Edition
published 1998

British Library CIP Data

Potter, Jeremy, *1922 –*
 Hazard chase.—Large print ed.—
Linford mystery library
1. Detective and mystery stories
2. Large type books
I. Title
823.9'14 [F]

ISBN 0–7089–5386–7

Published by
F. A. Thorpe (Publishing) Ltd.
Anstey, Leicestershire

Set by Words & Graphics Ltd.
Anstey, Leicestershire
Printed and bound in Great Britain by
T. J. International Ltd., Padstow, Cornwall

This book is printed on acid-free paper

to Tony Negretti

Author's Note

All the tennis players and other characters in this story are wholly imaginary. A factual note on Tennis and the Chase appears at the end of the book.

1

'Cocktails and real tennis,' announced the invitation cards when Alfred Pratt, the cockney tycoon, ceremonially reopened the large, ugly building beside the lake at High Cheney. The world's best tennis-players were honouring his newly-acquired country seat for the weekend, and a gaggle of local worthies had been invited to watch the opening exhibition match. On one side of the thick red curtains which divided the inside of the building a game was in progress: on the other Mr Pratt's lavish hospitality was being lavishly appreciated.

'Hazard worse than the door!' Lady Cheney repeated the marker's call peevishly. 'What *can* the fellow mean? Really, this is a most extraordinary party — and in what used to be one of our barns! We should never have sold the estate to That Man.'

She turned away from the chink in the

curtains, took a generous sip of her third dry martini and fixed Mrs Winterton with an angry glare.

'You had better tell me all about it,' she ordered. 'I dare say there will be no other topic of conversation at dinner tonight.'

Mrs. Winterton was timid by nature and daunted by titles. 'I'm afraid I know very little about the game,' she began nervously, 'and it has such a very complicated vocabulary. Hazard worse than the door is a sort of chase. The floor is marked in yards, you see, and I believe the idea is to hit the ball so that if the other person misses it the second bounce falls as near the back wall as possible. When that happens, the players change ends and the other player tries to get the second bounce of *his* shot nearer to the back wall than the first one's, if you see what I mean.'

Lady Cheney became her most aggressive self under the influence of gin, and it quickly became clear that she did not take kindly either to Mrs Winterton or to her explanation.

'Unfortunately,' she declared, 'being a stupid person, I do *not* see. Who or what is in hazard?'

'Oh dear,' said Mrs Winterton. 'They always serve from the same end of the court: that is called the service side, and the other one is the hazard side. But please don't ask me why. My husband gets very annoyed with me for not knowing these things.'

At this moment a burst of loud clapping broke out on the other side of the curtain, and Major Winterton himself stepped through in a state of great excitement.

'By golly,' he exclaimed. 'What a player old Nicholls is still! At thirty-all with better than half a yard against him he served a rattling fine chemin-de-fer which fairly fizzed off the penthouse and made a dead nick. Now he's won the chase with a backhand force off the battery wall into the corner of the dedans.'

The ladies received this information calmly.

'How absolutely splendid it is,' he went on, 'to have tennis played again at High Cheney! For the last fifty years courts have been closing all over the country, and now at last we have one opening again — after, it must be, the best part of a hundred years.'

For confirmation he looked enquiringly at Lady Cheney, who had to confess that she didn't know the exact date when the court closed.

'To be truthful,' she added, 'we were hardly aware that this *was* a tennis court. It had not been used for tennis for many years when I first came to High Cheney. In my husband's time — and, I believe, in the ninth earl's — it was in use simply as a farmyard shed. The game is a complete mystery to me, but Mrs Winterton was most kindly explaining it. I understand that you also are an authority, major?'

Lady Cheney spoke the words 'most kindly' and 'also' with distinct emphasis and glanced at Mrs Winterton as she did so.

'Hardly that,' replied the major modestly; 'though I do have the honour to be President of the Tennis Players Association, which is the governing body

4

in this country. Most people confuse the game with lawn tennis, of course: I only wish it were as widely played. There are so few courts left that an occasion like this is in the nature of a miracle. For a court which has been allowed — '

'It is certainly,' interrupted Lady Cheney, 'a very queer thing for Mr Pratt to have done. Very puzzling indeed. He does not play the game himself, I'm told.'

'I believe not,' said the major, 'but — '

'Nor any other game for that matter?'

'So far as I know, not. But even more than with most games one can find great enjoyment in watching other people play. Tennis is rather like chess in a way, and spectators can appreciate both the strokes and the tactics. Mr Pratt will undoubtedly have his reward for doing the game this great service.'

This last sentence might have been taken from the after-dinner speech which the major was due to deliver that evening. Mrs Winterton was about to express her loyal support for the sentiment when she was appalled to hear Lady

5

Cheney muttering, 'I hope not, I hope not indeed.'

'I beg your pardon?' she enquired.

'I did not speak,' declared her ladyship belligerently, and Mrs Winterton looked away in confusion.

They were in a room newly decorated in an ornate Victorian style. It formed an ante-room to the tennis court proper, and Mr Pratt's guests were packed tight, drinking, smoking and talking. There was just sufficient space for the waiters to squeeze their way through and keep the drink flowing, and Mrs Winterton apprehensively noted Lady Cheney exchanging her empty glass for a full one. Indeed so much alcohol was being consumed all round that the stand-up buffet lunch to follow might not be quite as stand-up as scheduled.

Through a gap in the heavy red curtains which served instead of a wall along the whole of one side of the room she could see into the dedans — a gallery filled with more guests, seated, aperitif in hand, while they watched the game through protective netting. Beyond

6

could be glimpsed the dark expanse of the court's black walls lit by tall windows high above the ground. At intervals two white-flannelled figures appeared, disappeared and re-appeared in Mrs Winterton's line of vision. Armed with rackets of medieval appearance, they were hitting a ball backwards and forwards between them over a net which drooped across the middle of the court.

At the end of every rally — which, the major repeatedly had to remind her, was not called a rally at all but (oddly enough) a rest — the score would be shouted, or else one of those incomprehensible phrases which her husband loved to mouth. 'Love Fifteen,' it went; 'Fifteen All'; 'Half a Yard Worse than the Last Gallery'; 'Pass'; 'Three and Four.'

Mrs Winterton sighed. She didn't like tennis and was coming to detest Lady Cheney. She rarely left home and wished she had not done so now. Usually the major was only too eager to leave her behind, but Mr Pratt had been insistent that he should bring her for what was to be a country-house weekend in pre-war style.

Lady Cheney also was looking around her. 'How much will Mr Pratt have spent on all this, do you suppose?' she enquired. 'He must be expecting a very great deal of pleasure from watching the game.' She took another sip from her glass and deftly smothered a hiccup in her handkerchief.

'I really couldn't say,' replied the major. 'And now if you will excuse us, Lady Cheney, I must go and have a word with our host, whom I see over there.'

Mr Pratt, a short, stout, flamboyant figure, was nearby, clicking his fingers and shouting what sounded suspiciously like 'Oi' to direct the waiters to a temporarily dry cluster of guests.

The major prepared to move, but Lady Cheney anticipated him, making her way in the opposite direction, and before the Wintertons could reach their host they were joined by a well-groomed but harassed-looking young man in his late twenties. He greeted the major anxiously:

'I came over to see how Mother was

getting on, but she seems to have vanished. Is she all right?' He ran a hand nervously over his blond hair, which was a shade or two too long.

'I don't believe you have met my wife, Gavin,' said the major. 'Lord Cheney, my dear. A member of my club.'

'How do you do,' said Gavin. 'I do hope — well — that Mother's not been saying anything she oughtn't.'

'Of course not,' replied the major far too reassuringly. 'She's quite all right — and in fine form. Isn't she, my dear?'

'Yes indeed,' agreed Mrs Winterton. 'She is showing a great interest in everything.'

Gavin became gloomy. 'That's just the trouble. Ever since father died and the estate was sold, she's taken far too much interest in it. You'd think in the circumstances she'd have been glad enough to settle down in the Bahamas, or at any rate come and live in London. But not a bit of it. She moves down to the dower house in the village and keeps an eye on everything the Pratts do. Not only that, but she goes round saying the most terrible things about them: that Mrs Pratt has been — '

He stopped abruptly.

'There you are,' he went on. 'I'm catching it myself. We shall be in the courts for slander one of these days, and they won't have much of a job proving malice. Mind you, I get on all right with them myself, but I can't imagine why they've asked us back for a rum junket like this.'

'It must be a very trying situation for your mother,' said Mrs Winterton sympathetically. 'And for you.'

But the major's thoughts had reverted to the game. Pratt was inaccessible in the middle of the room, and this was no time for idle gossip. 'Come on, Gavin my boy,' he summoned. 'We're missing some of the finest tennis we're ever likely to see. There aren't going to be all that more opportunities of seeing Old Nick play.'

On their way through the curtain to the dedans the major bumped into a stocky figure with a luxuriant moustache.

'Hullo, Gerry; how's it going?' he asked.

Gerry Montague's face was alight with excitement. An active player past his peak, he was a sporting journalist and tennis correspondent.

'Nick's tiring fast,' he replied. 'If he doesn't win this set he's had it. Young Timothy's playing a wonderful game. The old boy has had to give up his railroad, but he's still finding the openings. He's been in the winning gallery, let me see' — he consulted a piece of paper — 'yes, five times. And just listen to that. Straight into the grille.'

There was a loud crash of apparently shattered wood, followed by applause and appreciative comments from the spectators.

'Gerry,' said the major in a whisper, 'someone tells me you've brought the manuscript of Featherstonehaugh's Annals with you. Is that so?'

Gerry looked annoyed: 'As a matter of fact, it is. But I'm keeping rather quiet about it. It so happens that I've not had

11

it very long, but Pratt heard about it somehow and made a point of insisting that I bring it. He has a copy of the book in the library here, and naturally he's interested in the references to High Cheney and the Cheney family. Wants to check them over with the manuscript, he says.'

'I say, I'm interested too,' interrupted Gavin.

'I'm sure you are,' replied Gerry, 'still it's rather a nuisance for me. The thing is unique, after all. I keep it in safe deposit at the bank. Apart from checking through the pages I haven't even had time to examine it properly myself yet. However, with Pratt laying on this grand re-opening — exhibition matches, cocktail parties, dinners and so on — one could hardly refuse.'

The major's eyes were glistening. 'By jingo,' he said, 'you are a lucky fellow to have got hold of that. There's nothing I'd like to possess more than old Featherstonehaugh's manuscript. It must be devilish valuable. You will let me have a dekko, won't you?'

'Of course,' smiled Gerry. 'After dinner tonight perhaps.'

He moved on, and the others had barely taken their seats in the dedans when a ball flew into the netting within a few inches of the major's nose.

'Oh, good force, sir,' he applauded.

'Advantage. Hazard worse than a yard,' intoned the marker from his recess beside the net.

'Come along, Timothy,' called the major jovially to the nearer of the two players. 'Serve him one of his own dead nicks. It's your only chance with a hazard.'

The game had reached a crucial phase, and Timothy refused to let the major's banter break his concentration. With nearly thirty years' advantage over Old Nick, former world champion and the most famous player of his day, Timothy's policy was one of relentless attrition. Although himself the reigning amateur champion and holder of the Gold Racket, he knew that few of his strokes would make winners until he wore his opponent out.

Nick had won the first set 6-2 and run straight on to 3-0 in the second before Timothy's policy took effect. Then he began covering the court with slightly less agility and, to conserve energy, had been forced to abandon his famous service for a less effective long-neck giraffe. This had enabled Timothy to pull up to 5-5, but now the old professional needed only this eleventh game for the match. On the other hand, if he lost it, Timothy's youth would almost certainly be decisive in the final set.

The score had reached deuce, with Timothy now serving to defend two chases, one good and one bad. The good one Nick had just dealt with by means of a contemptuous volley hard into the dedans. It was his advantage; the next point would give him the match.

The major, suddenly realising the score, felt ashamed at his own levity. True, it was only an exhibition match, but one important enough to be reported in the press, and he knew that the two men disliked each other and were both determined to win. Indeed he could sense the hostility in the air. Nicholls was crouching to receive service with a shade less wooden expression than usual on his face, while Timothy moved into position tight-lipped and frowning. Jovial remarks were certainly out of place.

Timothy served. The ball struck the penthouse, humming with speed and cut. In a flash it had landed in the crack between the back wall and the floor and shot out into the court along the floor.

'Oh ho,' exclaimed the major, unable to restrain himself. 'Well served, sir! Dead nick! Pied sec! Taking my advice, eh?'

The players ignored him, and the dedans quickly became silent again. After a series of tense exchanges Nick laid down two short chases and the players changed ends amid appreciative applause for the old champion. As they crossed at the net they exchanged glances, and Nick muttered something to the marker.

'Deuce. One and two,' was called.

Nick served, and Timothy's return sped low across the court towards the forehand corner. Nick moved across to take it, hesitated and decided to leave it alone. The ball rebounded off the back wall and hit the floor for the second time a short way out.

'Won it,' called the marker.

'What!' shouted Nick.

'Won it. Advantage. Worse than Two,' declared the marker, awarding the point to Timothy and calling the next chase.

'Now then, Ted, have you gone blind?' Nick protested angrily and turned to the dedans to appeal for support. 'Are you refereeing, major?' he asked.

'There isn't an official referee,' replied the major, 'but I'm sure you'll both accept the consensus of opinion in the dedans. Unfortunately, so far as I am concerned, you were masking the ball. I couldn't see at all. Did anyone else notice where it fell?'

No one who knew enough about the game to venture an opinion had had a clear view, and Nick was compelled to appeal to his opponent.

'It fell chase two, Mr Forsyth. Didn't you see it?'

There was a short pause before Timothy spoke: 'It looked like chase a yard from here.'

'Advantage. Worse than Two,' called Ted again, in a get-on-with-the-game tone of voice. He was Old Nick's son and a professional like his father. They bickered continually; and he was enjoying a little revenge for past grievances.

Nick's face grew purple with fury. Instead of serving he took two balls out of the trough and lobbed them in turn high over his shoulder into the top gallery above the dedans.

'Fault,' called Ted. 'Double Fault. Game and Set to Mr Forsyth.'

'And Match,' added Nick. 'I'm retiring.'

He advanced to the net and the spectators could see him in angry dispute with his opponent and the marker. The dedans emptied quietly, the spectators shame-faced at the incident.

'I say,' whispered Gavin to the major. 'That's not quite the thing, is it? Who's in hazard now?'

17

2

Night had fallen over High Cheney.

In the moonlight the house looked everything it should have been — a legacy from the romantic past. There were mullioned oriel windows jutting out over carved corbels; there were gargoyles leering from the guttering, and terra-cotta plaques of Roman emperors dotting the wall round the baronial entrance; above, there were tall red twisted Tudor chimneys.

Lawns surrounded the house, and below it lay the lake, a crescent of silver water with its ducks, coots, moorhens and water-lilies all asleep. By the lake stood the tennis-court building, the Grecian portico of its facade upheld by six stalwart caryatids and surmounted by a gilded weathercock in the shape of a racket. Beyond, through the trees, could be seen the dim lights of the village: Abbots Cheney, recorded in William the Conqueror's Domesday Book and apparently undisturbed by anything that had happened since.

But moonlight can deceive. The lights of the village were dim because the villagers preferred to watch television in darkness. The writ of abbots had long ceased to run in Abbots Cheney; the last one had been hanged from his own sanctus bell-tower many years before. He had been dilatory in surrendering the abbey's treasure to the Crown, and the king's commissioner had found him so unhappy about the world he lived in that he had coarsely advised him to try the next one.

It was this royal commissioner who became the first Lord Cheney. As a reward for his desecrating zeal, he was granted the estate. The lake was then a small stream with the abbey buildings strung along its bank, and he used the stones to build himself a manor-house on the hill above. From being an adventurous hanger-on at court he rose to become a trusted friend of the great king — Henry VIII, tennis-player and

Defender of the Faith. There were limits to his loyalty, though. In addition to the estate he laid his hands on a sizeable quantity of the abbey's gold and silver and precious stones, much of which failed to find its way into the royal coffers.

This judicious piece of plundering had put the Cheneys among the 'best people' for more than four centuries: a substantial reward for a few days' enterprise. In time Capability Brown had been called in to elevate the stream into a lake of the then fashionable shape and size, and the eighth earl, not content with a genuine old-fashioned home, had pulled it down and replaced it with a grander conception of what a Tudor mansion should look like. But at last, eroded by death duties, high taxation and inefficient management, the estate had passed out of the family's possession.

The modern equivalent of the sixteenth-century commissioner was Mr Alfred Pratt, chairman of Pratt's Holdings, the development company which purchased the estate. Demobilised in 1945, Acting Company Quartermaster Sergeant Pratt had spent his gratuity on a few months' lease of a small office in Moorgate. To the amazement of his friends the office had rapidly become a complete block, and Alfred Pratt Ltd (authorised capital £100; paid-up capital £5) had spawned a multiplicity of associated companies, now under the aegis of Pratt's Holdings Ltd (£10 million not only authorised but fully paid-up). These ramified and percolated mysteriously through the nation's economy.

The villagers watched Mr Pratt set up his headquarters in the west lodge in person and waited with mild interest for the inevitable outrages: demolition squads in the house, trees cut down for timber, housing estates in the park, and light industry in the meadows. Certainly the local authorities were bombarded with plans for all these projects, and each letter, even for the same project, seemed to come from a different company.

But one day the letters stopped. Every development was shelved, the house splendidly redecorated, and Mr Pratt — heir to the Cheneys — moved in with Mrs Pratt, Miss Pratt, a butler, a cook, a chauffeur and four foreign girls, assisted by an army of local charwomen and gardeners. According to gossip, every man and woman of them was on the pay-roll of one of the Pratt companies. Even the massive tennis court had been repaired and refurbished, and a professional engaged. This, too, was said to be by courtesy of Mr Pratt's unwitting shareholders.

On the night of the tennis court's Grand Reopening, High Cheney was resplendent with light and life as it had not been since before the war. After some devastating years of occupation by the military and further years of neglect, the glory had returned. As the cars of the guests for the day were winding away down the half-mile drive, those who had been invited for the whole weekend were sitting down to a late dinner in the banqueting hall, under the gaze of the assorted male and female saints in the stained-glass windows.

Despite the size of the hall they made a select company of only twelve. The host was at the head of the table and Mrs Pratt at the foot. On Mr Pratt's right sat Lady Cheney, erect and alert, with the mustachioed Gerry Montague beside her. Opposite, on the host's left, were a beaming lady from Paris, Mlle Deschamps, and the young Lord Cheney. Beyond Lord Cheney sat Angel Pratt, daughter of the house; then Talbot B. Talbot, amateur tennis champion of the U.S.A.; and — on the right of his hostess — Major Winterton. Old Nick, the professional and former world champion, was placed opposite the major; while Timothy Forsyth, the British amateur champion, found himself in what would have been the best position of all if he had been in the mood to appreciate it — facing the comely Miss Pratt.

Awkwardly placed between Timothy and Old Nick was the third participant in the morning quarrel, Ted Nicholls, son of the old champion and himself the newly engaged tennis professional at High Cheney. Two guests were missing: the Australian representative, who had cried off by cable at the last minute, and Mrs Winterton, who had pleaded a headache and retired to her room.

After a long lie-down in the afternoon Lady Cheney, who privately considered this the strangest company she had ever been called upon to sit down with, was on her best behaviour. She complimented her host on the appearance of the house and the quality of the food, while keeping a sharp look-out for solecisms committed by the Swedish maids and the bogus-looking butler who was supervising operations.

'I'm very glad your ladyship likes it all,' said Mr Pratt, gratified. 'The redecoration cost a pretty penny, I don't need to tell you.'

'It must have indeed,' nodded Lady Cheney, 'but nothing of consequence to a man of your substance, I dare say.'

'My substance,' he laughed, leaning back and patting his stomach. 'If you're referring to money, you mustn't believe all you hear about me being a rich man. We have our ups and downs in the City, you know. Business is not as simple as some people think.'

'I for one would not have imagined so, particularly with taxation at its present disgraceful level.' Lady Cheney glared at her smoked salmon as if it were a tax inspector.

'Taxation now,' said Mr Pratt easily, unbuttoning under the influence of his own hospitality. 'You don't think I pay much of that, do you? Where do you imagine the wherewithal for all this comes from? Saved from the claws of those vultures in Somerset House, that's what it is. If you'd like some advice about your tax affairs, you've only to say the word and I'll send one of my men along. It's silly to pay more than you have to.'

Lady Cheney winced. Much as she detested paying her taxes, she detested people who didn't pay them even more. For four hundred years the Cheneys had been able to afford to be respectable, and the habit died hard.

'Now there's a real man of substance for you,' continued Mr Pratt, pointing unashamedly down the table with his fish knife.

'The American gentleman?'

25

'That's the one. The best amateur tennis player west of the Lizard, so they tell me, a Rhodes scholar at Oxford, and into the bargain vice-president and son and heir of Talbot's Dried Prunes of California. A very attractive commodity, prunes. Financially speaking.'

'Indeed,' observed Lady Cheney, refusing to be drawn into showing any interest in commerce. 'He seems to be making himself attractive to your daughter.'

'Well, between you and me' — here Mr Pratt ventured a wink — 'they're not sitting next to each other by accident.'

Lady Cheney winced again. She could feel the blood rising in her head. Much more of this man's vulgarity and she would lose control of herself again. Was he doing it on purpose, she wondered. And what exactly had she been saying when Gavin took her away from that ridiculous cocktail party before lunch in the tennis court? Not that it mattered. It was coming to something if a peeress couldn't behave as she pleased. Common people could think her eccentric if they chose. Gavin shouldn't pander to them.

Without warning she threw the small talk overboard and snapped: 'What did you do it for, eh?'

'Pardon?' enquired Mr Pratt, surprised and immediately suspicious. 'Do what for?'

But Lady Cheney had gone suddenly deaf and apparently transferred her attention to the Pre-Raphaelite saints in the windows. She had just noticed that Gavin was getting on rather too well with that dangerously overblown Frenchwoman, who must be the best part of twenty years too old for him. Was this another plot of that vulgar old tax-fiddler, who seemed to have arranged the table with such care? She had already noted that Gavin had Angel Pratt on his other side; news of the competition from dried prunes had therefore been a relief. Unfortunately she couldn't overhear what her son and the Frenchwoman were saying to each other.

This was no accident. Aware of his mother's interest and disapproval, Gavin was speaking in a deliberately low voice.

'Probably you'll think it rather callous of me,' he was saying, 'considering I'm the first head of the family for hundreds of years not to be living here, but if my mother didn't still have such an interest in the place I would hardly think about it at all, you know. I was brought up here, of course, but as you can see the house is far too large for these days. Apart from the expense, it's draughty and inconvenient and — well — not awfully easy on the eye, you know. A flat in Kensington's three times as comfortable.'

'Still,' insisted Mlle Deschamps sympathetically, 'it must have been a great sadness, a property like this leaving the family after so long. In my country also these things are occurring. But you are fortunate that Mr Pratt has decided to live here and has repaired the house so beautifully. An old house is like an old person; it appreciates attention.

Lord Cheney looked appropriately sad and grateful. 'Naturally it was a terrible wrench,' he said, 'but we had no choice in the matter. No one can accuse me of letting all those ancestors down: the whole bally place had to be sold for death duties, and that was that. If anyone is to blame it's poor old Father, who slipped up by not making provision against it.'

'But surely some arrangement could have been made with your government?'

'It should have been. The Treasury were pretty well talked into taking the whole estate in lieu of death duties. Then the National Trust refused to accept it because the endowment wasn't enough. And when a row blew up about it, they said anyway it wasn't of sufficient historic interest or architectural beauty. Rather humiliating, what?'

Mlle Deschamps expressed indignation. She was interested in châteaux — English as well as French, and hadn't she heard High Cheney referred to in the same terms as Chatsworth and Knole and Longleat?

'Great-grandpapa had a mania for rebuilding,' explained Gavin. 'He inherited a Tudor house tastefully jazzed up by Inigo Jones and left this gigantic pile of Victorian red brick. So it's hardly in the Chatsworth class, I'm afraid. The Victorian Society makes a great fuss about it, but no one else does. There's nothing here now more than about a hundred years old.'

'Nevertheless it is charming and must have cost your ancestor much money.'

'Yes, he was loaded with the stuff when he started, then he ran right out and had to marry an heiress. She was the daughter of a railway king. Even so he got through just about everything she had by the time he'd finished.'

At this point Gerry Montague, dabbing his moustache with a napkin, interrupted to ask what the tennis court had been like before it was done up.

Gavin laughed. 'My dear fellow, after what we've seen today you'd never believe it. It was a large shed for the farm. There was an enormous doorway in the end wall for a start: haycarts were parked there. In that spectators' gallery you call the — what is it? — dedans there were chickens. And I can remember bundles of hay stacked on the floor, cows being milked in one corner and stables for carthorses along one side. The top gallery was a loft, and we used to scramble up a ladder and play secret games there. Mr Pratt has certainly done a largescale conversion job.'

While he was speaking, Mlle Deschamps had asked for some more wine. As it was being poured out, the glass suddenly tilted and half its contents cascaded on to her lap. With an exclamation she jumped up and, after a word to her host, left the room.

Conversation at the other end of the table was flowing less readily. Mrs Pratt found the major a stodgy old stick, and he regarded her ('with all that frizzed-up unnatural blonde hair,' he grumbled to Mrs Winterton afterwards) as a mutton-dressed-up-as-lamb barmaid type. Old Nick was morose and flushed with drink after his fit of tantrums in the morning; Ted did not aspire to social graces; Timothy was taut with nervous tension on which several glasses of wine had no apparent effect. Around him and Old Nick there was an air of conspiracy mixed with the hostility.

In the middle Talbot B. Talbot occupied himself agreeably by keeping Angel amused, until her father despatched her in search of mademoiselle, who was being unduly slow in returning to the table. He then became involved with Gerry Montague in a discussion about the various countries in the world where tennis had been played.

Joining in from a distance, the major announced that tennis was the touchstone of civilisation: when people were civilised they had leisure and spent it on the finer things of life such as tennis; where there was no tennis, there was no civilisation. With all respect to the absent lady, France was the best example of this. Although the cradle of tennis in the good old days, the game there had been killed by the Revolution. It was the same (he said) in Russia, where no tennis had been played since 1917. Tennis should be made an Olympic sport. The Russians would then take it up, and there would be some hope for the world again.

Gerry, as a reporter of the game and its would-be historian, disagreed with the major's thesis. In his view, tennis had been on the wane in France long before the Revolution: in 1600 there were as many as 250 courts in Paris; fifty years later fewer than half that number.

'In the heyday of the game,' he went on, 'it was even said that there were more tennis courts than churches in France and more tennis-players in France than beer-drinkers in England. But that was two centuries before the Revolution. In the seventeenth century the *paumiers* found they could get more money by hiring the courts out as theatres. Molière was always performing in them. In fact . . . '

Here, since the two missing ladies had now returned to the room, he broke off and appealed to the Frenchwoman.

'Mlle Deschamps, as the official representative of French tennis here tonight you are the very person we need. Please adjudicate between Major Winterton and myself in a little argument which has broken out. Just how much effect did the French Revolution have on the playing of tennis in your country?'

The conversation was now general, and

33

all eyes turned to Mlle Deschamps. She seemed flustered. Her dress had been changed, but the new one bore signs of having been put on in haste. Although earlier she had experienced no difficulty in conversing with Gavin in excellent English, it now looked as if she did not understand the language well enough to appreciate the meaning of the question.

'Tennis' — she spoke after a brief hesitation — 'has an honoured place in the story of our Revolution. You will have heard of the famous oath in the tennis court at Versailles. There is a painting in commemoration by Jacques-Louis David, and the court is now a museum.'

'Disgraceful,' interjected the major, adding courteously: 'if you will allow me to say so. I mean it is disgraceful that the court should be a museum. Not only that, but the Tuileries courts have now been desecrated by pictures.'

'If you are referring to the Museum of the Impressionists at the Jeu de Paume . . . ' began Mlle Deschamps heatedly, but Mr Pratt interrupted by enquiring tactfully whether tennis was still played outside Paris.

'Yes indeed.'

'Whereabouts?'

'Oh, in Fontainebleau. And Bordeaux. And Pau. And Deauville.'

'But surely,' Gerry protested, 'tennis hasn't been played at Pau or Deauville or Fontainebleau for many years.'

'But yes,' she replied sweetly, and returned pointedly to the business of catching up on her eating.

'That's very interesting,' murmured Gerry, exchanging glances down the table with the major. 'But even if we agree that France is a doubtful case, there is still the question of Russia. Here there is no doubt. The St Petersburg court, which is the only one I can trace, was closed by 1870, years before the revolution.'

'How clever of you to know these things!' put in Mrs Pratt, who was growing jealous of the attention attracted by the Frenchwoman. She herself had dressed and made up with special care that evening; Angel was looking as nubile as any mother could wish for; yet the men were taken up with this foreigner who must be forty if a day, however much she tried to conceal it by smiling all the time into her wrinkles.

'Not really.' Gerry deprecated the flattery. 'Featherstone-haugh published his Annals in 1870 and he refers to the court being recently closed. So far as I know, it has never been re-opened.'

'The Annals!' exclaimed the major boisterously. 'Be a sport, Gerry old son, and let us have a look at the manuscript. It'll be just the thing over the port.' And when Gerry appeared reluctant he insisted: 'Go along, there's a good fellow. Your host and hostess will excuse you for a moment, I'm sure. I shan't believe you about St Petersburg until you produce the evidence.'

'There's a copy of the book in the library, where we shall all be going in a few minutes,' Mr Pratt pointed out. 'Tomorrow will be a better time for the manuscript.'

The major, heavily supported by Timothy and Talbot, won his point, however, and Gerry gave in graciously;

which is more than could be said for Mr Pratt, who continued to protest that they ought not to run the risk of having wine spilt on something so precious. But Gerry left in spite of him.

His absence from the room was a short one. When he returned he was white-faced and empty-handed.

'May I ask,' he enquired angrily from the doorway, 'who has borrowed the manuscript without my permission?'

'Borrowed indeed!' declared Lady Cheney roundly, breaking a startled silence. 'Stolen, you mean! You'll never see that again, young man.'

3

Angel Pratt was in bed. With the yellow nylon pillow-case doing service as a halo she looked like a slumbering saint of the Sienese school. But though exhausted by the day's excitements she was still awake and far from other-worldliness. The phosphorescent glow of the alarm clock revealed that it was four o'clock, and with an unsaintly exclamation she suddenly jumped out of bed, crossed the room to the washbasin and shook herself a couple of aspirin tablets from a bottle on the shelf.

She slept with her curtains drawn back, and the room was faintly lit from outside by the moon. It was stuffy, and she sat on the side of the bed wriggling her toes into the pile of the carpet. Her mind was keeping her body from sleep, for she couldn't stop thinking. What a day and all, with those odd people and that extraordinary game! That sweet boy Ted was jolly well going to have to teach her how to play it.

Unlike her parents, Angel was completely without consciousness of class. Neither her father's origins — seventh child of a Deptford bricklayer — nor an education at one of the most expensive boarding schools in the country had affected her in the slightest. Her speech was neither common nor lah-de-dah. She was as interested in the company of her father's tennis professional as in the eleventh Earl of Cheney. She took them as they came. If they amused her she encouraged them; if they didn't she would avoid them, however tearfully her mother might point out that they were royalty or Rockefellers or what-have-you.

Armed with this egalitarian approach, Angel was able to study her father's weekend visitors dispassionately, and her favourite guest bar none was the one her mother called the Ogress. So far from scaring Angel, Lady Cheney kept her constantly intrigued guessing what she was going to do or say next. And in spite of Angel's reputation as the representative of a classless society the feeling was evidently reciprocated. Lady Cheney had been reported by one of the charwomen from the village as referring to 'that interesting Pratt gel.'

Angel yawned. What a lark that drama at the end of dinner had been! What a turn-up for the book, if that wasn't quite the wrong expression! There was poor old Dad cantering home along the straight after a day's triumph scattering largesse to all the nobs, when bingo! someone pinches that manuscript and brings the old man down with his nose just an inch or two short of the post. It had certainly put a damper on the after-dinner small talk, and anything might happen if it wasn't retrieved. In a family conference at bedtime Dad had said it was the Ogress who'd snitched it, and Mum said nothing but looked as if she thought Dad had done it himself. Angel had her own ideas.

She stretched and strolled over to the window before lying down for another attempt at some sleep. Perhaps she should have taken a dose of stomach-powder instead of aspirin. The most peculiar rumblings were going on inside her, and she cursed herself for an idiot in not sticking to the hock. Not only had she had a glass and a half of claret (the half before she could stop Higgs topping her up), but Dad had failed to get rid of the ladies before the port (Mum being partial to a drop) and she had even had a glass of that terrible stuff. Vintage or not, red ink wasn't in it.

Outside, on the wall of the west wing, the orange berries of a straggling pyracanth glistened in the moonlight and caught her eye. Colour was her passion. She should have stayed on at the Slade and become an artist instead of being lured down here by the glamour of country life and the prospect of endless riding. Probably she hadn't the talent; certainly she didn't have the powers of application or that single-mindedness which they all needed and which had uprooted Papa Gauguin in middle-age. Still, better a bad painter than no painter at all.

Her chain of thought was broken at

the moment of turning back to bed. In surveying the now familiar landscape of lawns, shrubberies, park, wood and lake her eye had taken in something unusual. A second or two elapsed before the impression transferred itself to the brain, and immediately her eyes flashed back to the spot. Yes, the lights were on in the tennis court!

Angel climbed back into bed even further from sleep than before she had taken the aspirin. She closed her eyes and was trying to resolve the problem of who was doing what there and whether she should do anything about it, when a board creaked in the corridor outside. She sat up with a jolt and felt for the light switch above the bed. Silence; and then a sinister sound of shuffling and tiptoeing.

She looked round for a weapon. There was none within reach, and no bell. As the tiptoeing came nearer she opened the door of her bedside cupboard and seized the china object by its handle. If she didn't like the look of whoever it was when he opened the door she would hurl it at him. It was a heavy pre-1914 model with pink roses round the rim and would at any rate smash when it hit the floor. That should sound an alarm and frighten the enemy off.

But the door did not open and the sound receded. Instantly deciding to go over to the offensive, Angel jumped out of bed, opened the door herself and peered out into the corridor. She was just in time to see a white figure turn down the stairs.

Nearly twenty now, she simply didn't believe in ghosts, and anyway if there were such things she wanted to see them — the second Earl was reputed to stage periodical come-backs in search of a lady-friend whom his wife had poisoned and disposed of in the kitchen garden. Racing down the corridor in her pyjamas, she reached the head of the stairs too late. The figure had vanished, and nothing broke the silence except the ticking of a grandfather clock in the hall below.

Disappointed but not feeling in the mood for further pursuit, Angel returned to her room, jumped into bed again and pulled the blankets round her ears for warmth. If it wasn't the amorous second Earl, then presumably it was a tennis-player fighting a tennis duel an hour before dawn in accordance with some Knights-of-Yore etiquette she had never heard of. Come to think of it, though, Gerry Montague had been telling her before dinner that Charles II, of all people, used to play at an ungodly hour before breakfast. She had shocked the press representative by replying that she would have thought the Merry Monarch much more the one for a long lie-in after all that dalliance with his assortment of mistresses. The white figure might, of course, be Mr Montague himself, disguised as a ghost, searching for his blessed manuscript.

The hock, claret and port now seemed to be making free with her inside as a battle-ground for some internecine feud among the wine family. Whether this unsettled state of her stomach or some temporarily-acquired power of extra-sensory perception caused it Angel could never afterwards decide, but a sudden sensation of tragedy crept over her like early-morning mist billowing up the lawns from the lake.

She got up, pulled a yellow roll-top sweater over her pale blue pyjamas, worked her feet into some pink moccasins and even at this moment paused to admire the colour scheme in the wardrobe mirror. If the corridor was dark the stairs were a pool of total blackness, but she negotiated them safely, felt her way through the hall and out of a small garden door, picking up her riding whip from a lobby on the way.

Clouds now shielded the moon, and in contrast to the warmth of her room the night was as cold as a September night can be. A narrow gravel path led across the grass down to the dark silhouette of the tennis-court building, with lights blazing out into the night from the long stretch of its ten giant windows on either side. On the way she thought she glimpsed a lurking figure and heard the rustle of clothing in the shrubbery, but it could have been the shadow of a bush and the wind stirring its leaves.

On the threshold Angel became really frightened for the first time. The silence was as complete as the silence outside: no smack of ball against wall; no one shouting the score; no sign of human occupation except the blaze of the lights and the door ajar with the key in it.

Angel pushed it open and waited for something to happen. Nothing did. The door of the ante-room stood open and she could see that the room was empty. Passing it, she stepped warily across the entrance-hall and walked noiselessly down the side gallery so that she could look into the court itself. The dressing-room doors were closed, but she gave them one or two nervous glances and gripped her whip at the ready before turning her full attention to the court.

On the hazard side there was nothing to be seen, but at the service end a long ladder stood propped against the wall above the dedans, its top reaching almost up to the gallery above. Near its foot a figure lay spread-eagled on the floor.

Angel instinctively crammed a fist into her mouth to choke back a scream.

Dressed all in white — shirt, sweater, trousers, socks and plimsolls — the figure sprawled against the end wall. The head was half-hidden by an arm and the face invisible.

Steeling herself, she entered the court and was crossing the floor for a closer inspection when something else caught her eye. Along the wall a few feet from the figure stood a row of empty bottles. Each bottle had a tennis ball carefully balanced in the neck, and each ball had a letter roughly drawn on it. The bottles had been arranged in two groups and the letters spelt out the words, DEAD NICK.

In contrast to the bright lights of the court, the recesses of the dedans and side galleries stood deep in shadow. Peering round as she went, Angel tiptoed across to the body and stooped over it. The message was accurate in one respect: it was certainly Old Nick. His face was placid but very grey compared with its purple hue at dinner. The rest of the message could well be true too: the head was bent at an unnatural angle, and

Angel could detect no sign of breathing. Another sensation stole over her, as the certainty of tragedy had in her bedroom. This time it was panic, rising to her chest and forcing its way up into her throat.

A sound reached her from the dedans and she looked up to see a back disappearing through the curtains. They swished like a snake's hiss as they swung back into position.

She seized on Old Nick's racket as a stouter weapon than her riding whip. Then she set off at high speed for the return journey to the house. As she ran she brandished her weapon like someone attacked by a swarm of wasps. Out of the court she rushed; along the gallery into the hallway; out of the building on to the path; from the path to the sweep of the drive; across the drive and in at the garden door; through the hall and up the stairs; along the corridor to her parents' room. And not until she was clutching the door-handle did she feel safe again. She had not looked round once, and her breath was coming in short, irregular jerks.

Inside the room heavy snoring guided her to her father's side of the bed. At first she tapped him gently on the arm, then she dug her fingers more insistently into him. 'Dad,' she whispered. 'Dad!'

If Mr Pratt took some time coming to, he was alert the moment he did. Dressing-gowned and slippered, he accompanied Angel into the corridor without waking his wife. Together, after a few words of explanation, they made their way to the tennis court, Mr Pratt taking the precaution of arming himself with a shot-gun from a cupboard in the hall.

The scene in the court was exactly as Angel had left it. Mr Pratt's first concern was to check that Old Nick was really dead. Then he took the balls off the bottles and put them into his dressing-gown pockets. The bottles he replaced on a pile of empties in the corner of the ante-room where they had evidently come from. They were mainly sherry and gin bottles, remnants of the previous day's party, but one still contained some whisky. From this he took a large swig and, despite protests, made Angel do the same. She also protested at the dismantling of the evidence, only to be told, in a brusque paternal manner, to shut her trap.

'And what's more, my girl,' added Mr Pratt, 'you're to keep it shut, do you see? Permanently shut. You haven't been here at all, not even with me. You slept heavily all night and didn't hear a thing. Right?'

'It's not right at all. For one thing — '

'For one thing nothing. You've not been here. Understand?'

'All right, if you say so, but I don't — '

'You don't need to,' Mr Pratt interrupted again. 'Now hop along to bed, while I have a word with that undersized good-for-nothing, Ted Nicholls.'

A cough behind him caused Mr Pratt to forget his bulk and leap round with shot-gun raised. In the doorway stood the undersized good-for-nothing in person looking puzzled, diffident and dishevelled.

'I just came to see if everything was in order, sir,' he muttered. 'Something woke me up, and I saw the lights on in the court. The key was gone, so I came down to find out . . . ' His voice tailed away as he caught the glint in his employer's eye.

'The key was gone,' mimicked Mr Pratt, working himself into a rage. 'You're lying. What the hell do you mean by allowing people to use the court at night? Don't tell me you don't know all about it. What was it I warned you when you were hired?'

'Mr Pratt, I — '

'Just answer the question, you little bastard. What was it I warned you when you were hired?'

Ted gulped. 'You said the court was never in no circumstances to be open unless I was here myself. That I was to keep the key and let no one else have it. And that I would be — wouldn't keep the job if you ever found the court open and me not there.'

'Don't bully him, Dad,' Angel intervened. 'After all . . . '

She gestured towards the body, and with a cry of sudden recognition Ted ran across the court, bent over his father

51

and burst into tears.

They had little effect on Mr Pratt, though he now spoke more gently. 'There, there!' he said: 'Stop caterwauling. I never noticed you being fond of your dad before. You can keep all that snivelling for later on. Meantime if you don't want to be booted out straight away, just remember that Miss Angel isn't here, will you?'

Ted, who was still sobbing, was not very quick on the uptake at any time. He gaped at Angel, who put an arm round his shoulders to draw him away from the body while she murmured some words of sympathy and then explained that her father wanted her kept out of any enquiries.

'Of course, of course,' agreed Ted eagerly. 'I understand, miss. Just as Mr Pratt says.'

'All right then,' continued Mr Pratt. 'Put your overcoat over him in case there is any hope. Turn off the lights. Lock the door behind us without touching anything. When you get back to the house, telephone for a doctor. When the doctor arrives, let me know. I'll be in my room.'

Ted showed some embarrassment over removing his overcoat in Angel's presence. He took it off bashfully, uncovering a pair of Charing Cross Road pyjamas decorated with scantily attired female figures. In the act of leaving with her father Angel hardly noticed the pyjamas, but she did see, as he knelt, that Ted was wearing white socks and tennis shoes.

'What about the police, Mr Pratt?' Ted enquired huskily after their retreating backs.

Mr Pratt sprang round infuriated. 'I said a doctor, didn't I?' he shouted.

Then, prompted by an angry glance from Angel, he added: 'I'm sorry, boy. I know I shouldn't speak to you like that with your father lying there, even if you didn't get on with him. Just get the doctor. Don't you know an accident when you see one?'

4

If the most important thing in life is to choose one's parents wisely, Angel had been lucky. They squabbled from time to time, of course: what family didn't? But as far back as she could remember she had been loved and allowed to do most of the things she wanted to. Nowadays they all jogged along amicably in luxury, and whenever there was a crisis the three of them drew together into a tight family trinity.

There was a crisis now, and Angel and Mrs Pratt were settling down after lunch to talk it out in private. The morning had passed in a flurry of uncertainty and rumour; the doctor had been and gone, but Mr Pratt had issued no statement. Most of the guests had kept to their rooms until lunch, when the conversation was confined to formal regrets and desultory small talk.

Mother and daughter sat in the summer

house on the far side of the lake enjoying the last of the year's sun — if enjoyment were possible after what had happened. Angel was suffering from lack of sleep and the horrors of the night, while Mrs Pratt looked up continually from her knitting to keep a sharp eye on the landscape, as though expecting a policeman or a murderer to appear at any moment. She had just had a full account of the night's goings-on for the first time.

'So he was really murdered?' she gasped.

Angel nodded grimly. 'He couldn't have done that gruesome business with the tennis balls himself, could he? And after he was dead no one else would be likely to do it unless they wanted to gloat over doing him in.'

'Then it must be a madman,' sniffed Mrs Pratt, clicking her knitting needles frantically to prevent herself losing control and breaking down. 'Good heavens, Angie, we're none of us safe! Can they hear us from here in the house if we scream? One of these people we've invited is stark raving mad.'

'I don't think it's as bad as that,' said Angel.

'Don't you, darling? Well, I do. You say it looked like an accident, but whoever did it went out of his way to tell everyone that it wasn't. I only hope Alf did the right thing in taking those balls away.'

'If he hadn't, the police would be here now.'

Mrs Pratt shuddered. 'Don't mention the police, dear,' she begged. 'You know I can't bear to have them mentioned. Still, if it's them or being murdered in our own beds . . .'

'Dad must know what he's doing. He always does, and he's avoided a scandal so far. According to Ted, the doctor was a push-over. He was quite prepared to certify that death was due to a broken neck after an accidental fall off the ladder. He said the alcohol in Old Nick's blood-stream might set up an all-time record, and Dad delivered one of his persuasive spiels about the importance of discretion in view of the world-wide reputation of the dead man etcetera, etcetera. Apparently it all went through as smoothly as a shareholders' meeting. The inquest oughtn't to be more than a formality.'

A tear furrowed its way through the make-up on Mrs Pratt's cheek. 'Poor man,' she sighed, 'I only really spoke to him once and that was in the corridor upstairs before dinner last night. He said what a wonderful place High Cheney was and kissed me.'

'Kissed you!'

'On the cheek, mind you. Nothing vulgar, darling. Though his breath did smell a bit ginny. Then your father came along and gave him a dirty look.'

'I'm not surprised,' said Angel indignantly. 'And a dirty look for you too, I should hope. Pecking in the corridors with someone you've never even spoken to before!'

'You young girls are all prudes these days. Or perhaps it's the education we've given you, Angie. A kiss doesn't mean anything; it's just a way of saying hullo nicely.'

'Dad didn't think so, did he?'

'Men have funny ideas about these

things, and Alf's no different from the rest of them. What about if he'd been doing the kissing? It wouldn't have meant anything then, I'm sure! Where is he anyway? Why hasn't he told me all about this himself? I want to talk to him.' Mrs Pratt grew nervous again and querulous.

'He's in the tennis court I think. After the doctor left he took Ted's key off him so that no one else could get in until he'd had a good look round himself. I expect he's looking for clues. You stay here and I'll go and fetch him.'

'You'll do no such thing,' ordered Mrs Pratt sharply. 'He won't want to be disturbed and I'm not going to be left alone with a murderous nut at large. Who is it, that's what I want to know. And why doesn't Alf send the whole lot packing? You must have guessed who it is; you're a sharp girl. No, don't tell me; I know. It's that blue-blooded old bitch from the village. She's as mad as a March hare.'

'Mum, really! Don't be so hysterical. Lady C. may be a bit odd, but she's not a homicidal maniac. Can you see her getting up in the middle of the night and pitching people off ladders?'

'Yes I can. And what's more, I can easily imagine her setting up those empty bottles so carefully, taking the balls out of the basket, scrawling letters on them — there's a pen and ink beside the visitors' book in the ante-room, isn't there? — and then doing a triumphant jig round the body when she'd arranged them all nicely. She's an evil old bag and she's after something and won't stop till she's got it. It's too horrid to think about!'

Here Mrs Pratt finally burst into tears. She shook her head vehemently when Angel enquired what it was that Lady Cheney was supposed to be after. Then she blew her nose several times and spent some minutes repairing the damage to her face.

Suddenly she screamed. 'Look Angie! There's a man coming this way. He's lurking over there behind that bush.'

Angel looked up and saw Gerry Montague. He was strolling rather than lurking and was followed immediately by Gavin, with whom he was deep in conversation. By the time they reached the summer-house Mrs Pratt had resumed the role of chatelaine and put on the highly refined voice which she kept in reserve for the benefit of the high-born and socially superior classes.

'Oh, it's Mr Montague — and Lord Cheney.' She acknowledged their presence graciously. 'This is a very tragic affair. I trust we can rely on the press being discreet.'

'So far as I am concerned, you can of course,' replied Gerry, who as tennis correspondent was reporting the weekend's play for the one or two newspapers interested in such esoteric proceedings. 'It's a terrible end for one of the greatest tennis-players of all time, and I'm as keen as anyone in seeing that a sensation isn't made of it.'

'Still,' Angel pointed out, 'if he'd had the choice he might have preferred to die on the court.'

'Perfectly true,' Gerry agreed. 'He certainly would have. I've made the same point in the obituary I wrote this morning. The tragedy is that he still had several more years of good tennis left in him. His epitaph was spoken by the major as soon as he heard the news: 'He went before his time, but at any rate he fell better than half a yard,' he said. Almost a dead nick, in fact, from what I hear.' He gave a grim half-laugh and ran a finger nervously over his moustache.

At the mention of 'dead nick' Angel blanched and enquired whether the major had used that phrase and what exactly it meant. Gerry explained that it referred to a ball falling in the 'nick' or crack between the wall and the floor and failing to rise: Nicholls had specialised in 'nicks'; hence, in part, his nickname. Mrs Pratt declared with a shudder that in the circumstances she had never heard of anything more ghoulish. She supposed the court would be shut up and put out of commission for a time.

'On the contrary,' said Gerry: 'It has just been decided to carry on with the programme. This is what Old Nick would have wished; we're all agreed on that.

I'm on my way to the court to get changed now.'

During this conversation Gavin had been standing outside the summer-house, politely attentive. From time to time he ran his eye over Angel, who was wearing a fetching pair of scarlet jeans despite its being Sunday afternoon on what her parents had hoped was to be a formal pre-war-style country-house weekend. She had put on jeans for fear of a cold after her nocturnal expeditions through the grounds, and scarlet ones because she needed cheering up. Gavin's glances did not escape Mrs Pratt's notice and she seized the opportunity presented by Gerry.

'In that case,' she said, 'since Mr Pratt is in the court already, I'll walk round with you.'

No sooner had she spoken than it crossed her mind that either of these two escorts might be the murderer if Angel was right about the Ogress. Gavin might have inherited a streak of insanity from his mother, or might be in league with her. Mrs Pratt paused in the act of rising from her chair.

'What about your manuscript, Mr Montague?' Angel enquired. 'Has it turned up yet?'

'I'm sorry to say it hasn't. Gavin and I were just discussing the matter. I told Mr Pratt before lunch that unless it is returned by this evening I shall have to ask for the police to be called in. It's a most unpleasant thing to have to do, but the loss is quite crippling for me. Apart from the financial side — and Mr Pratt has generously offered compensation out of his own pocket — the manuscript is an invaluable source for the history of the game which I am writing. There are quite a number of passages in it which for one reason or another never appeared in the printed book.'

'Oh dear!' exclaimed Mrs Pratt. 'We simply must avoid having the police on the premises. We should never live it down; you know how people gossip in the country, and particularly about men in my husband's position. I'm sure there must be a mistake somewhere. None of the servants would do anything like that — they wouldn't know the value of a manuscript or how to dispose of it. It must have got mislaid somewhere. If you will allow me, I'll search your room myself before tea.'

As she still remained seated when she had finished speaking and Gerry made no comment, Angel urged her on. 'Go on then, Mum, if you're going to the court first. I expect Mr Montague wants to get changed for his game.'

Reluctantly she picked up a large work-bag, popped her knitting into the top of it and stood up. Gerry's offer to carry the bag was turned down, and as they disappeared slowly through the rhododendrons he had reassuringly changed the topic of conversation and was complimenting her on a fine display of dahlias visible across the lake.

'Well, your lordship,' said Angel with as much of a twinkle as she could muster. 'Pray be seated.'

'Thanks,' said Gavin. 'Not a bad afternoon, is it?'

Angel considered the question for a moment and decided on a qualification.

'For the time of year,' she said.

'Yes, of course. For the time of year.'

A silence followed, broken by Angel, who asked, with only the faintest suspicion of mockery, whether she had the correct impression in imagining that Lord Cheney wished to speak to her.

'For heaven's sake call me Gavin, won't you? Yes, there are a lot of things I want to talk to you about, but it's difficult to know where to start. The most important thing, though, is who's got that manuscript.'

'Why on earth should you think I know?'

Angel's eyes opened so wide that Gavin involuntarily muttered, 'I say, that's funny. I thought your eyes were blue.'

'Well, aren't they?'

'No, they aren't. They're dark grey. Did your father take it?'

'What an idea!' Angel pretended to be indignant. 'Only a minute ago my mother was telling me that it was your mother who pinched it.'

Gavin laughed shortly. 'No dice,' he said. 'The Cheneys haven't pinched anything for nearly four hundred and fifty years. They haven't had to.'

'But perhaps they've reached the point where they are having to start again.'

Gavin was no longer amused. They flashed looks of mutual suspicion at each other and she apologised.

'I can answer for my mater,' said Gavin. 'She didn't do it.'

'Well, I can't answer for Dad, but let's assume he didn't do it. Who's the most likely suspect then?'

'Nearly everyone here seems to have a mania for tennis. Whether that's sufficient to turn one into a criminal I wouldn't know, not having it myself.'

'To judge from the look on his face, that manuscript means as much to the major as the crown jewels.'

'But majors don't steal,' Gavin protested.

'Don't they? I bet they do. Wasn't that chap who once made off with the crown jewels a captain? That's near enough. Anyhow, even if the major doesn't steal he's just the sort to set his wife on to doing the dirty work. She was playing possum upstairs all through dinner last night when the coast was nice and clear.'

Gavin shook his head. 'Agreed she could have done it, but I don't believe she did. She seems to have a pretty genuine cold.'

'All right then. What about the enchanting Parisienne? Spilling something over yourself as an excuse for leaving the room is the oldest trick in the book.'

At the mention of 'enchanting Parisienne' Gavin blushed, as Angel had intended he should. They were both aware that la Deschamps had cast a spell over him during dinner. In the cold light of retrospect he was conscious of having been taken for a ride. She had dazzled him with a display of charm and carefully regulated glimpses of that well-upholstered bosom.

'I don't know what to make of her,' he admitted.

'Don't you? I thought she was telling you all about herself when she was rummaging around and taking that cameo off her décolletage or whatever it's called. So far as I could overhear, it belonged to one of her grandmothers, who was descended in a complicated and not very legitimate way from the Counts of Foix.'

Gavin blushed again. 'That wasn't the point at all,' he said. 'We were discussing English and French portraiture, or rather she was. It seems she's interested in art. English art especially.'

'Such as the Victorian splendour of High Cheney?'

'Certainly she was rather over-enthusiastic about the house. But the French always like that sort of thing. It's Gainsborough and artists of that sort she really admires. I told her we once had a Holbein in the family and she wanted to know all about it. I couldn't — '

'Holbein's nothing like Gainsborough,' interrupted Angel, 'and he wasn't English. That woman is a fraud. Didn't you notice that she doesn't know anything about tennis either? Gerry Montague caught her out properly.'

'Yes, but even supposing she is, how could she know Gerry was going to bring the manuscript? Or do you mean she came just for the purpose of laying her hands on anything valuable that happened to be around?'

'I'm not suggesting anything, just speculating. Do you think she's capable of murder?'

'Murder?' Gavin was caught completely by surprise, or appeared to be. Angel was watching him closely and decided on the spur of the moment to risk her father's anger and let him into the secret.

'Yes, murder.' She made him swear never to tell anyone else and then gave him the details of the night's alarms and excursions. When she had finished he was aghast and kept muttering: 'I simply can't believe it; it can't be true.'

'Why ever not? People do get murdered, you know.'

'Because there's no one here who would do such a thing.'

'There was one person Old Nick looked like wanting to murder only yesterday, and the feeling might have been reciprocated for all we know.'

'You mean Timothy Forsyth after that fiasco at the end of the match? My dear girl, it's absurd. Timothy would never murder anyone. We were at Eton together.'

'That's not an alibi. And where's he been all day? Reported to be in his bedroom suffering from a hangover. It's after three o'clock and he hasn't put in an appearance yet. If someone's got to be a murderer he's behaving suspiciously enough.'

'Oh I say! There's nothing suspicious about a hangover. He was drinking like a fish last night. If it's got to be someone it's much more likely to be that young professional, Ted Nicholls. He was quite as much involved in yesterday's row; more than Timothy in fact. He and the old man never got on. Everyone knows that.'

It was Angel's turn to be angry. She sprang to Ted's defence. 'Ted's a nice boy. It's awful to accuse someone of killing his own father. You oughtn't to have said that.'

'I'm sorry, but he's as likely to have done it as Timothy. Still, when it comes to the point, one can't believe any sane person could commit murder.'

'Exactly. That's why I'm looking for someone who isn't sane.'

A guarded look spread across Gavin's face. He went over to the doorway and stared out into the distance, frowning heavily. In a nearby bush a pair of blackbirds were squawking at each other. Eventually he turned round.

'Or it could have been done,' he said, 'by someone who loses his temper easily — someone pushing the ladder over in a fit of rage when Nicholls was at the top. That's much more probable than a madman.'

Angel rose to her feet abruptly. 'I know who you mean,' she said coldly. 'He was asleep.'

In silence they made their way along the lakeside to the tennis court, where the afternoon's programme was due to start. As they were taking their seats in the dedans, Gerry, the major and Ted came onto the court with Talbot, the American, for a four-handed game. They were all subdued, and Ted looked pale and hollow-eyed. He stooped and picked the ball-basket out of its recess in the floor beside the net. Carrying it, he crossed the court towards the dedans.

Angel knew that this was routine. Tennis was played with a set of five or six dozen balls. Before the game started they were tipped from their wicker basket into a trough on the court side of the dedans netting, where they lay handy for the server. As the game proceeded the balls gradually accumulated at the net in the middle of the court. It was the marker's job to collect them in the basket and replenish the server's trough when supplies were running low.

The simple routine was almost too much for Ted. In coming across he involuntarily shied away from the place where his father's body had lain, and his hands were trembling as he upended the basket. He shouldn't have been asked to come into the court at all, thought Angel indignantly.

The balls began tumbling out of the basket, clattering into the wooden box. Then suddenly they stopped and from the bottom of the basket fell a snowstorm of scattered sheets of manuscript.

5

Light sparkled from the crystal chandeliers in the Long Gallery. Log fires crackled and spat in each of the two Adam-style hearths. Along the wall between and beyond them hung a set of enormous faded tapestries depicting battle scenes, coronations, apotheoses and the like. According to the major's calculations the gallery was about two cricket pitches in length, and the wall opposite the tapestries gave the magical appearance of one long endless mirror. By day it contained seven windows interspersed with gilt-framed looking-glasses; at night, instead of curtains, panels of mirror-glass were drawn across the windows, making the narrow room seem as spacious as it was long.

In the true stately-home tradition this gallery still did service as the state drawing-room at High Cheney, and here Mr Pratt's guests were gathered for coffee

73

after dinner on Sunday.

Although the evening was mild, they clustered naturally into two groups on and around the chaise-longues which faced each of the fires. Mr Pratt himself stood under the central tapestry between the two. Above his head a stout lady in a Roman helmet, attended by other stout ladies, garlanded and toga-ed, sat with her foot resting on a dormant leopard. Beside the leopard sprawled one or two half-clad male bodies clutching swords and spears. Whether the triumph was historical or allegorical no one now alive could say. The lady might be a classical or biblical heroine; she might be Britannia or Liberty; she might even be the Cheney family or an earlier countess. All that was now certain about her was the fact she was woven at Mortlake.

Mr Pratt cleared his throat in the approved manner of professional chairmen and waited for the conversational hum to die down. He stood with his legs aggressively apart, stirring a saccharine tablet into his coffee until everyone was silent and expectant.

'Ladies and gentlemen,' he said, 'it is impossible for me to find words which can express adequately the deep honour I feel at being privileged to entertain such a distinguished company at High Cheney. I am sincerely grateful to all the eminent gentlemen from the tennis world — not forgetting the fair representative from our neighbours in France' (he bowed in Mlle Deschamps' direction) ' — and above all to the President himself' (here he nodded to the major) 'for gracing this occasion with their presence.'

'It is also,' he went on, 'a source of the greatest satisfaction to my wife and myself to welcome under our — I nearly said, humble, but that won't do at all — under our magnificent roof the head of the Cheney family and the Dowager Countess, who will, we earnestly hope, continue to regard this as the ancestral home with which they will always have — and will certainly be felt by us to have — a very special link.'

This sentiment drew a ripple of applause, during which Mr Pratt remarked, less formally, to anyone who could hear him that at this point his secretary had put in something in Latin which he had described as 'just the job', but that he (Mr Pratt) was blowed if he could pronounce it and wasn't going to try. Instead he went on to the more serious, and extempore, part of his speech.

'I'm sorry the weekend has been marred by misfortune. Mr Montague's manuscript, we're all happy to know, is back in his safe keeping, and we'd better draw a tactful veil over that little episode. Mr Montague wants no more to be heard of it. The matter is closed.'

Some stirring took place on the Chippendale chairs and settees at this announcement, and the speaker paused. One or two glances were exchanged, but Gerry Montague remained silent and no one else ventured a remark. Mr Pratt proceeded.

'Regarding the other incident — the tragic death of Mr Nicholls, a sportsman of world-wide fame — we can only express our most sincere sorrow. We all know how much he will be missed; and all our sympathy goes to Ted. It's nothing more than a gesture, but you may be interested to know that I'm going to present to the Tennis Players Association a Nicholls Memorial Cup to be competed for annually on terms which the committee can decide. I will see you all again in the morning before you go, but let me say a formal 'thank you' once more now.'

During the latter part of this speech a diversion was caused by the American, Talbot B. Talbot. He was sitting at some distance from the others, smoking a cigar and resting his elbow on the shoulder of a negro servant boy in coloured porcelain. Moved by something his host said, he seemed about to interrupt, but was hushed into silence. When Mr Pratt had finished he made no further attempt to speak, but sat thoughtfully puffing smoke-rings into the black boy's grinning face.

The major at once took the floor. His funeral oration on Old Nick covered most aspects of tennis for the preceding fifty years and lasted rather more than twenty minutes by the Long Gallery's Tompion clock. Finally, after associating himself and the club of which he had the honour to be President with the sorrow expressed by Mr Pratt at the accident which had led to the untimely termination of a career without parallel in the long annals of tennis, Major Winterton formally acknowledged the generosity of the donor of the Nicholls Memorial Cup and ended by proposing a vote of thanks to their host and hostess for a supremely hospitable weekend.

The proposal being carried with acclamation, Talbot B. Talbot then put up his hand and enquired in a slow, casual voice whether it was in order to ask a question.

Mr Pratt assured him benignly that this was not a public meeting. High Cheney was Liberty Hall. Guests could say or do anything they pleased, subject only to the canons of good taste and, of course, the laws of the land; neither of which, he felt certain, Mr Talbot intended to infringe.

'Then I would like to ask why you and Major Winterton here are so sure that Nicholls' death was an accident.'

A hush settled on the company. From

one end of the Long Gallery to the other you could have heard the string of a racket snap.

'Because,' the major retaliated sharply, 'it *was* an accident. What are you implying, sir?'

Talbot B. Talbot was still lounging comfortably in a chair which had been so constructed by an eighteenth-century craftsman as to make this an almost impossible feat. His figure was a loose, gangling one, more like a Texan's than that of a long-distance commuter between New York City and Berkeley, Cal. It was a second or two before he took the cigar from his mouth and replied with deliberation:

'I am implying, sir, that it was not an accident.'

'If it was not an accident, what was it?' demanded the major.

'You tell me.'

The major, who was already boiling over with indignation, had no reserves available for this sort of effrontery, and Mr Pratt took over. His temper, too, flared periodically into the most formidable firework displays. Unlike the major's, though, it was often secretly under control — one of the various weapons in his well-stocked armoury.

'Are you accusing anyone of anything?' he asked, regulating his voice to a fine mixture of blandness and menace.

Talbot ducked the direct question. 'I'm not so familiar with the laws you have over here,' he said, 'but back home the police would need to investigate something like this.'

'But, Mr Talbot,' intervened Mrs Pratt, 'the doctor examined poor Nicholls and found that he had broken his neck after falling off the ladder. I don't like to say this, but Mr Nicholls did have a great deal to drink. You may have noticed it at dinner last night. The coroner will hold an inquest, but if the doctor is satisfied the police will be too, I'm sure.'

'I see. And the doctor was provided with all the facts?'

'All the facts were on the ground before him, Mr Talbot. Just as my husband found them.'

'It was your husband who found the body, ma'am?'

Mr Pratt eyed the American ruminatively. 'Yes,' he replied shortly, 'something woke me during the night; I saw the lights on in the court, discovered the body and summoned Ted, who locked up the court and sent for the doctor. That's right, isn't it, Ted?'

Sitting ill at ease, as if he had strayed above stairs from the servants' hall, the young professional flushed and nodded: 'Yes, Mr Pratt. That's quite correct.'

'And was there anyone else with us?'

Ted gulped. 'No one,' he declared hoarsely; and then more vehemently: 'No one at all.'

Talbot bent his head back and closed his eyes. Smoke from his cigar curled upwards to the heavily stuccoed ceiling. 'Not Miss Pratt, for example?' he enquired softly.

All eyes were immediately on Angel, who looked across to her father for support. If Talbot is the murderer, she thought, what is he stirring things up for? If he isn't, how on earth does he know?

'Why should you think my daughter was there?'

'Because I saw her.'

These four words created almost as much stir as if the speaker had lobbed a plastic bomb on to the Aubusson carpet. Even Lady Cheney was roused out of what had seemed to be a sound nap. 'Explain yourself, Mr Talbot,' she ordered regally.

'That's easily done. Like Mr Pratt, I too was disturbed during the night. In my case it was by an outside door shutting. I looked out of the window and saw what I took to be Miss Angel going towards the tennis court, which was lit up. Thinking something might be wrong, and she might need some help, I tailed her.'

'When I reached the building everything was quiet, so I tiptoed into the dedans. The lady was standing in the middle of the court in some distress, and I was wondering how to make myself known without scaring the daylight out of her when something creaked in the ante-room and I dived through the curtains to see who it was. Whoever it was, he made tracks mighty fast. He was out of the building before I was through the curtains. I chased him across the grass — saw he was in white. But I lost trace of him when he reached the house.'

'It's all perfectly true,' confessed Angel, ' — about me, I mean. And there *was* someone in the dedans. But I was very upset, and Dad thought I shouldn't be involved in any questioning. I hope that satisfies you, Mr Talbot.'

'Thank you; I wish it did. I hate being an outlandish boor in such elegant and hospitable surroundings, but would I be wrong in suggesting that some other highly material evidence is being suppressed?'

The question hung in the air.

'Nothing of any importance has been suppressed,' stated Mr Pratt at last.

'That might be a matter of opinion, sir,' Talbot pointed out midly.

Lady Cheney was less mild. 'If we are being asked to observe discretion in order to avert a scandal, then the least we should be offered in return are the full facts. We may then determine for ourselves whether by not summoning the police instantly we are becoming accessories after the fact in some dreadful crime.'

'I do so agree with Lady Cheney,' ventured Mrs Winterton. 'Aren't we running a terrible risk by not calling the police at once?' She sniffed and blew her nose.

'You'd better tell them, Angie,' said her mother. And, Mr Pratt making no sign, Angel related the story of the bottles and the balls and the writing on them. Another long, tense silence followed.

It was broken by Mr Pratt calling on Ted to confess.

'Confess to what, sir?' asked Ted, as if groping for a lead.

'To being up to some prank or other. There's no one else it could be.'

'I don't know anything about them bottles and balls.'

'Are you going to deny that you appeared suddenly in the court when Miss Angel and I were there? And that you gave us the impression that you knew nothing of what had happened?'

'Yes; that is, no. I mean I don't deny it.'

'Do you deny you were the person Mr Talbot chased?'

Ted looked cornered and on the verge of tears.

'It was me,' he snivelled at last. 'I woke up and found the key gone. It hangs on a hook in my room. The door had just shut; that's what woke me. I knew what was going on and that Father must have pinched it, so I wasn't too worried at first. But after a bit, when I couldn't get back to sleep, I did begin to worry, knowing your orders that no one was to use the court without me being there. So I changed and went across. It was awful spooky down there with all those lights and no one playing, so I got frightened and crept into the ante-room. Then there was a funny noise from the dedans and I ran for it with someone after me. That's all I know. Honest it is.'

'You're a darned good runner,' said Talbot appreciatively. 'And now come clean about the bottles.'

'I don't know nothing about them bottles and balls,' wailed Ted for the second time, his grammar slipping with his self-confidence. 'It was a dirty thing to do, and I wouldn't never have done it — to my own father or anyone else. He ought to be ashamed of himself. That's what he ought.'

'WHO ought to be ashamed of himself?' Lady Cheney's first word came not far short of a bellow.

For answer Ted turned towards the chesterfield where Timothy Forsyth and Mlle Deschamps were sitting side by side. Timothy had made his first appearance of the day at dinner and answered enquiries about his health with non-committal politeness. He was looking grey and withdrawn.

'Perhaps I should explain what happened,' he began apologetically, feeling himself now the general target.

'It would be such a relief to us all if you would, Mr Forsyth,' said Mrs Pratt in the encouraging voice of someone begging to have a magic wand waved over the whole unsavoury business.

'You see, it wasn't till dinner-time just now that I learned about Old Nick being dead. You can imagine what a shock it was and how I feel about it. In the dressing room after the match yesterday he challenged me to a return match — a proper game, he called it. I pointed out that it wouldn't be possible to fit it into the programme and he at once started implying that I was scared of a re-play. He then said that we didn't need any spectators and he certainly wasn't having Ted as marker again, so we could play after dinner when everyone else had gone to bed. I still hesitated — it seemed an idiotic idea — and he became offensive, saying that he proposed to get as tight as the whole House of Lords but I could stay stone-cold sober and take fifteen and a bisque. He seemed determined to force me into accepting the challenge, and eventually, against my better judgment, I agreed — refusing the handicap, of course.'

He paused and stared at length into the fire waiting for comments, but no one spoke.

'At dinner I decided to show him that the game was going to be played on strictly level terms, and I drank with him glass for glass. It was a damn silly thing to do, especially since his capacity was greater than mine. By bedtime I wasn't in any condition to play; nor was he. We agreed to sleep it off for a few hours. He had an alarm clock and would wake me when he was dressed. Then he would take the key from Ted's room and go ahead to open the court and make it ready for play, while I dressed. We had both brought our tennis things across to the house.

'It seemed about two minutes after I'd gone to sleep that he woke me up. I knew it was madness and I'd never be able to play properly, but it was like being talked into a duel — I didn't see how I could get out of it. I managed to dress and stagger across to the court. By the time I got there I felt thoroughly resentful at being forced into such a ridiculous schoolboy escapade, and when I saw him lying there on the floor my only feeling was delight that he was incapable of playing. I was in a pretty fuddled state and it never even crossed my mind that he was seriously hurt, let alone dead. I imagined he had found he couldn't climb the ladder and had simply lain down in a drunken stupor and gone to sleep. My only thought was to establish the fact that I had been there ready for play and then nip back to bed as fast as I could move. Setting up the bottles and balls was a juvenile type of joke, I admit. They were intended as a message that I'd been there, so that he could see for himself as soon as he came to that I'd not defaulted. That's all there was to it.'

'Might one enquire how you happened to use such regrettably accurate words in your message, Mr Forsyth?' The question came from Lady Cheney, who had been following the narrative attentively.

'It sounds silly now, but he was lying right up against the wall. Dead nick is a tennis term for when the ball falls in the crack: Nicholls was famous for the number of times it happened with his shots. And then, of course, he was lying there dead to the world — unconscious, as I thought. It was a pun, that's all, but rather a macabre one in the circumstances, I'm afraid.'

His voice tailed away and Talbot expressed himself sorry if Timothy had been put on the spot. He was satisfied (so he said) about the death being accidental, and now of the opinion that no good purpose would be served by any further investigations.

Mr Pratt resumed command and thanked him. 'Mr Talbot has relieved our minds of any doubt about what happened to Nicholls during the night. Clearly he was already dead when Mr Forsyth found him: the doctor said that death must have been instantaneous when he hit the floor. While I would be the first person to notify the police of any suspicion of foul play if it proved necessary, in this instance a great deal of inconvenience and undesirable publicity would result, all to no purpose. And we do, after all, owe it to the dead man to keep his reputation clean. The police will need formal statements before the inquest, but if news of a special enquiry leaked out to the press — as it would be bound to — goodness knows what rumours would soon be circulating. Mr Talbot has handsomely declared himself satisfied and I'm sure you will agree that there's no necessity for causing Mr Forsyth further embarrassment. May I take it that agreement on this is unanimous?'

The prospect of publicity in the popular press filled most of the gathering with alarm. It would be bad for the Pratt business interests, bad for the game of tennis, bad for the Cheney family and devastating for all their private lives. There were murmurs of assent and only one further question.

'The ladder,' enquired Mlle Deschamps. 'One may ask for what purpose Mr Nicholls was climbing the ladder?'

'Certainly,' replied Mr Pratt easily. 'The ladder is kept in the corridor outside the court. The approach to the gallery above the dedans is from outside and rather unsafe, so we keep the door up there locked. Whenever the upper gallery has to be reached, we find it simpler to use the ladder. Ted will confirm what I say.'

'Yes, Mr Pratt. Dad hit a couple of balls into the gallery during the game yesterday. I expect he was filling in time until Mr Forsyth came by going up to fetch them.'

'Thank you,' said Mlle Deschamps. 'That seems a most likely explanation.'

And she placed the very faintest emphasis on the word 'seems'.

6

Later the same evening the famous manuscript made its belated official appearance. It was a large pile of yellowed paper densely covered with faded writing. The sheets, once bound together, were now loose and, due to their recent adventures ending in the ball-basket, in some disarray. Gerry Montague produced them ruefully, like a priest unveiling a desecrated idol.

Grouped with him round the table where the manuscript lay, Mlle Deschamps, Talbot and the major sat in admiration. Angel and her father and Gavin Cheney completed the company. The others, including a distraught Timothy, had retired to bed.

Gerry and the major were engrossed in a historical survey of what the major described with fervour as 'the king of games and the game of kings'. Angel learned that tennis had been

93

mentioned by Chaucer two hundred years before Shakespeare put the game on the literary map; that Erasmus devoted a colloquy to it; that Rabelais made Pantagruel play tennis at Orleans; and that people playing tennis were a feature of Swedenborg's vision of Heaven. These items of information were supplied by Gerry: the major showed greater enthusiasm for the royal aspects of the game and passed round for admiration a print showing Charles IX of France at the age of two with a tennis racket already in his hand.

'At one time, do you know' — he picked on Angel as likely to prove a sympathetic audience — 'all the kings of England and France played. Except the weaklings, that is. All the Louises from X to XV inclusive, for instance. And their nobility.'

'Not to mention some ordinary people,' put in Gerry, 'when the kings didn't make laws to stop them.'

'And then the French Henrys,' continued the major, less interested in the lower orders. 'Henry II, Henry III and Henry IV all played. In fact I don't mind wagering that Henry of Navarre could have played Louis XIV with all the openings barred and still beaten him.' He was fond of this form of speculation and looked eagerly round for a challenger.

'Henry II was the best of the bunch, though,' said Gerry. 'He was championship class and, what's more, he wouldn't have come to the throne but for tennis. He was Francis I's second son, and the Dauphin died from taking an iced drink after a game of tennis.'

'Ah, Francis I!' The major hailed him with warmth. 'There's a king for you. He even built a tennis court on one of the ships of his fleet. But would he have beaten our Henry VIII? That's the question. One of the great unsolved riddles of history. It's disloyal to say so, I know, but it's my firm conviction that he would.'

'Wouldn't the match have gone to whoever was playing at home?' enquired Mr Pratt cynically. 'Presumably the markers knew which side their bread was buttered.'

'You've a point there,' agreed Gerry. 'One might run into a charge of high treason if one's sovereign liege didn't have the benefit of all doubts. Though, as a matter of history, Henry VIII lost a lot of money at tennis; perhaps that's why he had to dissolve the monasteries. Come to think of it, there's an old story about him and a marker. I can't remember what it was, but didn't High Cheney come into it somewhere?'

'My dear fellow,' the major protested, 'it couldn't possibly have. The court here wasn't built at that time. What you say about him losing money confirms what I've always thought about Henry VIII: he wasn't nearly as good as he's cracked up to be. It was the Stuarts who were the true tennis-players in this country. I bet Rupert of the Rhine was a dab hand at straight forces. He was the best, but they all played. Except, of course, for James I.'

'Why of course?' asked Angel.

The major ignored the interruption, since by that time he had swept on to bemoan the Hanoverian succession.

'What a tragedy for the country that was,' he said fiercely. 'Not a tennis-player among them. It's a good indication that the Germans have never been really civilised. The Prince Consort and Edward VII played about half a dozen times each, and that's the dynasty's entire record in two hundred and fifty years.'

'Don't forget Poor Fred,' Gerry admonished.

'He may have played, I grant you,' snapped the major. 'But if he did he was so weak he died of it.'

'What about other countries?' Gavin enquired.

The major considered. 'I hope Gerry's researches are going to throw fresh light on the subject. Meanwhile we are not too well off for information. In Scotland the game developed even earlier than in England. I believe I'm right in saying that James IV and James V played. In Spain — let me see now — there was Henry I of Castile, and later a whole succession of crowned players. Queer chaps! They used white walls and black balls. Philip II didn't play,

97

though — lucky for us — otherwise that little affair with the Armada might have turned out very differently. You wouldn't find a tennis-playing monarch sitting at home when his fleet sailed. He would have been in command. Think of it: a tennis-player against a bowls-player. Bound to have gone the other way.'

Innocently Angel asked why, and received an answer that went on for some minutes. From it she gathered that the strategic and tactical skill necessary to win a battle was child's play to anyone who had developed his court craft. Gustavus Adolphus was a player, she learned, as were Napoleon and the Duke of Wellington (who built his own court). To the major's intense regret 'Boney' and the Duke had never played against each other, although they had both used the Fontainebleau court. But the result of the battle of Waterloo provided conclusive evidence that the Duke was 'at least half fifteen and a bisque better.'

The silence which followed this dissertation was disturbed by another of Talbot's bombshells. 'Say, Gerry,' he began, eyeing the manuscript, a passage from which had started them on their historical enquiry, 'are you sure you've got the whole darned thing back? Mr Somebody might have frozen on to a page or two.'

This remark caused almost as much consternation as his questions earlier in the evening. The major was openly aghast, showing everyone who cared to look in his direction that, in his opinion, this finally proved his contention that foreigners could never qualify as gentlemen, however rich they might be, and even if they were champion tennis-players and had been to Oxford. Mr Pratt's face, on the other hand, remained the model of a poker-player's.

The American continued unabashed: 'And why the blue blazes don't you keep it out of sight instead of spreading it out like this in front of the whole gang of us? If you don't watch out it'll be gone again by the morning.'

'Really!' expostulated the major. 'It was brought down at my earnest request.

There's no question of its being mislaid a second time.'

'You're mighty certain,' Talbot retaliated.

'Of course I'm certain. We can all put two and two together, can't we? Why he did it I cannot conceive, though, and as things stand we must just regard it as some obscure prank. The poor fellow!'

Mlle Deschamps flashed her well-curled eye-lashes in excitement and asked, 'Do you imply, Major Winterton, that Mr Nicholls was the thief?'

The major humphed in the back of his throat in pained deprecation. 'No, no, no!' he said. 'I didn't mention the word 'thief', mademoiselle, and I hold it to be unfair to the memory of the dead man to use such a word. In this country a man is presumed innocent until he is proved guilty in a court of law. Your system in France is different, I'm aware, and I pass no comment on it. It is my belief that Nicholls took the manuscript, yes; but for what reason or with what intention it's impossible to say. Certainly it is most improper for us to assume that he intended to keep it. Rather, from the place in which it was discovered, I think we may reasonably deduce that he intended nothing of the sort.'

'It still beats me why you're so certain he was the culprit,' said Talbot persistently.

'Heavens above, man!' exploded the major. 'It's obvious, isn't it? We know he was roaming about in the middle of the night. He could easily have gone into Gerry's room. Was the door unlocked?'

Gerry nodded.

'Exactly; there you are,' the major went on, as if this proved his case. 'Nicholls bagged the manuscript when he was fuddled, carried it down to the court with him and hid it in the basket. It must have been for some kind of practical joke against Timothy, since the thing would have been found before they began playing.'

Talbot shook his head at the major reprovingly. 'The snag about your theory, major,' he said, 'is a small matter of timing. The manuscript was missing at the end of dinner, long before Nicholls started prowling. You remember that, don't you, mademoiselle?'

The Frenchwoman was startled by this sudden appeal, Angel noticed, but made an excellent job of disguising the fact. Talbot rated as no fool: his apparently direct approach was subtle, even sinister. Without so much as referring to the matter he had recalled to everyone's mind mademoiselle's departure from the dinner-table the previous evening. Angel realised that she had been underestimating the American.

Giving a curt nod, Mlle Deschamps kept silent, while Mr Pratt came to the major's assistance. 'That's true, of course,' he agreed, 'but it doesn't disprove the major's theory. I came across Nicholls wandering through the upstairs corridors before dinner last night. He was nowhere near his own room. It did cross my mind at the time to wonder what he was doing. But he plainly had such a load of alcohol under his belt that I didn't really give it much thought.'

'So that sews the whole business up neatly,' murmured Talbot. 'Nicholls took the manuscript and then slipped off the ladder. Finis.'

'That is unquestionably the situation,' said the major firmly.

'And in case any of you have any further worries about the manuscript,' announced Mr Pratt good-humouredly, 'you may like to know that Mr Montague has been issued with a key to his room for tonight. There's no drain-pipe or creeper leading up to his window, and no one can jump onto the sill from a handy piece of guttering. No doubt he will be sleeping with the valuable document under his pillow or in some other safe place. He may or may not have firearms.' Mr Pratt smiled at the company and rang the bell for night-caps.

At this moment Gavin, who was gingerly fingering the sheaf of paper with all the respect due to a valuable piece of someone else's property, remarked: 'I say, Gerry, it's in the most frightful state of chaos. How can you possibly be sure it's all here?'

'It never occurred to me to doubt it,' Gerry replied, 'until Talbot raised the question a few moments ago. I was simply worried whether any of the sheets were damaged. As you say, they're all upside down and in the wrong order, but none of them is actually torn or mutilated. Believe me, I was so relieved after I had skimmed through to find out. They were carefully wrapped before they were taken, and I was afraid they might have been roughly handled by Nicholls in his cups.'

'Well,' said Talbot, 'Lord Cheney has repeated my question. Can you be sure you've got the whole bag of tricks there?'

Gerry glanced briefly from face to face before replying. They were all tense except for Mr Pratt's. As befitted a host, he sat benevolent and relaxed. But Gerry suspected that this was the mask he wore at the crucial moment in a big deal.

'No,' he said.

'But aren't the pages numbered in any way?' asked Gavin.

'You can see for yourself there are no folio numbers. And look at the size of the pile. In print it runs into three volumes.'

'I'm surprised you didn't go right through and number each sheet when you first got it,' remarked the major, his tidy mind offended.

'When I said no,' Gerry replied, 'I meant not for the moment. Naturally I examined the whole thing carefully as soon as I'd bought it, but I decided not to mark it in any way. Instead I made some notes. With the help of those and going through the printed edition chapter by chapter I could almost certainly find out whether the manuscript is still complete. But it will take me hours and I can't do it until I get home.'

'I don't know why anyone should imagine that any of the pages are missing,' said Mr Pratt after a pause during which they all digested the implication of Gerry's remarks. 'Nicholls would have had some idea of the value of what he had taken, and there is no suggestion, surely, that he was actuated by malice.'

'Would some of the sheets have a special value on their own?' asked Talbot.

'I can't say.' Gerry frowned and

then went on: 'The importance of the manuscript lies in a certain amount of information and a number of anecdotes which were suppressed for one reason or another when it came to publication. Rumour even has it that old Featherstonehaugh invented some discreditable stories, showed them in confidence to the families concerned and made quite a good thing out of accepting considerations for keeping them out of print. He was a wily bird off the court as well as on it.'

'God bless my soul!' exclaimed the major. 'But he was a clergyman.'

'And nearly a bishop too,' nodded Gerry. 'I expect the blackmail was done very delicately as between gentlemen.'

'How many of these stories have you found?' enquired Mlle Deschamps.

'None properly so far,' said Gerry. 'I do wish I'd had time to read the thing before bringing it down here. I simply ran my eye down each page checking roughly.'

'It's my fault,' declared Mr Pratt, 'and I apologise for pressing it on you. I ought never to have asked, and you can't know how badly I feel about what has happened. But this game of yours intrigues me. I dipped into the Featherstonehaugh in the library and was told that there might be some further references to High Cheney in the original manuscript.'

Gerry stroked his moustache as an aid to thought. 'I believe there are, too,' he said. 'Didn't that business about Henry VIII and the marker have something to do with the first Lord Cheney? I'm almost sure that's where that story caught my eye.'

'It's no use asking us anything, old boy,' said the major.

'I thought Gavin might know about it.'

Gavin's response to the appeal was to turn pink. 'I honestly can't say,' he answered vaguely. 'Mother would know if anyone did. She's the one for family history, you know.'

'Well, never mind about it now,' said Mr Pratt, as the butler entered with a decanter and glasses, followed by one of the maids carrying a tea-tray. 'The manuscript needs thoroughly sorting out, I can see, and it's too late tonight to start hunting for references and comparing passages with the book. When you've had time to put it all in apple-pie order and study it, I hope you'll forgive me and satisfy my curiosity.'

'There's nothing to forgive,' Gerry assured him. 'You can't be held responsible for what was probably nothing more than a piece of mischievousness.'

'You are still reckoning,' persisted Talbot, 'that you have the whole manuscript there. What if you haven't?'

Mr Pratt looked annoyed, but said nothing.

Gerry hesitated. 'If it should materialise that some part of it is missing, however small,' he announced, 'I'm sure everyone will understand that this would invalidate our agreement about nothing more being heard of the matter. I should feel obliged to place it in the hands of the police.'

'That,' said Mr Pratt, 'might cause us all a lot of trouble in connection with Nicholls' death. However, despite Mr Talbot's doubts, I'm convinced it won't be necessary. Angel, will you pour out a cup of tea for Mlle Deschamps unless she wants anything stronger? And perhaps the gentlemen would like to help themselves to whisky. All the usual trimmings should be there, including some ice for our American friend. Now will you excuse me for a few minutes while I give the servants instructions for the morning?'

Mr Pratt left the room, and attention was turned to the less controversial subject of liquid refreshment. With a shudder at the prospect of drinking tea at all, let alone late in the evening, the Frenchwoman opted for a small whisky and went over to join the men. Angel, alone with her cup of tea, sat down beside the temporarily deserted manuscript and looked with interest at the spidery clerical writing on the top sheet.

'Etiquette,' she read. 'It is etiquette for you as a player:

(1) Not to force for the Dedans when you are between the Net and the Line of the Last Gallery on the Hazard side, unless you (a) send a Boasted Force or (b) are taking a Service or

(c) are absolutely sure that you will not hit the ball near your opponent.

N.B. — The modern tendency to force straight from close to the Net is despicable. Some Courts have a positive rule against such ungentlemanly conduct.

(2) Not to serve before your opponent is ready.

(3) Not to baulk your opponent in any way: for example, by delaying before you serve.

(4) Not to swear, or use objectionable language, which will include any expression of anger at the decision of the Marker or Referee.

(5) Not to refuse to take proper Odds.'

Angel was fascinated. What pious words from a hypocritical old Christian blackmailer! So this was the sort of thing all their guests were going goofy about. Would she really catch the bug too when she'd had a few lessons from Ted?

Her father returned to the room breathing rather more heavily than usual, Angel noticed, and carrying a file of papers under his arm. He took in the room at a glance and moved briskly to his daughter's side.

'Angel my dear,' he said, 'you shouldn't sip tea and look at Mr Montague's manuscript at the same time. You might spill a drop and stain the pages. Here let me — '

He leaned across her as though to move the cup and saucer. Instead he knocked the top sheets of paper off the pile onto the floor and dropped his file at the same time. Loose papers shot out of the file on top of the manuscript sheets on the carpet.

'Whoops! Sorry,' he cried, hastily grabbing the cup of tea and transferring it to another table. 'Very careless of me, but no harm done. We don't want any more trouble with this blessed manuscript. I think Mr Montague had better take it away and lock it up before it suffers any further mishap.'

He assisted Angel in picking up the sheets and allowed Gerry, who had hurried over, to satisfy himself that they all went onto the pile on the table, while the other papers were replaced in Mr Pratt's file. When they had finished Gerry bore his property away with him, bidding the company a terse good-night on the way out.

Angel stood regarding her father with dark and ill-concealed suspicion. He was also the object of other inquisitive looks, but seemed quite oblivious of them.

'Now this is what I was bringing in to show you,' he said, spreading the papers all over the table. Ostentatiously he emptied the folder so that everyone could see that it contained nothing belonging to Gerry Montague as a result of the recent confusion. 'These are the original drawings for the tennis court, with all the dimensions and elevations.'

'By Jove, isn't that interesting?' The major sat down agog to examine them in detail. He made exclamations of surprise as he turned them over: 'Floor length 98 feet! That must make it the longest court in the country — only a foot or so short of the old Fontainebleau one. Aha! And the tambour's two feet five inches, is it? I reckoned it must be narrow.'

While he became absorbed, the others uttered polite expressions of interest and one by one retired to bed. The last of the guests to go was Mlle Deschamps, who appeared to be lingering in the hope of a private word with her host; but he showed no sign of moving from the major's elbow, and the major was evidently set for a long session.

'Good-night, Mr Pratt.' In crossing to the door she paused to thrust a shapely arm in his direction. He took her hand in his and gave the back of it a hearty peck, at the same time bending low to make a show of Gallic courtesy.

'Bon soir, mademoiselle,' he enunciated in a Churchillian accent. 'Or, since I'm old enough to be your father, might I call you — '

'Emilienne,' she replied scarcely above a whisper. She glanced sidelong at the major, who was to all appearances engrossed, muttering to himself about the width of the grille bandeau.

'After this evening, mon cher Monsieur Pratt,' she added softly, 'you may count me as one of your admirers. Bon soir.'

'And me as one of yours, Emilienne,' he countered gallantly, opening the door for her and planting a quick, wet kiss on her cheek as she passed through.

7

An air of disuse hung over the library. On three sides of the room the spines of the morocco bindings formed a solid, cheerless phalanx from floor to ceiling. His eye ran over the M's. Molière, Mommsen, Motley: they were respectable names, stirring even — but plainly unread. In an access of suspicion Talbot even pulled out a volume or two at random to make sure that real books lurked behind the gold-tooled lettering.

He sat himself down in the one comfortable chair and read Nicholls' obituary in the morning paper. Credited to 'our own tennis correspondent', it was a warm and erudite appreciation of the old champion — his life, his play, his place in the history and development of the game. The brief introductory phrases — 'died yesterday at High Cheney aged fifty-eight, his long and distinguished tennis career terminating fatally, as he would perhaps have wished, on court' — were discretion itself. The notice concluded with a personal anecdote: 'Only the day before his untimely death the great champion told your correspondent, in all modesty, that he had been playing tennis for forty-five years and believed that he now knew 'about half of it'. *Sic transit victor ludorum*.' Gerry had done Old Nick proud.

In the library sepulchral quiet prevailed, no sound penetrating from the rest of the house. Most of the other guests had already left, and Talbot himself was due to go before lunch. Before doing so he wanted to see more of Angel. At breakfast, on asking for prunes, he had been snubbed by the butler for the third morning running, much to her amusement.

'I'm so sorry, Mr Talbot,' she had apologised. 'Mummy specially ordered some of your dried prunes from the village stores on Saturday, but your Abbots Cheney representative is not earning his keep. They were quite unobtainable.'

He had promised jocularly to order his European general manager over from Paris to open up the Abbots Cheney market in person. Then he had suggested a stroll in the grounds, but she had pleaded an appointment to go riding.

While recalling this he left the armchair and found himself circling the room, eyeing the shelves again. What was he after? Yes, of course — the Featherstonehaugh. The books being arranged in strict alphabetical order, the hunt was soon over and the handsome dark-red Volume I of The Annals of The Royal Game of Tennis lay in his hands. He turned to the title-page, where the subtitle read: 'An historical enquiry into the King of Games and Game of Kings' (so that was where the major had picked up the slogan) 'containing many Curiosities concerning Tennis and Tennis-players, by the Reverend Samuel Featherstonehaugh MA, Fellow of St John's College, Oxford, sometime holder of the James Street Silver Racket.' The gentleman himself was shown in a sepia frontispiece, a resplendent beard almost hiding his clerical collar, a racket in his hand, and a positively unholy glint in his eye.

Talbot read a page or two and learned that on the first of May 1802 Joseph Barcellon of Paris beat Philip Cox of London, although conceding fifteen for two bisques, and thereby won a hundred guineas; which couldn't have been peanuts in those days. Another passage informed him that Charles IX of France, on being interrupted at tennis on the twenty-second of August 1572 by the news of the assassination of Coligny, had exclaimed, 'Par La Mort Dieu! Will they then never leave me at peace?' A monarch after the major's own heart!

There was no index in the first volume, so he turned to the chapter headings to look up the references to High Cheney. These were shown as falling in Volume II, but the shelf revealed nothing but a gap between Vols I and III.

The gap annoyed him. Maybe there was nothing particularly sinister about Volume II being missing; in fact it could be argued that, of the whole collection of books in the room, this was the most likely one to be in use. Even Mlle Deschamps hardly looked a Molière fan; despite his special interest in history the major was unlikely to spend his spare moments on the rise of the Dutch republic; and as for Mommsen . . .

Nevertheless, in his moment of annoyance Talbot suddenly decided not to leave England until the events of the weekend had been unravelled to his satisfaction. Something fishy was going on — he was pretty sure of that; and he was darn well going to bring it out into the open.

As a first step he decided to search out young Ted Nicholls. This would kill two birds with one stone, since he was in need of exercise. He would have a couple of sets with the boy and then pump him and snoop around the court a little. Perhaps he would meet up with Angel, too.

But when he reached the tennis-court building the door was locked. He rattled the handle impatiently. No sound of movement came from inside. Preparing to return to the house, he met Ted coming along the path.

'Just the man I'm looking for,' Talbot hailed him. 'I need one helluva good hard single to work a weekend's overeating out of my system. You can take half thirty, and five pounds if you win.'

'It can't be done, sir,' said Ted, crestfallen, 'Mr Pratt has forbidden the court to be used.'

'That's because he figured we'd all be leaving right after breakfast. Just you nip over and tell him I've asked for a game before I go.'

Ted shook his head. 'It won't work. The old man's in a mood, I can tell you. He's even taken my key away.'

'You mean you can't get into the court yourself?'

'That's right. I'm on my way to help out with a bit of gardening. Sweeping up leaves, I shouldn't be surprised. Still, if you're on the payroll you've got to do what you're told and there's no point in moping. Ask him for the key yourself if you like — I'd be glad of a game, Mr Talbot. But you won't get it. I know him when he's in one of his moods.'

'Of course I'll ask him,' said Talbot sharply. 'And I don't understand what you mean by his moods. He's very hospitable and you shouldn't talk about your boss like that.'

This drew Ted into justifying himself; as Talbot had intended. 'Hospitable!' he exclaimed viciously. 'Maybe, but he's a proper bastard to me. Bawls me out for this, that and the other all the time. You can't make the sort of money he's made if you're nice. I'd have left after a week if the pay hadn't been so good. Now I don't know what to do. They might give me Father's job in London, I suppose.'

'Mr Pratt bawled you out on Saturday night, didn't he?'

'How do you know?' Ted was instantly cautious. 'Were you listening?'

'As a matter of fact I was,' admitted Talbot. 'You don't think I went back to bed after chasing you, do you? With that poor girl all by herself in the court.'

'Miss Angel's a brick. I won't have a word said against her.' Ted suddenly became pugnacious. 'And if you repeat anything I've said about Mr Pratt I'll deny it.'

'That's okay,' Talbot assured him. 'I agree about Miss Pratt and I've no interest in repeating what you said. All I want to do is to find out what happened on Saturday night or early on Sunday morning that you haven't told anyone yet. You're holding something back, aren't you?'

Ted thought for a moment, shuffling his feet on the gravel. 'How much is it worth?' he asked.

'A hundred pounds if it's important,' replied Talbot without a second's hesitation. His father had instilled into him early in life that if you want something in this world you've got to pay for it, and 'if you need it bad you'd better pay good.' The Talbot Californian Dried Prune Corporation was a fair-sized testimonial to the effectiveness of this philosophy.

Ted looked startled at first, then crafty. 'Tax free!' he muttered. 'But who's to say whether it's important?'

'We can agree on that, I guess. And if

it's really important there'll be a bonus.'

Greed shone through the boy's eyes. He couldn't be more than eighteen, Talbot estimated: a short, shifty lad with the impossible handicap of being a great man's son. According to the obituary, his mother had died when he was born.

'What do you know already?' he asked.

'After you beat it,' said Talbot, 'I tailed Miss Pratt back to the house without her knowing. She was so scared, poor kid, that if I'd said 'Pardon me' she'd have kicked the bucket. Then I saw her come back to the court with her old man. I was going to offer to help when the funny stuff about removing the bottles started, so I lay doggo. Then you showed up again. What made you do that?'

'I . . . I'd rather not say.'

'That's mighty unBritish, I must say, when I've gone clean through my own programme for free.' Talbot jingled a few coins in his pockets enticingly.

A struggle was in progress inside Ted, and the American waited confidently for cupidity to win. Ted was a weak character, sometimes ingratiating, sometimes aggressive, but always with a watery eye on the main chance. He was a worm, Talbot reckoned, but one capable of turning.

'When are you leaving, Mr Talbot?' he asked at last, reverting to his Uriah Heep voice.

'Right now if I can't organise myself onto this darned court.'

'If we play I'll tell you after the game, but Mr Pratt's sure not to part with the key. If you give me your address in London I can find you there.'

'I'll be putting up at the Savoy. But don't leave it too long, sonny, otherwise I'll be back home in the States by the time you feel a yen for that hundred pounds. The offer's not open indefinitely.' He walked off slowly and glanced back before turning the corner of the building.

Ted watched him with the expression of a man staring at a gold-mine disappearing from sight. He was biting his lip and made as if to speak.

Talbot stopped in his tracks. 'Two hundred if it's real good,' he called out.

With something between a sob and a moan Ted vanished in the direction of the house, leaving Talbot cursing himself for not having made it three hundred and brought the deal off. He moved on round the corner reflectively and was halted by a voice.

'Good morning to the Ivy League,' it said.

On a wooden seat under an oak-tree sat Mlle Deschamps. A pad of drawing paper lay on her knee, and she gave the impression of being busily engaged in sketching the landscape in front of her, nine-tenths of which, Talbot noted, was not the English countryside but the tennis court.

'Or are you from Missouri?' she laughed.

'Neither, but a bit of both, I guess,' he laughed. 'You've been to the States?'

'From time to time I am there. On business.'

'Is it in order for me to ask what kind of business? To judge from that professional drawing, you might be an architect.' He peered closely over her shoulder at a detailed pencil sketch of the tennis court. Abruptly she snapped the pad shut.

'One may always ask,' she said.

'In that case,' he went on, ignoring the rebuff, 'there's another question I would rather put. The only thing anyone here seems to know about you is that you are a very charming person who doesn't have much knowledge of tennis. What I would like to be told — although it's none of my business — is what in the name of glory you're doing here at all.'

'Thank you for the 'charming',' she said; 'and your question is easy to answer. My father is a good friend of the President of our tennis confederation — the Major Winterton of France, you may say. At short notice the President himself was unable to come — through indisposition. He could not quickly find a substitute from his committee and asked me if I would be his representative. I was delighted to oblige him and visit this beautiful place. But naturally I would not wish to reveal that I have little familiarity with *le jeu de paume*.'

126

'Naturally.'

'But since you are so inquisitive — curiosity is an American characteristic, is it not? — and because I believe Mr Pratt has been telephoning to Paris this morning to unmask me, I have no objection to sharing my little secret with you. I was above all pleased to come here because antiquities enchant me. This house, its furnishings, its setting, the tennis court, as you see — they all fascinate me. My father and I are art dealers, and these things mean much to us.' While producing this item of information she was watching closely how it affected him.

'Uh-huh,' he said dead-pan, casually taking a penny from his pocket and seeing whether he could throw it over the oaktree. This gambit was in conformity with another of Talbot senior's precepts, emphasising the advantages to be gained by doing something unexpected to conceal one's reactions.

'Darned great cartwheels,' he murmured, as his thoughts worked over what the Frenchwoman had said. 'At least we know our cents and centimes aren't worth anything, but the English still have delusions of grandeur about their currency. I assume a penny bought something once, but it's not worth the wear and tear on the pockets of one's pants these days.' He took out another one and threw it after the first. 'So you're an art dealer. Would my native curiosity allow me to ask, without being too rude, whether you're here primarily on business or pleasure?'

'Talking to you is a pleasure,' she smiled. 'But my journey is not entirely one of pleasure. I have business to do in London.'

'I guess I mustn't grumble,' he replied: 'that's all the answer I deserve. But let me tell you what's eating me. Outside of America I've never met such a bunch of frank, open individuals: Mr Pratt — a blunt man of affairs; Lady Cheney — outspoken if anyone could ever be called that; Major Winterton — not a person to mince words; friendly young folk like Angel, Gerry and Cheney; and, of course, your charming self. Yet I've a hunch, which is rapidly expanding into a complex, that I'm the only one who doesn't know what's going on round here.'

'Indeed?'

'Indeed indeed. Why, right now I became so desperate that I even offered young Ted £200 for some information — and didn't get it.'

'Indeed!' repeated the Frenchwoman. 'What information?'

'Just the full facts about Saturday night.'

Emilienne Deschamps put the pad under her arm and stood up. She had a fine fleshy figure and was not above flaunting it. 'You are not as ignorant as you would have me believe.'

'I most certainly am,' protested Talbot. 'You can have no idea how ignorant I am.'

'No one here is completely ignorant,' she replied. 'Some know precisely what they are looking for; others don't. That is the only difference. Perhaps you are in the second category.'

'Nope.' Talbot was emphatic. 'Not

even that. But I'd be glad to join you in whichever category you're in.'

She moved away. 'You must excuse me,' she said. 'We are both business people and you can hardly suppose that I would give away information freely when you have a moment ago told me that you are offering money for it.'

'Okay,' he said. 'How much?'

The Frenchwoman laughed softly and unpleasantly. 'The stakes are too high for — what do they call it? — chicken-feed, my dear friend. Excuse me please. I wish to view the inside of the court once more before I leave for London.'

But before she could go Mr Pratt had joined them. Dressed in country-squire tweeds, he was carrying a double-barrelled shot-gun and looked decidedly menacing. Now the weekend was over the benign host had vanished with it.

'You have your own transport, I think, Mr Talbot,' he said without preamble. 'Or my car is taking Mlle Deschamps to the station in a few minutes if you care to make use of it.'

'That's kind of you, but I have a hired

car. And if Mlle Deschamps is making for London I'd be honoured to have her come along with me.'

'Thank you,' she said shortly, 'but my arrangements are made.'

'As you wish.' Talbot turned back to Mr Pratt. 'I was on the point of coming to hunt you out. Before going I want to have a last game with Ted, and he tells me that you have the key.'

'The court is closed,' said Mr Pratt. 'I'm sorry, but there it is.'

Talbot flushed and mentally confirmed the decision he had taken in the library. 'That's ridiculous,' he said.

By contrast Mr Pratt became icy. 'I'm advised the top gallery may not be secure. There has been one accident already and I cannot risk another.'

'But we played there yesterday, after the accident, and there was nothing wrong then.' By jiminy, thought Talbot, Ted was right about him being an old s.o.b.

'It has been examined since.' Mr Pratt's tone was arctic.

'There can be no objection, I presume,'

131

interposed Mlle Deschamps, 'to my having a quick farewell look round the inside of the building.' She gave him a soft feminine look calculated to remind him of the previous night's kiss.

'There can and is,' snapped Mr Pratt, recognising the look and rejecting it out of hand. 'I have no wish to be inhospitable, but some City associates of mine are arriving before lunch for an important and confidential conference. I must request you both to leave without delay.'

'That's plain enough,' Talbot snapped back. 'And if I ever doubted there was something here which needed looking into I don't doubt it now. You needn't think you can push us all out like this. I know where I'm going now.'

'I don't care a brass farthing where you're going, and if you are threatening me you'd better watch your step. That goes for you too, Emilienne' — here Mr Pratt rounded on the Frenchwoman — 'worming your way into my house under false pretences. I've found out a thing or two about you all right, and

I'm asking Major Winterton to write to the French tennis authorities for an explanation. You're up to plenty of games I daresay, but tennis doesn't happen to be one of them.'

Together the three of them marched across the handsome lawns, for all the world like a gamekeeper escorting two poachers off the premises. It even occurred to Talbot to wonder whether Mr Pratt's gun was loaded and if so whether a discharge in the right direction would be lethal. On reaching the house he made for his bedroom to collect his belongings and be gone.

The stone porch outside the front door was supported by fluted Corinthian columns. Under it Mr Pratt's Rolls was waiting with the Frenchwoman's luggage aboard. The chauffeur opened the door and stood with an astrakhan rug over one arm. It was a Hollywood scene of life in rural England.

In the act of climbing in, she turned. Her handsome bosom was heaving with pent-up hatred, but she controlled herself.

'Thank you for such an interesting

weekend, Alfred,' she said in sugary tones. 'It is Alfred, isn't it?'

'Not to you it isn't,' he retorted sharply, ending the brief flirtation with a bang.

'You low-bred pig,' she exploded, and suddenly spat onto the tiles at his feet. Some spots landed on the toecap of one of his boots. Instinctively he raised the barrel of his gun.

8

'Why come to me? No doubt they have told you I am mad.'

Lady Cheney sat very upright and spoke with dignity and composure. She was wearing a deep purple dress, a closefitting hat and a three-string pearl necklace. Despite the mild weather a fire blazed in the hearth and the room felt stuffy. Talbot wondered what the reaction would be if he were to ask permission to take his jacket off. She might stalk out of the room in a huff, or she might tell him brusquely that he could take off anything he liked for all she cared. He decided not to risk it.

They were sitting in the first-floor drawing room of the Cheney dower-house. The windows gave a wide view of the park and a glimpse of the tennis-court roof. A mellow Queen Anne building standing on the outskirts of the village, this was as far as Lady Cheney could be induced to move after the estate had been sold.

Talbot had come here on an impulse directly after his eviction by Mr Pratt. Though small, the house certainly had style about it. An iron gate with a gilt monogram led into the garden; the lawns and dahlia beds were well-kept; white paint gleamed from the outside wood-work, except the front door, which was a shiny black. Even to an alien's eye there were indications of class as well as money. What had surprised him was a large brass notice on the door proclaiming: 'No solicitors'. He knew that the English equivalent of this American sign was 'no hawkers', solicitors in England being people you couldn't afford to insult.

Shown upstairs by a middle-aged female retainer, he had been received by Lady Cheney as though expected, and a decanter of sherry on a silver tray appeared almost before he was seated. She brushed aside the conventional preliminaries, and he asked her straight out who she thought was responsible for the unauthorised borrowing of the Featherstonehaugh manuscript.

When she said, 'they have told you I am mad,' she stressed the 'they' so heavily that he wondered whether 'they' were right and she was suffering from a persecution mania. He hastened to deny that anyone had told him anything about her.

'Perhaps it is true,' she insisted. 'I have been in homes, don't you know.'

'I didn't,' he replied. 'I hope you are better now.'

'Better!' Having brought him out in the open, she rounded on him. 'There has never been anything wrong with me. Never!'

'I can see that,' he said hastily. Not that he could see anything of the kind. But if provoked she might even start throwing the china around, and the room was cluttered with bowls and small bric-à-brac and Chinese temple dragons of all sizes.

'Far be it from me,' she said, 'to lower this country in the estimation of one who is — well, not an outsider but, shall we say, a blood-relation.' She broke off. 'You are Irish, are you not?'

'My family came from Ireland, yes ma'am.'

She muttered something suspiciously like 'poor boy', but drowned it in a gulp of sherry.

'It grieves me to tell you this, but our country has fallen into the hands of lawyers. No one is safe from them. Not content with robbing us of High Cheney, almost stripping the clothes off our backs in their anxiety to hand everything over to that Cockney money-grubber — who paid them well for it, I don't doubt; not content with this, they had the impudence when I stood upon my rights, to suggest that I must be out of my mind and have me trundled off to what they call a rest cure. That is the phrase: a rest cure. Couldn't even call a lunatic asylum by its proper name.'

With a sniff of derision she handed him a silver box containing Turkish cigarettes. He refused and lit up a Camel from his own pack. 'Lord Cheney stood by you, I'm sure,' he said.

'Gavin did what he could, naturally, and they were forced to release me after a few weeks. But he was a minor at the time and they took him in with their stories. All estates in England are run by lawyers nowadays, Mr Talbot: dukes are allowed pocket money out of their own income. These men call themselves trustees and executors and fancy names like that. But that does not mean they are to be trusted or that they look after anyone's interest but their own. Once upon a time lawyers and doctors and such like were kept in their place. They used the servants' entrance and one did not invite them into the drawing room any more than one would invite the butcher. Now they are the masters, and we who should be running the country are reduced to this.'

With a sweep of the arm she expressed total destitution. Talbot followed the gesture — from a Ming vase to a Boule desk and back across the Persian carpet to the pearls round her neck. She was still a little way from the bread line.

'It's a terrible state of affairs,' he

sympathised, 'and if it's any consolation things are the same way in my country. Believe me, you're sane enough, countess.'

This was graciously received. She nodded, pleased, and returned to his original question. 'Mr Pratt took the manuscript. Whom else would you suppose?'

'What makes you so certain?'

'He asked for the manuscript to be brought. He had an interest in the contents. He is a criminal type. He was even noticed returning the last pages in a clumsy way, so Gavin tells me. What do you imagine he bought High Cheney for?'

'As an investment, I reckon, or an advertisement.'

'Young man,' she declared, vigorously jerking her head at him: 'Young man, you know very little. You will be telling me next that you believe the cock-and-bull story of Nicholls falling off the ladder. You who made so courageous a stand yesterday evening! I admired you very much, Mr Talbot, if you will permit me to say so. That is why I am talking to you so frankly now.'

Talbot took leave, privately, to doubt this last statement. He could imagine no circumstances in which Lady Cheney would fail to speak frankly. But he appreciated the compliment and said so.

'That evil Cockney money-lender' (she was speaking less sedately now) 'or whatever he is — he is not even an honest manufacturer, it seems, but merely juggles with other people's money — he deliberately pulled or pushed that unfortunate tennis-player to his death. Of that there can be no doubt. And you and I must be the ones to see that he is punished. I believe,' she added with a glint, 'if there is robbery in it he can still be hanged.'

'If that's the case, shouldn't you telephone the police right now?'

'The police!' As soon as she uttered the words Talbot knew that they belonged alongside the lawyers and doctors. 'They positively eat out of that man's hand. No doubt he pays them well. They cannot be called in without irrefutable evidence. And it won't be easy to obtain. Mr

Pratt is a clever man. Look at the way he invited me for this weekend, in the hope that I would lead him to what he is looking for! No; we must do what we can do without the police, and while we are doing it we shall need to be very careful. One or two more 'accidental' deaths would be of no great consequence to our friend.'

'You implied just now that he had been in goal. Is he a known convict then?'

'It is not generally known — and perhaps not by the local police — but he and his wife (if she is his wife) have both been in prison.'

Talbot stubbed out his cigarette and sucked through his teeth reflectively. 'What you say certainly confirms my own suspicions. That man is a shady operator if ever I saw one.'

'Then it may also interest you to learn — the sherry is on the table; thank you, I will — that there are some very peculiar clauses in the deeds relating to the sale of High Cheney.'

'Such as?'

'Such as this. Mr Pratt bought not

only the house, the park and the farms and other buildings on the estate, but all the furnishings and movables belonging to the family. Except the few Gavin and I managed to remove from his reach. The lawyer's jargon about goods and chattels covered every single Cheney possession in or on the estate at the time of purchase, whether known or unknown. They tried to stop me reading it all. Said I wouldn't understand.'

'I see,' said Talbot; though he didn't.

'However,' Lady Cheney went on, 'I read it attentively enough to notice also that it was Mr Pratt's company which was buying the estate, but Mr Pratt personally who was purchasing the goods and chattels. And at an absurdly low figure.'

'I see,' said Talbot again; and this time he was beginning to. 'But didn't your lawyers object to any of these provisions?'

Lady Cheney pursed her lips. 'They said that the overall price was so satisfactory it would be unwise to object to anything. They said, too, that the arrangements between Mr Pratt and his company were no concern of ours. I pointed out more than once that the clause about Cheney possessions known and unknown was intolerable and should have been struck out.' She banged her glass down on a console-table. 'They took no notice of me — for reasons you can guess.'

'You mean . . . ?'

'I certainly do. There is an odious modern phrase for it: money talks.'

'If I gather the gist of this rightly, countess, you believe there is some valuable heirloom on the premises?'

Lady Cheney greeted the question with an arrogant stare which reminded him of a Beacon Hill mandarin. Indeed, here sat the prototype of all those toffee-nosed New Englanders his great-grandfather had worked for. Yet he was developing quite a fellow feeling for her, scatty or not. She didn't daunt him; after all, Oxford had introduced him to this sort of thing, and he was conscious that the Talbots could buy up all the Cheneys had left several times over and not notice it. And they had a common bond: they both had it in for Pratt.

Evidently the prolonged stare had ended in a favourable judgment. She had decided to trust him.

'You must promise me,' she commanded, ' — and since you were at Oxford they say, I know I can rely on your word as a gentleman — not to pass on this information to anyone. Anyone at all.'

He promised and she went on: 'Before the Reformation High Cheney was an abbey. The estate and the abbey treasure were both given by the Crown to the first Lord Cheney. Some people who are jealous of the family say that he had no right to the treasure, but that is malicious gossip. He was the royal commissioner and entitled to the reward for his services.' A thought struck her. 'You are not a Roman Catholic I trust, Mr Talbot?'

'You trust wrong,' he corrected her, 'I am a Catholic — but a bad one. You won't offend me.'

Lady Cheney grunted and continued,

but more guardedly. 'When it was not in use in the sanctuary the treasure was kept in safe custody in the abbot's lodgings. After the dissolution the family continued the tradition of keeping it concealed on the same spot. No one else knew this of course, but it went on even after the original building had disappeared. Do you follow me?' She shot him a sharp, searching glance.

'Certainly I follow you. This is the reason you've been paying such close attention to Mr Pratt's activities since he came to live at High Cheney. You think he is looking for the treasure and if you can anticipate him and cart it off the premises secretly it will belong to you and not him. That is, if there is really any treasure left.'

This summary proved too candid for Lady Cheney. She specialised in candour herself but relished it less in others.

'There is not the slightest doubt about the treasure being there,' she snapped, 'nor about whom it belongs to. None at all.'

'How come he's taking so much time

then? He hasn't started digging anywhere yet so far as I saw.'

'You are not as quick-witted as I took you for, Mr Talbot,' she reprimanded him. Rising, she beckoned him to the window and they surveyed the early autumnal scene. The leaves had barely begun to turn, and the park was exhibiting a lush variety of greens. 'There!' she gesticulated.

Talbot bestirred his Irish blood. He wasn't a great one for landscape, but obligingly agreed that nothing as green as that could be other than beautiful — only to have his head bitten off.

'Idiot!' she exclaimed. 'The tennis court! Don't you see it through the trees? It is on the site of the abbot's lodgings. Why do you suppose there has been all this fuss about tennis? Do you think for one instant that a man like that would entertain the smallest interest in a ball game unless he had some financial motive in the background? Why do you imagine he came to live in the house instead of pulling it down? If you had the millions of pounds he is reputed to be worth you would choose somewhere more comfortable than High Cheney, wouldn't you? A slum boy from the back streets of the East End can have no feeling for the history or grandeur of a place like this. If he had he would be ashamed of defiling it with his presence.' She blew her nose with a masculine amount of noise and sat down.

He ignored the rhetorical questions. 'Since I'm so slow-witted, Lady Cheney,' he said, 'would you tell me why Mr Pratt should go to the trouble of restoring the tennis court instead of pulling it down and excavating the site?'

'That has puzzled me,' she admitted. 'He must have come across some clue, otherwise he would never have developed an interest in the tennis court at all. It was built in the last century by the eighth earl, who was said to be eccentric. That is how he was described by the common people. In the light of Mr Pratt's activities one must conclude that he has reason to believe that the eighth earl had a repository built into the fabric of the court, and he is frightened of demolition in case it is never found or the contents are stolen by a workman while his back is turned. When the restoration was being carried out he haunted the place, I can assure you. The murder of Nicholls makes two things plain: that the treasure is there all right, and Mr Pratt has still not discovered it.'

'That squares with his closing the court and turning so rude.'

'Rudeness is native to him, but he uses it for a purpose. Also he works fast. If he closed the court this morning, he will have a barbed wire entanglement round it tomorrow and trenches the day after. I have taken you into my confidence, Mr Talbot, and we must act at once.'

'We? What about your son? Won't he help you?'

'Gavin, I regret to say, is impressionable and easily imposed upon. It has been a Cheney failing for several generations now. He places too much reliance on other people's words. The lawyers have persuaded him that the treasure no longer exists, and he is too young and good-natured to understand other people's villainy. He is still in the village, but he intends to return to London today and I despair of making him see the seriousness of the situation. You must have been sent by Providence.'

'Whatever it is must be mighty valuable to interest a man worth all that money. What have you in mind that I should do?'

'There is only one thing to be done. To break into the court, find the treasure and bring it here.'

Talbot rubbed his chin. 'Three questions occur to me,' he said, 'or rather, four. One, would it be theft? Two, where do I look? Three, what am I looking for? And four, why the hell should I do it anyway?'

'Kindly do not use that sort of language,' Lady Cheney replied. 'It is quite unnecessary. And you can dismiss from your mind any idea that handing family heirlooms to the family could be called theft. Mr Pratt can have no claim once the articles are this side of the lodge gates.'

'Unless he were to claim that they were

discovered on his property.'

'Which he would not be able to prove,' she answered crisply. 'As for where you look, the eighth earl was a tennis-player and so are you. I don't understand these grilles and tambours and what they are for, but he may have taken advantage of the peculiarities of the court. The top gallery which Nicholls was making for is the most likely place. What you are looking for I need hardly describe to a Roman Catholic. Only one individual item is known: Pope Boniface's chalice, given to the abbey by the Pope in gratitude for the abbot's assistance in securing his release from the Tower of London. He was imprisoned there many years before he became Pope, and the abbot responsible had died. But he remembered the abbey with this gift, which was famous throughout Europe. It is made of gold with a giant ruby embedded in the stem.'

'Wow!' Talbot exclaimed. 'Gold chalices and giant rubies! At last I can understand what everyone is getting so steamed up about. Miss Deschamps was right. She said the stakes were high.'

'The French hussy! Does she know?' demanded Lady Cheney.

'It's a certainty she knows something. She's an art dealer and she didn't come for the tennis. When was this chalice last seen?'

'It has not been seen outside the family since the Reformation. But there have been a number of references to its being in our possession, the last as recently as 1745.'

1745 was not Talbot's idea of recent, but he let it pass.

Lady Cheney was expressing some anxiety about Mlle Deschamps. 'This makes it all the more important to act now.' She became emphatic. 'You will do it, won't you, as soon as it is dark? And since you are a Roman Catholic I promise that Gavin and I will sell the chalice to the Vatican if they want it. There! Does that give you an inducement?'

Talbot laughed. 'It might help in the confessional,' he said.

9

Something glittered in the night — a gleam which vanished as soon as seen. Talbot pulled up short and peered uneasily in front of him. A breeze was rustling the leaves; nothing else broke the dark silence.

He had climbed the wall which ran round the park, choosing a point at some distance from the main gates and lodges. With the aid of a flash-light bought in the village that afternoon he snaked his way in and out of a copse. At every step twigs cracked under his feet like rifle fire. But he pressed on, confident of having that outlying province of the Pratt domain to himself.

Now, without daring to use the torch any more, he had skirted the lake and could not be far from the tennis court. The night was so black that he began to wonder whether he would be able to locate it. He was wearing a dark-blue sweater, grey flannels and tennis shoes. The shoes were glaringly white, but on balance the best of his available footwear for the job.

An empty haversack was slung on his back. If his mission turned out to be successful the loot could go in there and he would still have both hands free for climbing or an emergency. On reflection he had turned down the idea of bringing a largesize spanner from the boot of his car. He was in fairly good athletic trim and packed a useful punch; in case of trouble he would rely on natural resources. In fact, while stealing along the path he had been thinking how much he would like to squelch a fist into Mr Pratt's flabby features. He wouldn't be averse, even, to a quick jab of the knee into the folds of that outsize paunch.

He stood stock-still and alert until his eyes started to prick with the strain, but the cause of the gleam remained a mystery. He racked his brains to recall what it might be. The seat la Deschamps had been sitting on in the morning was not metallic, he was pretty sure of that.

And he wasn't quite at the court itself; otherwise there would have been some indication of the bulk of the walls. The only other possibility which occurred to him was that it might be the glint in a bovine eye belonging to one of the herd of grazing cattle astray from the other side of the lake.

Should he edge forward or should he risk the torch, which he had been determined not to use once he was out of the trees? The light would be visible from the house, but was it likely to be noticed in the small hours?

After a few seconds' thought he switched on the torch. No sooner had he done so than he drew in his breath in amazement and snapped it hurriedly off. Then he squatted on his haunches for a session of more concentrated thought. Lady Cheney was more of a prophetess than he had bargained for. A fence stretched across his path — a fence which had not been there that morning. The wire was not barbed, but now that his ear was nearer the ground he could hear in the distance a soft, ominous ticking which told him that the strands were electrified. He flashed the light on a second time. Even for someone of his height, the top strand was too high to be certain of jumping it without catching a foot as one went over. The bottom strand was too low for him to roll underneath without touching it; and a middle one effectively prevented any climbing through.

The wily old rogue! After following cautiously round the entire circumference of the fence and satisfying himself that the court was well and truly sealed off, Talbot ruefully handed it to Mr Pratt for a mighty slick operation. If anyone asked what it was in aid of, he would be sure to have some pat story about stopping a prize short-horn from knocking its head against one of the tennis-court walls. Gloomily Talbot tried to guess how many volts Mr Pratt had arranged to send through the wires. If they were not going to give him more than a mild shock he would clamber through and to hell with it, but he had a nasty inkling that his former host was the sort of man to have hotted up the normal through-put.

Should he give up? Why should he of all people get involved in plucking the Cheney chestnuts out of Mr Pratt's fire — chestnuts that rightly belonged to the Church in any case? Wasn't he simply being used as a stooge by that old ramrod of a countess? He had taken up her suggestion on impulse, just for the hell of it. What was it to do with him anyway?

He decided, first, that he was being a sucker and, secondly, that he was darned if he would give up. For better or worse, he wasn't the giving-up type. There were two courses open: either to take a flying jump at the fence and hope for luck or to nose out something to climb on and drop down the other side. He must have done higher high jumps in his day, but under more favourable conditions — and without an electrified crossbar.

An idea occurred to him. He made his way back to the bench, which he had passed on his circumambulation. It had proved to be wooden, and he now tipped it so that it stood up on end. If he could mount and stand on this it would provide him with the necessary height for a jump.

He tried it once and then again but the seat had no proper balance on its side. It was impossible to climb up without its toppling. He became livid with frustration and nearly jammed the seat onto the top wire in a fit of temper. Wood was not a conductor, but it would be bound to set off an alarm.

At last he hit on the notion of making use of the oak-tree. It stood outside the fence, but by climbing up to a bottom branch, swinging along it hand over hand and hanging monkey-fashion he could poise himself, not the right side of the wire, but at least above the up-ended seat. He did this, dangled for a moment, then dropped onto the seat and immediately sprang off into the air. He felt the seat wobbling under him and his leap was in the nick of time. As he propelled himself forward he thrust back with his legs and the seat fell backwards away from the fence. He landed at the same instant, sprawled in the grass, but inside Mr Pratt's defences.

Triumphantly he rose to his feet and listened for any reactions to the thud of the falling seat. Nothing disturbed the silence except the distant bumble and rattle of a goods train on the far side of the valley. It crossed his mind that he had left himself no method of getting out, but that problem could be faced later. Meanwhile he was in!

As expected, the door was locked. He was loth to break a window but determined not to allow respect for Mr Pratt's property to stand in his way now. If no other means of entrance offered itself he would break into the ante-room, where the windows came near enough to the ground to be vulnerable. But what he had planned was to find the outside approach to the top gallery. This was a steep flight of wooden steps leading to a duck-walk with a hand-rail which ran the length of one side of the building. Barring the use of a ladder from inside, it would be the only means of access to the high windows lighting the court.

The steps were decayed and unsafe,

Talbot knew. They were kept out of use by a wicket gate at the bottom, which stood permanently locked. This proved no obstacle; he scaled it in a few seconds. Then he moved cagily up the steps, guiding himself with the torch and avoiding the middle of the treads. The duck-walk at the top was broad and reasonably secure. It must have been in use occasionally by Ted Nicholls, who would have to come up to open the windows on hot days or retrieve balls caught in the wire netting which protected them or attend to the arc-lights which had been installed for night play.

To avoid the outside steps Ted's normal procedure would be to use the ladder which his father had fallen off. This took him into the top gallery and from there a small door led out onto the duck-walk. The discussions after the old man's death had taught Talbot this, and the small door was his next objective. He prayed it would be open.

It wasn't. He tugged and twisted the handle sharply, but so far as he could judge it was firmly held by top and bottom bolts on the inside. There was only one thing for it. He slid the end window ajar, edged sideways through the gap onto the inside ledge at its foot and managed to detach the lower part of the netting from its hooks on the wall.

He did this on the side nearer the top gallery, which was a few feet away and at the same height. This gave him a cramped but free take-off for another unorthodox jump. He directed his beam down into the black stone well of the court and felt as though he were inside some enormous rifled sarcophagus. The penalty for failure this time would be at least a broken leg. The sloping roof of the penthouse above the dedans would break the fall and might prevent anything worse.

A slight scratching noise attracted his attention to the nearby gallery. He turned his beam instantly in that direction and ran the spot over the wall. Nothing! Old buildings tended to creak at night, he told himself, or it could be mice.

The gallery had a low parapet for spectators to lean over. After stowing the torch away in his pocket Talbot took a deep deliberate breath and leapt for this, only to discover as he landed that the top was not flat. Fortunately it sloped the right way for him — towards the gallery. He slithered onto the floor at the small cost of a bruise or two. But there his luck ended.

An eye glinted in the darkness.

As he leapt round, something struck him squarely on the head.

The blood surged up behind his eyes and he struggled all he knew to retain consciousness. His knees caved in, and the shock upset the balance of his thoughts as well. What had happened? Groping through a labyrinth of bewilderment, he focussed a clear picture of someone lurking in the gallery and knocking him cold — and that someone could be none other than the sinister, odious Pratt on sentry-go in person.

Fury at the idea of being worsted by That Man gave him strength. Without warning he lunged forward in a football tackle, grabbed a pair of legs and brought his assailant to the ground. Caught off guard, the man fell with such a thump that the floor boards shook and it seemed possible that they might both drop through the ceiling of the ante-room. Desperately Talbot grappled with him, but a violent kick in the face made him relax his grip, and the other broke away.

There was total silence now, apart from the sound of his own panting, which he kept as low as he could. Gingerly the American slid inch by inch backwards across the floor until his back pressed against the wall. He was between his assailant and the door. He could afford to take time to regain his strength and wits, confident that the other had no escape route without passing him. In a moment he would make certain that it was indeed Mr Pratt. Then, once he had relieved him of that murderous weapon, they could have a frank little chat. If Pratt wouldn't talk he would knock the daylight out of him.

His torch was still in his trouser pocket. He took it out and pressed the button. Nothing happened and he shook it anxiously. A faint tinkling noise reached him: the bulb was broken.

While he was still cursing under his breath the second attack was launched. A wild flurry of arms and legs pounded against him and he received a sharp blow on the shoulder which sent a spasm of pain running down his left arm. The man was threshing about homicidally with a heavy stick.

Talbot rose groggily to his feet and closed with him. The effort caused jagged stabs of pain to shoot through his head, but he had to keep at close quarters and not give him room to swing. Locked together, they floundered all over the gallery.

As they did so, it dawned on Talbot that his opponent was too agile for Mr Pratt and much too narrow round the waist. Who could it be? For an almost fatal second he faltered and loosened his hold. The other struggled free and delivered another blow. This time it caught the side of his head and sent him reeling against the wall three parts stunned.

Through the daze he heard the gallery door being unbolted, followed by the sound of footsteps running along the outside planks and descending the rickety stairs.

He groped vaguely round the floor on hands and knees until he had covered the entire area of the gallery. All he came across was what felt like the handle of a broom, which he appropriated; it would be better than nothing if there were further rounds to be fought. Then he leaned dizzily against the parapet to test his equilibrium. He could just discern the outline of the net across the centre of the court. Should he risk dropping onto the penthouse roof and try to find a light in the ante-room to carry out his search? The expedition had been futile if he didn't, but in his present condition he couldn't raise much relish for the prospect. Alternatively, was it safe to leave by the way he had come and break into the ante-room from outside?

Suddenly through the middle of the night a scream burst out, a full-throated male scream followed by the urgent clanging of alarm bells. Someone else was in trouble and so would he be. Staggering upright and leaning heavily on the broom-handle, he lurched to the door and tugged it open. The fresh air braced him, but twice he nearly stumbled off the duck-walk into the darkness below. He descended the steps like a drunk pursued by an imaginary policeman. The wicket gate held him up for what seemed an age: by the time he had climbed over, the alarm had lapsed into silence and there were lights on in the house. Already a party was setting off from the front door in his direction.

Talbot zigzagged across the grass. He was caught inside the wire and, with his torch out of action, couldn't even see exactly where it was. His assailant was lying doggo or electrocuted or had made off, but the real Mr Pratt was now in sight approaching at speed with the butler. A bright light which the butler was carrying illuminated them and the surrounding landscape for some distance. In Mr Pratt's hands was his shot-gun, held in front of him ready to raise to the shoulder at a second's notice. His determined stride made Talbot feel like a caged animal watching the arrival of its vicious keeper.

Thinking as sharply as he could bring his mind to focus, Talbot reckoned that his only hope was to run for it. In view of the fortifications he had penetrated, explanations of any sort were out of the question, and if he stood his ground he wouldn't put it past Pratt to take a pot shot at him out of malice, pretending that he had not been recognised. What the butler's evidence would be in that case was not in much doubt.

The wire was now lit up by the approaching light, and Talbot lumbered instinctively towards the farthest corner. The spot where he had climbed in was exposed and anyway the seat lay inaccessibly outside the fence. It was too late even to examine the gateway which he could now see that the Pratt posse was making for. He started to run, and as he ran his head became less fuddled.

The area enclosed by the wire was not large and he was already within a few yards of the bottom stretch. He continued to run; in fact, he ran faster. Just short of the fence he jammed one end of the broom-handle into the ground and took off, levering himself up into the air. It was a perfect pole-vault. He even landed on his feet, a yard or two from the edge of the lake.

At that instant the gun went off and shot spattered the ground beside him. Recovering his balance, he doubled along the lakeside. It felt like being in the war. He was too young for that, but he had learned about evasive action and zigzagged erratically to confuse the enemy's aim. When the second barrel went off he did not so much as hear the shot falling.

10

At a more godly hour that same morning Old Nick's last adversary, Timothy Forsyth, stood on the towpath at Hampton Court watching the river swirl round the bend towards Kingston and the sea. The water was swollen with recent rains and the ducks paddled sideways, working hard to stay where they were. Through the arches of the Lutyens bridge nestled the by-water of Molesey lock, and from behind the bank opposite him the Mole crept in unobtrusively to join the main stream. The sun was trying to shine, but the piers and huts announcing boat-fares to Richmond and Westminster had already been abandoned for the winter.

Timothy had wanted to be a diplomat. He offered the civil service commissioners four blues and a third-class honours degree in history. When they expressed interest in foreign languages he threw in G.C.E. French and a promise of further study. This had not tipped the scales. Yet tall and reserved, good-looking and well-spoken, he was all the world's idea of an official Englishman. When his hair greyed like Gerry Montague's no one would look more like an ambassador. Yet odd neuroses festered under the surface, erupting from time to time in the form of violent quarrels and drinking bouts and causing him to gamble compulsively beyond his means.

Unenthusiastically he had taken up the only other job in sight: a desk in the family firm of City solicitors. He was qualified now, but bored to distraction. His uncle resented his boredom and kept him at conveyancing work, which decreased his interest even further. They clashed spasmodically about the amount of time he took off to play games, and he would never have got away with it but for his prowess. Even to Uncle Sam playing cricket for Middlesex and being amateur tennis champion meant something. Nevertheless, the old boy niggled away at the stack of correspondence and dog-eared deeds in

Timothy's pending tray, and a certain degree of subterfuge was necessary to keep him from breaking out into an ultimatum.

Today, for instance, Timothy had telephoned the office and left a message with the girl at the switchboard that he did not feel well and would not be in. Would she tell Mr Samuel that he had picked up some food-poisoning over the weekend, but hoped to be in the next day? She had the impudence to make unconvincing sounds of sympathy and slily ask whether he would like to be put through to Mr Samuel. It didn't matter that she disbelieved him — his stock stood low in the office anyway — but she would certainly have delivered the message in such a way as to enrage Uncle Sam. There had been enough grumbling about the Monday absence which his weekend at High Cheney entailed. Now Tuesday as well!

It couldn't be helped. But he must remember that the old boy would be likely to puddle round to his flat after work to try and catch him out; they lived not far from each other in Chelsea. Timothy sighed and threw a votive stick to the river god. He would have to be in bed, then, by seven o'clock to humour a tiresome uncle, who could cut up very rough indeed when he felt like it. Timothy was not yet a partner. That was Uncle Sam's weapon: unless he observed a certain minimum of attendance and efficiency the partnership would be withheld. It was as bad as being at school again, feuding with his tutor. His nerves couldn't stand much more of it.

All this friction and uncertainty were dangerously relevant to the events of the weekend. If Nicholls' death became more than a routine police enquiry, bang would go his chances of a partnership. Should a real scandal blow up Uncle Sam might even banish him. They had legal connexions in New Zealand, and these had been mentioned at the time of some previous quarrel. If it came to the point, though, he would insist on Australia — Victoria or Tasmania, where at any rate there were tennis courts and a reasonable standard of cricket. Even so the prospect was far from enticing. He had too many friends and roots in England and several more years of top-flight games-playing ahead.

Usually he played tennis at Queen's, but driving into Town from High Cheney the day before he had felt in urgent need of a day by himself, away from social and business commitments and the bustle of central London. In the afternoon there was a mid-week meeting at Kempton Park, so he had arranged for a game with the professional at Hampton Court in the morning. He would have lunch at the Mitre and be on the spot for the racing afterwards. With this programme he could relax and think things out a bit. And food poisoning was not so far from the truth. He had had to spend most of Sunday in bed with a dicky stomach and even now didn't know whether he could face his favourite Mitre dish of langoustines flambées.

Hampton Court and the river round its doorstep always soothed him. His feeling for history went deep — though it was not, unfortunately, the sort of history the examiners at Oxford were much interested in. The economic consequences of the medieval wool trade left him unmoved, as did constitutional documents written in Latin or Old French. As a subject history seemed to have been captured by economists and political scientists. What took Timothy's fancy were the activities and influence of royal mistresses, details of battles in the Wars of the Roses, the fall of old families like the Bohuns and the rise of new ones like the Russells and the Cecils.

The bricks of Hampton Court breathed history of this sort: the lives of important people of the past, not economic trends. Timothy was generally thought to be a snob, but the man he most admired in history was the butcher's son from Suffolk who became an archbishop and a cardinal, founded Timothy's college at Oxford and built the palace here. What could Timothy, with all his advantages of birth, hope to leave behind him to compare with Christ Church and Hampton Court?

Reflecting on his own ambitions and

frustrations, he left the river-front, crossed the moat between the ranks of royal beasts and turned off the first courtyard to take a short cut past the Tudor kitchens into Tennis Court Lane, where he had parked his car. After collecting his tennis clothes he went through the long stone corridor, a dank, indestructible tunnel of the kind only found in stately homes, public schools and dungeons.

The tennis court, built by Henry VIII in the suspiciously appropriate year of 1530, was the oldest in existence. The massive stone slabs of the floor had borne the weight of the bluff king himself and survived him by more than four centuries. Most of the rest had been rebuilt when Wren restored and added to the palace. Painted on the wall above the net was the elaborate monogram of Wren's double-headed monarch — William-and-Mary.

To Timothy a game at Hampton Court represented a double experience. This was not only the most historic court; it was also the best. The walls and floor were fast, and if you cut the ball properly it would screw down sharply before your opponent had a hope of getting his racket to it.

Dykes, the professional, had ginger hair and played a flamboyant, aggressive game. He could beat every amateur in the country except Timothy, whom he coached assiduously while being steadily outplayed. They discussed Nicholls' death, but Timothy was unwilling to be drawn into details and hurried into the court to avoid interrogation.

Immediately they became absorbed in the subtleties of the game. Dykes miraculously scraped up and returned Timothy's shots off the back wall, and Timothy retaliated by volleying Dykes's forces crisply into the grille. At the hazard end Dykes was wearing himself out protecting the tambour and grille. Timothy, on the other hand, played with a cool ruthlessness, perfectly relaxed, every movement co-ordinated, every worry forgotten. Oblivious of Old Nick and Uncle Sam, he concentrated his mind on the tactics and grand strategy of the game, swinging his racket automatically in the characteristic tennis manner from high above his head.

Most tennis players have to learn and re-learn the unnatural tennis swing, but to Timothy it came instinctively as soon as the racket was in his hand. The lawn tennis swing is from the shoulder, rackets and squash strokes are mainly wrist-work, but in tennis the racket has to describe a peculiar arc, and the secret of it lies in the elbow. The swing is a forearm one, speeding the ball with the weight of the racket's head and at the same time dragging it back with an undertow of cut. Timothy never gave a moment's thought to this while playing a game, nor to the positioning of feet and body which made it possible, but Dykes, whose job it was, watched every detail of his opponent's play as well as the ball.

'You'll lock your wrist if you let your thumb move round the racket like that, Mr Forsyth,' he admonished, after Timothy had beaten chase better than two with an apparently immaculate shot on the floor.

'A little tighter grip for the volley, sir,' he called out a few strokes later, although

Timothy's shot had found the winning gallery with surgical precision.

Timothy showed no resentment. Far from it: he paid for Dykes's services and was never too proud to pick up a tip. All the same these criticisms tightened his determination to win. One long chase to beat and he would have the first set. Then the professional's extra years would begin to tell.

The chase to be played off had fallen half a yard worse than the last gallery. Dykes would serve a railroad and expect him to go for the last gallery if it didn't come off or the forehand corner if it did. Timothy decided to move a couple of yards up court as soon as the service was struck. He would volley for the main-wall side of the dedans, straight or boasted according to how it came: that should fix it. He crouched in expectation.

But in the act of serving Dykes lowered his racket. A movement in the top gallery on the hazard side had distracted him.

'That gallery is not in use, madam,' he called sharply, 'I must ask you to come down.' And in a lower voice he

178

added to Timothy: 'How did she get in, I wonder? Nothing to do with you, sir, is she?'

Timothy, about to shake his head, turned to look upwards first. When he saw who it was, his peace of mind vanished. Mlle Deschamps was standing aloft exuding feminine charm like a queen on a public balcony.

Plump and trim in a cut-away coat and matching hat, she came down and sat composedly in the dedans while they finished the game, treating Timothy like an old friend and Dykes as yet another interesting male. Timothy became eaten away with apprehension, his enjoyment gone, the rhythm of his play disrupted. He lost the second set disastrously and, the hour being up, they left the game drawn. Dykes retired to the changing room for a quick smoke before his next game, while Timothy put on his sweater and decided to face the Frenchwoman in the dedans.

She at once turned a Mona Lisa smile on him, ostensibly friendly but enigmatic. 'Good morning, my dear friend,' she greeted him. 'You did not expect to see me here, I think?'

He confessed that the pleasure was unanticipated, and she continued: 'For me too. As you see, I have become interested in tennis courts. They are cold and perhaps not beautiful. But of great interest.'

She stared into his face intently, and he had to restrain himself from shuffling along the bench away from her. Although chic and faintly seductive, she could be quite menacing at close quarters. Heavens, he thought, these Frenchwomen certainly know how to get themselves up for the benefit of the male animal, but they've got hard centres all right.

No sooner had the thought passed through his head than she said softly: 'I am going to make a statement to the police.'

'What!' he exclaimed. 'That would be most unwise. Mr Pratt and Ted Nicholls will have to, since they found the body, but no one else need. You really shouldn't, you know.'

'It is my duty,' she declared, half-closing her eyes and looking at him from under a luxuriant set of false eyelashes. 'You agree, M. Forsyth? Englishmen have a big sense of duty, I perceive.'

'Of course,' he replied, 'but in this case it is our duty to say nothing. The complications and publicity would be most unfortunate for everyone.'

'For me, no. But for you perhaps?'

'I was thinking of the Cheneys and the Pratts and Major and Mrs Winterton — everyone.'

'Including M. Forsyth?'

'Myself too, naturally. I would be shown in a very unfavourable light.'

She brought her soft laugh into play. 'Evidemment,' she smiled. 'Such a fact had occurred to me. I had intended to make enquiries at lunch-time about your address and come for a little visit to your house. This is a rendezvous arranged by fate. If you do not wish me to go to the police I have a proposition.'

Blackmail! Timothy felt sick.

'I don't know that I can consider anything like that,' he said.

She pulled him up sharply: 'Don't play the haughty English gentleman with me, young man; otherwise you will regret it. I give you an opportunity to save your skin. What I need is the smallest piece of information. If I obtain it I do not go to the police; if I do not obtain it — ' she drew her hand viciously across her throat as though Timothy were liable to be guillotined for the murder of Nicholls.

'What sort of information?' he asked coldly.

'What sort of information?' she mocked. 'You know well enough what I mean. Where is it?'

'Where is what? Do be less mysterious and more precise.'

'Very good,' she sneered, 'very good indeed, Mr English Gentleman Forsyth. You stupid, stuck-up assassin! You can have thirty seconds to tell me or else it's the police.' Theatrically she drew back the sleeve of her coat and exposed her wrist-watch.

Ten long seconds of silence passed. Timothy's emotions — rage and fear — took over and he found himself incapable of working out a proper response. He could half-throttle her and tell her he would complete the job later if she went to the police, or he could humour her, or he could simply get up and go. Wolsey would have made short work of her. So would Henry VIII: Catherine Howard had screamed for mercy unavailingly more or less on this very spot before being shipped to the Tower for execution. To dare was a mark of greatness. Ten more seconds went by. He moved towards her, his eyes ablaze.

She recoiled, retreating along the bench with surprising agility. But she had merely moved herself into a dark corner: he was still between her and the only exit. He lunged forward to reach her before she started screaming.

As she raised a row of pointed fingernails to fight him off, a voice interrupted them. The professional stood in the doorway. His next opponent had failed to turn up and he was enquiring whether Mr Forsyth was going to have a bath before he locked up.

The tension died away. Mlle Deschamps opened her bag and set to work with a powder compact and lipstick. Timothy stood awkwardly and said yes, he was just coming and could he introduce Mr Dykes to Mlle Deschamps from Paris. She nodded curtly to him, and Dykes, who thought he had interrupted something quite different, asked whether tennis interested her.

With an effort she became all charm again. She had been at High Cheney for the weekend, she told him. It was there she had met Mr Forsyth. While there she had also heard of this wonderful court of Mr Dykes's and had found her own way in from Tennis Court Lane. She hoped he would forgive her, because she had been told that the court was closed to the public for the year and knew she was being naughty.

'Any friend of Mr Forsyth is welcome here at any time,' said Dykes gallantly; 'though I'm afraid the dedans is a bit poky, as you see.'

The Frenchwoman looked round her and politely admired the pictures.

'Just a few photographs of past champions,' Dykes told her, adding: 'We'll have Mr Forsyth up here one day if I've anything to do with it.'

'That one's not a photograph,' she pointed out, her sharp eyes settling on a blackened oil painting in the darkest corner.

The professional stood corrected. 'Funny you should notice that,' he said. 'That's a previous Lord Cheney presented by himself. There's a hundred pounds a year for the professional here as long as it hangs in the dedans. His lordship wasn't all that good as a player and wanted to buy his way into the hall of fame, I suppose. A hundred a year must have been quite a lot of money before the First War. I keep the old geyser over there in the dark, even though I do rely on him for beer and fags. We can't have him beside Peter Latham and the Honourable Alfred Lyttelton, can we?'

He showed signs of leaving, and Mlle Deschamps made a hasty departure first. Before going she handed Timothy the address of her hotel and announced with a scowl that she would be expecting to hear from him very soon.

In his bath Timothy nearly fainted. Unable to face any lunch at all, let alone the brandy-fried langoustines, he abandoned the racing and drove back to his flat, where he placed his bets by telephone and then went straight to bed.

At any rate it would appease Uncle Sam to find him there.

11

The door-bell rang with a half-hearted whirr. Gerry Montague, sitting at the desk in his study, reminded himself to buy a new battery. Strewn over the desk and the surrounding chairs and floor lay a jumble of miscellaneous papers which included the pages of the Featherstonehaugh manuscript, volumes of the printed work and his own typewritten notes. It was an hour or two since Timothy Forsyth had retired to bed on the other side of London and less than twenty-four since Gerry himself had returned from High Cheney. The whole of that period, apart from time-off for eating and sleeping, he had spent working his way through the manuscript. By now he felt sure that there were no sheets missing. In another hour he would be able to put the manuscript back into apple-pie order. Then after tea he would comb systematically through for the references to High Cheney.

Gerry lived at the top of an Edwardian block of flats standing on high ground near the heath at Hampstead. It rated as a first-class residential area and was handy for Lord's. From his windows he could see the sprawl of the ugly old eyesore of a metropolis, from the heights of Greenwich beyond the river, the cross on the dome of St Paul's and the stone slab of the university building, right round to Battersea power station and the distant outlines of the Brentford and Harrow gasometers.

London was the subject he had been ruminating on when the bell rang, for in front of him, in the late Reverend Featherstonehaugh's ornate hand-writing, lay a copy of a document discovered by his reverence in the archives at Petworth. It listed fourteen tennis courts in London in 1615.

Two stood in the palace buildings at Whitehall, and this was before Charles II built his new court there, where Pepys had watched him at play. Under the list was written a sentence taken from the Diary: 'To the Tennis Court and there saw the King play at tennis and others; but to see how the King's play was extolled, without any cause at all, was a loathsome sight, though sometimes, indeed, he did play very well, and deserved to be commended; but such open flattery is beastly.'

Somerset House and Essex House in the Strand each had a court, and all the others seemed to be within the City walls: Fetter Lane, Fleet Street and Blackfriars; Southampton, Powles Chain and Charterhouse; Abchurch Lane, St Lawrence Pountney, Fenchurch Street and Crutched Friars. Gerry already knew Racquet Court off Fleet Street and Tennis Court off High Holborn; for the history he was preparing he would need to trace the site of all the others.

The door-bell whirred again, and he went to answer it reluctantly. Frosted glass filled the top half of the front door, and a blurred figure was discernible on the other side. It might be man or woman. For some time he had been on the point of installing a strip of that deceptive modern glass which was a mirror to the person outside but could be seen through from the inside. Then he would know whether or not to be at home, and no offence caused.

He opened the door. Mrs Pratt stood there, bright and effusive.

'I was afraid you must be out,' she said, stepping briskly across the threshold. 'I was going to tell you that I'd found myself passing and popped in on the spur of the moment, but that sounds rather silly after climbing all those stairs, doesn't it? Hadn't they heard of lifts when these flats were built?'

While she talked they were walking along the passage. She looked inquisitively into every room as they passed.

'Everything's in a fearful mess,' he apologised. 'My wife is away with the children until the end of the week. They always finish the summer holidays with relatives before going back to school.'

He was hoping to distract her attention and steer her safely past the study to the drawing room, but the study door was wide open and she shot a momentary but comprehensive glance into the room.

The drawing room and its view met with her approval. 'It's a very nice flat,' she complimented him. 'The rent must be on the hefty side. I never realised a journalist could afford a place like this.' Mrs Pratt believed shamelessly in the direct approach.

Vulgar old bag, thought Gerry and replied stiffly: 'Writers aren't all penniless, you know. And as a matter of fact we have other money.'

'Money,' said Mrs Pratt, 'is what I came to see you about. You surely haven't got so much of the stuff you can't do with more?'

'I beg your pardon?' He offered her a cigarette and she accepted one after a moment's scrutiny.

'You've got all those papers spread out next door, I noticed,' she went on. 'I suppose you've found what you're looking for?'

He blew some smoke out through his nostrils and said nothing.

'Come, come,' she coaxed, 'you mustn't feel bad about Alf pinching that old manuscript — though he's a naughty boy, I admit. When he wants something he just goes and takes it. He says it's what's called capitalism. They all do it in the City, and Alf beats them at their own game. Really fly he is. Everything's all right if you're prepared to pay: that's the system. And he offered you a lot of money for that manuscript, Mr Montague, you've got to admit that.'

'I'm not denying it,' Gerry answered. 'But it so happens that the manuscript is my property and not for sale. I had my suspicions, but I'm surprised you should come here and tell me in so many words that your husband is a thief.'

'Not a thief,' she protested. 'He only wanted to borrow it and keep it out of circulation for a while. All the same, I was livid the minute I realised that he'd done it. That's no way to treat a gentleman like Mr Montague, I told him. Then what is, he asked. Offer him some money for any information and help he can give, I said. That's the proper way to do things.'

She paused for Gerry to say something, but his experience as a reporter told him that she needed no prompting.

'Angel fair gave him hell at dinner last night. That kid's got character, you can't deny it. I'm ashamed of you, she told him — inviting all those nobs down for the weekend and then going in for a bit of common burglary in your own house. You set yourself up as a country squire; you're worth millions, we're always being told; yet you can't keep your hand out of a guest's pocket. It's mean, deceitful and downright unnecessary, she said. Mind you, Alf comes in for quite a bit of criticism now and again — the papers are always on about his take-over bids, and they even asked questions about him in Parliament once. But it doesn't worry him in the least. When I give him what for, too, it simply bounces off like one of your tennis balls — and I haven't been married to him for twenty-five years without knowing where to aim. But Angel's another matter. When she turns the heat on he curls right up. And did she turn it on last night!'

'Most interesting,' observed Gerry drily. But sarcasm was wasted. Mrs Pratt, who had been so silent at High Cheney, was in full flood now that she was away from her husband.

'So — I'm coming to the point, Mr Montague — Alf said that if Angel felt like that we could cut you in, and when it was safely in the bag you would have a share of the proceeds. What about that? I swear neither Angel nor I knew what was going on at first. When we heard we were amazed, and Angel at once said it was only right to bring you in on it. Mind you, between ourselves she also thought the Cheneys should have a share, but Dad scotched that one. They've no claim, and one can't go spreading it too thin, can one?'

Gerry made no reply, and Mrs Pratt went garrulously on to impress him with the danger of the situation and the need for secrecy. 'Alf is emphatic that we mustn't tell a soul. Not a soul, Mr Montague; you do understand, don't you? If we're not careful that Frenchwoman will be on to it. Or that nervy young man, Timothy Forsyth, who behaves so strangely. The major probably knows something, and even the American is beginning to suspect. As for her aged Ladyship, she's not as gaga as she pretends to be — not by a long chalk. The moment Alf told me about it I realised what she had been up to all this time. And we're even having to keep a sharp eye on Ted, you know. They're none of them to be trusted.'

'And why do you think I am?' Gerry asked.

'Because I know a gentleman when I see one,' said Mrs Pratt. 'That's why. Also it's in your interest to come in on our side — that's where the money is — and you're sensible enough to see it.

'Well?' she added after a moment's silence.

Gerry stood up. 'You will excuse me, I'm sure, Mrs Pratt,' he said, 'but I have to go out in a few minutes. I'm due to play tennis with Mr Talbot at Lord's. Meanwhile it's impossible for me to agree to anything since I don't understand what you are talking about and if I did I suspect it might not be quite on the right side of the law.'

'Not on the right side of the law!' Mrs Pratt repeated indignantly. 'What a thing to suggest! Of course any arrangement would be legal and above board. What sort of people do you take us for? Do you think my husband doesn't employ the best lawyers? I can see what's eating you, young man. The financial details. That's it, isn't it? Well, there's no need to worry about that. There's plenty of money in it, and you'll be treated fairly. Here's one of Alf's cards. All you have to do is to give him a tinkle and he'll have an agreement drawn up. It'll safeguard your right to a certain sum when the blessed thing is finally found.'

'I see. But what thing?'

'Pardon?' Mrs Pratt seemed genuinely taken aback.

'I asked, what thing.'

'I heard you first time,' she said, suddenly brisk again. 'I'd better leave my husband to talk to you about that and all the other details. Like you, I must be going. It's been a most useful chat. We can count on your discretion, I'm sure. Gentlemen never give away confidences, do they? No; please don't bother. I can find my own way out.'

Despite this he insisted on showing her out. Manners apart, there was no knowing what she might do on the way if left to herself. She tried to throw him off by asking to use the lavatory, but he stood resolutely outside the door until she came out. Making the best of it, she beamed her way out of the flat. He closed the front door on her firmly before dashing back to the drawing room to answer a summons from the telephone.

It was Talbot's voice, sounding apologetic and somewhat incoherent. He had just booked in at his hotel, it seemed, after undergoing an experience not to be mentioned on the telephone. He was in no shape for a game of tennis, but desperately wanted to talk to Gerry. If he had been feeling better he would have come out to Hampstead. As it was, would Gerry mind awfully coming to the hotel to see him. The business on the agenda was mighty urgent.

Obediently Gerry took the underground to the Strand, walked from there to the hotel and asked for Talbot at the reception desk. He was shown up into a spacious room over-looking the river, where the American sat in an armchair by the window gazing gloomily at the iron girders of Hungerford Bridge in the middle distance.

They shook hands formally, and Talbot pushed a bottle of Polish vodka across the table. He had bought it at a roadhouse on the way into Town and claimed that it was the only thing keeping him alive. Gerry doubtfully poured himself a small tot and downed it with a bottle of tonic water. Vodka at four in the afternoon was exotic even for a Fleet Street man.

'What the devil has happened to you?' he asked. 'You look as if war had broken out.'

'Correct,' said Talbot succinctly. 'That's precisely what has happened. War! We don't know each other very well, Montague, but you are a decent fellow and I want you on my side.'

Gerry was startled. Here was a counter-bid coming up already! 'You mean a battle of wits, I presume,' he said. 'Not a shooting war.'

'That's where you are wrong.' Talbot glared down at the river. 'This is no sissy affair. I've been knocked black and blue and shot at.'

Gerry laughed. 'You don't mean it, do you? That someone has been trying to kill you? It's absurd.' He was beginning to believe that Talbot had a hang-over which was developing into persecution mania. For all he knew, this might be a standard symptom of over-indulgence in vodka.

But Talbot proved sane enough. After apologies for cancelling the game and putting Gerry to the inconvenience of coming to the hotel, he gave a lucid account of the events of the previous day and night: his attempt to use the High Cheney court in the morning, the meeting with Mlle Deschamps, their expulsion by Mr Pratt, the visit to Lady Cheney and the whole saga of the nocturnal expedition to the tennis court. While he talked he prowled purposefully round the room like a captive lion. When he had finished he took a large neat tot of vodka and dashed it down his throat in the best European style.

'Pope Boniface's chalice!' Gerry exclaimed. 'It sounds utterly fantastic. In all my twenty years in Fleet Street I've never heard of anything quite as unlikely — and that's saying something, I can tell you. Where is it supposed to be? Bricked up in the walls? It can hardly be anywhere else. I don't imagine there's so much as a cupboard in the top gallery — they're usually completely bare.'

'So far as I could make out from crawling all over it in the dark,' admitted Talbot, 'you're right. But there must be a clue in that manuscript of yours. I want you to dig it out of your bank's safe deposit and let us have a complete run-through.'

Gerry nodded: 'Nothing could be easier. It's not in the bank: I've been working on it all day. But for coming here I would probably have unearthed the reference by now.'

'Not in the bank! You mean it's in your flat? Unguarded?' It was a reprimand from the younger man and Gerry flushed.

'My dear chap,' he protested, 'this is not Chicago, you know. It's perfectly safe.'

'That's no way to talk after what's happened to me,' Talbot observed grimly. 'So far as I'm concerned, Chicago has nothing on rural England when it comes to violence. But it's the Pratts I'm interested in. So long as they're not in Town . . . '

'But they are! At least Mrs is. She's just been to see me.'

'She's what!' Talbot went speechless, and Gerry continued.

'With a cash offer. Join the Pratts and make a fortune. No need to worry, though. I as good as told her that poor-but-honest was more in my line.'

'But the manuscript!' Talbot was manifesting signs of anxiety neurosis. 'Did she see it? You didn't leave her with it, did you?'

'Of course I didn't leave her there.' Gerry spoke brusquely; he was growing anxious himself now. 'In fact I took special care to show her safely off the premises. But she certainly noticed it and that may have been the reason she wanted to show herself out. All the time she was with me I thought she was play-acting a bit and . . . Oh, my God!' He broke off.

'Go on, man,' shouted Talbot. 'What's the matter?'

Gerry's face had gone as grey as his temples. 'What a fool I am,' he said. 'The penny's just dropped. She came to me with a proposition because they believed I would have read the relevant passage in the manuscript. Then at the end I asked outright what it was everyone was hunting for, and she must have realised that I hadn't. That would account for her change of manner and her making off so abruptly.'

'Look,' said Talbot, thumping the table with his fist and making the vodka bottle bounce, 'contrary to normal practice, I'm just about being kept on my feet by this Polish fire-water. Before I die or collapse later this evening I want to find out what old man Featherstonehaugh says about the Papal chalice that was so interesting it was held out of the published book. We'd better get up to your place right away before Pratt comes along and takes it off you at the point of his shot-gun. There's been someone in the flat while you've been here, I presume?' he added sharply.

'Not a soul,' confessed Gerry miserably. 'Not only that; I remember telling the woman when she arrived that my family were all away. Then later I let on that I had a date to play you at Lord's. She would know that the coast was clear for a couple of hours.'

With a groan Talbot rang down for a taxi. Together they dashed out of the hotel into the waiting cab. The driver countered Talbot's instruction to step on it by announcing sourly that they needn't think they had hired a helicoptor. The rush-hour snarl-up reduced them to pedestrain pace, and only after crossing the Euston Road did they speed up, to arrive at Hampstead with some semblence of urgency.

Talbot took the stairs by threes and Gerry behind him reached the top landing breathless. One look at his front door and his heart sank. The square pane of glass immediately above the Yale lock was smashed. He never used the mortice key except for securing the place when they went away for holidays. It would be easy for anyone to put a hand through the gap and open the door by pulling back the catch on the inside.

This he now did himself and hurried along the corridor with the American at his heels. The study door was closed; though he had left it open. They glanced at each other, simultaneously struck by the thought that the intruder might still be inside. Talbot brandishing a fist to indicate that he hoped it was Pratt.

Gerry turned the handle and flung open the door. The room was empty. The printed volumes of the Annals were stacked precisely in the centre of the desk, but the chaotic litter of papers he had left when interrupted by the door-bell were no longer there. A brief, unhopeful hunt through the flat uncovered no sign of them. The manuscript and all his notes had disappeared.

12

Caught in the headlights of the car, the lodge gates looked wet and sullen. They were open but inhospitable. The cold and dampness of the night heralded winter.

Gerry's face was set with tiredness and determination. An easy-going man who had been pushed too far, the second disappearance of his prized manuscript left him ice-cold with anger. Lost again — perhaps not to be recovered this time — was the raw material for what he had every intention of making the new classic work on the game: Montague on Tennis. With the approach of middle age, a backwater journalist and long past his peak as an athlete, his ambitions were few; but this was the crown of them.

It made matters worse that he had only himself to blame for leaving the manuscript unprotected after Mrs Pratt's visit. Knowing that the Pratts were responsible for the earlier theft, he should have taken precautions. Mrs Pratt had told him in so many words that her husband had no scruples, and he now saw that she hadn't either.

After discovering the loss and searching the flat vainly he and Talbot had gone downstairs to question the porter. Walk-in thieves were not uncommon in Hampstead, and one of the man's duties was to keep an eye open for unfamiliar faces on the premises.

Yes, he said, as a matter of fact he had noticed a woman going out of the main doors carrying a fair-sized bundle under her arm. She appeared to be a lady and not one of the charwomen, and he had started after her to see whether he could help her through the swing doors, but she had been too quick for him. She must have come from one of the upstairs flats, and the time tallied with Gerry's absence. Only her back had been visible, and the porter could say little more than that she didn't seem to be a young girl — 'too thick' was his description.

This was enough for them. Gerry threw some things into an overnight bag and went round to the garage to fetch his car. In a few moments they had set out for High Cheney together: a thick-set, grey-haired Englishman with moustache bristling and a young, lanky American with a swollen and bruised face.

They did not stop, even for a meal, until they reached Abbots Cheney, and then only to book rooms at the hotel. Talbot fell asleep while they were still on the North Circular. The stop at the Cheney Arms did not wake him, and Gerry dug an elbow into his side as the house loomed ahead of them.

Talbot came awake like a cat — instantly alert. He peered through the windscreen and drew in his breath. 'Here already! This is a pretty speedy return to the scene of my attempted crime.'

'How are you feeling?'

'All right, I reckon.' He paused for a check-up. 'And spoiling for a fight,' he added.

They drew up outside the baronial entrance, which was lit by a mock-antique lantern above the door. Gerry tugged the bell-pull and they waited.

The door was opened by the butler, who showed no sign of recognition.

They wished to see Mr Pratt? Would they come this way and he would enquire whether Mr Pratt was in? That's rich, thought Talbot — at nine o'clock in the evening.

They were led, not to the drawing room, but to the library. Heavy crimson curtains were drawn across the windows, but the room remained chilly and cheerless. The books looked unfriendly as well as unread. Their minds shared the same question as they stood expectantly in the centre of the room: would Pratt admit it, deny it or bluster?

The door opened and they swung round to confront him. It was Angel. They looked hostile, for she flinched momentarily.

'Hiya,' she greeted them. 'This is a surprise. Dad's temporarily mislaid. I've sent out a search party for him. Is there anything I can do meanwhile?'

Gerry considered. 'I'm not sure there is,' he replied. 'Is your mother in?'

'Mother's been to Town. We're

expecting her back any minute now. Why don't you come into the drawing room where it's warmer and tell me all about whatever it is?' Angel smiled, which was an attractive sight, and Talbot's rancour melted a little. But Gerry brusquely declined the invitation.

'Thank you,' he said stiffly, 'but we're not here for more than a few minutes. I've come from London to collect my manuscript, which your mother stole from my flat this afternoon.'

'Oh no!' Angel's manner altered, and she looked apprehensive.

'Oh yes, I'm afraid,' retorted Gerry.

'It isn't true. It can't be. Dad will explain.' Angel appealed to Talbot.

'You know what the Arabs say?' He spoke with a drawl, swinging backwards and forwards on the balls of his feet, his hands in his trouser pockets. 'Something like: it is a good thing to know the truth and speak it, but it is a better thing to know the truth and speak of palm trees. There's been a certain amount of palm-tree stuff going on round here in the last few days, and I'd prefer to talk about them to you, Angel, just until your old man shows up.'

'It isn't true,' she repeated, 'you must see that. Mum has had some trouble with the police in the past — nothing at all serious — and she would do anything to avoid any more. Can't you see how anxious she's been all along to keep the police out of this business?'

'The facts are against her,' said Gerry. 'What sort of trouble has she been in with the police? It's not a point in her favour.'

'It was nothing of this sort,' Angel assured him. 'If you must know, it was a malicious charge of shoplifting — '

'Light fingers,' murmured Talbot pointedly, and Angel rounded on him in a flash of fury.

'Who are you to talk?' she demanded. 'A dirty little sneak-thief in the night! A hired burglar! You're lucky to be this side of prison bars yourself and you come barging in here uninvited making slanderous remarks about my mother. You've a nerve, even for a Yank. Now get out of the house and keep your hands

210

off the silver in the hall on your way out. Go on, get out! The pair of you.' She flung open the heavy oak door with a flourish.

In the doorway stood Mr Pratt, apparently in the act of entering. 'Hullo, 'ullo, 'ullo,' he called out. 'What have we here? The long and the short of it, eh?'

He eyed them up and down and then looked at Angel, who subsided into tears and ran off down the corridor without speaking.

Mr Pratt turned on the visitors, addressing himself to Talbot in a voice usually reserved for recalcitrant employees and debtors: it was like a cobra's kiss, silky and steely.

'I don't know what you've been saying to my daughter — we'll come to that later. But I'm surprised you have the effrontery to set foot on these premises after what occurred last night. Perhaps you've come to offer some explanation?'

Talbot could recognise a dangerous man and judged it better to duck the question. It certainly was a nerve, and what could he say? Moreover, most of his mind was still occupied with Angel. Really, he thought, that girl looks mighty pretty when she gets steamed up; the flushed cheeks and sparkling eyes did something for her. It was more than six months since his second spouse had taken a transfer to a Los Angeles baseball player and he was becoming increasingly conscious of being between wives.

'Creeping about my grounds like a poacher,' Mr Pratt went on, with controlled venom. 'You might very well have been shot, and you'll be lucky if I don't send for the police now. You *and* that parchment-faced old harridan down in the village. They'd lock you both up. I know you went to see her and I dare say she filled you up with the usual Cheney poppy-cock. What a man with a father as rich as yours wants to get himself mixed up in petty theft for, I can't imagine. And who was your pal last night, eh? Was it young Gavin? I'll take it out of that young man if it was. Peer of the flipping realm or not, he needs to keep his blue-blooded hands off my property. And that goes for you too. I'm warning you, and I'm not a man who warns more than once.'

'That's okay then,' replied Talbot easily, 'because I'm not a person who ever takes any notice of warnings. I'm not interested in your big-mouthed threats. You call the police if you want to. This is a free country, they tell me. Go right ahead; there's the telephone.' He crossed to it and picked the receiver up. 'Nine-nine-nine, isn't it? Or would you prefer to talk to Montague here for a few moments first?' Mr Pratt making no move, he contemptuously slammed the receiver back onto its cradle.

'I'm the person who'll be needing to use that telephone,' declared Gerry. 'Either I leave this house with my manuscript or it's the police. And the sooner you hand it over the better: I'm fed up with hypocritical havering.'

'What do you mean?' Mr Pratt turned on him like a bull confronted with a fresh torero.

'Exactly what I say,' snapped Gerry. 'Not content with stealing my manuscript once yourself, you send your wife up to London to steal it again.'

'You're lying.' Beneath his mask Mr Pratt was as taken aback as Angel had been — or seemed to be. 'Come off it,' he said roughly. 'What are you trying to pull?'

'Neither of us is trying to pull anything: I simply want my manuscript. Mrs Pratt visited my flat this afternoon, as I dare say you know. She confessed on your behalf to the earlier theft and offered some kind of financial deal which seemed to me, shall we say, not quite above board. I refused it and in my absence your wife broke in and removed the manuscript.'

'What a preposterous story!' exploded Mr Pratt. 'I — '

'Quit blustering, Pratt,' interrupted Talbot. 'Either give the man his manuscript or let him telephone the police. But cut the cackle: I was out late last night and I'm feeling tired.'

Glaring, Mr Pratt seized the bell cord with both hands as if it were the American's neck. When the butler came he asked him whether Mrs Pratt had arrived back from London yet. She had that moment come in, the butler said, and he was despatched to fetch her.

Forewarned apparently, Mrs Pratt blew into the room like a tidal wave. 'Well?' she demanded.

'My dear,' Mr Pratt informed her, 'you are being accused of stealing this press rat's precious manuscript.'

'Nothing Mr Talbot said would surprise me in the least,' she replied angrily, 'but I thought Mr Montague was a gentleman.'

'You deny the theft?' asked Gerry bluntly.

'It's worse than untrue,' she flamed, 'the very idea is ridiculous. And now let me ask you whether you deny repeating our confidential conversation to this' — her favourite word 'gentleman' going against the grain, she settled instead for 'prune merchant'.

'There was no agreement about keeping your extraordinary proposals this afternoon confidential, and I'm not answerable to you for what I say to my friends. I'm only sorry I didn't call the police in straight away and tell the whole story to them instead of wasting time like this. This'll lead to a full-scale enquiry into Nicholls' death too, I expect.' Gerry moved towards the door.

Mrs Pratt anticipated him. 'Ted,' she yelled into the corridor. 'Come here. Wait a moment, Mr Montague,' she ordered. 'A sergeant and one of the men from the local station spent four hours here yesterday afternoon. My husband gave them every assistance. They went down to the court and took a long statement from Ted. They're perfectly satisfied. So there!'

Ted was wearing a dark suit and black tie. He looked sheepish, but nodded a greeting to the visitors before turning to his employers.

'My husband needed the chauffeur, so Ted drove me to London today,' Mrs Pratt explained. 'You may ask him any questions you please.'

Under interrogation Ted remained adamant that Mrs Pratt had made only a single visit to the flat in Hampstead. If genuine, his evidence also precluded any possibility of her lurking in the hall and returning to the flat. After the visit they had driven to the West End for shopping — he listed shops and approximate times — and then home, stopping on the way for dinner. The story sounded authentic, but Ted was shifty and might have been coached.

In conclusion he said earnestly to Gerry: 'It's the truth I'm telling you, sir.'

'If so,' Gerry asked Mrs Pratt, 'how is it my manuscript should have disappeared so rapidly after your call? You showed a good deal of interest in it, and no one else knew it was there.'

Before she could answer Mr Pratt gave an ironical laugh. 'My wife is not the only person interested, and anyone might have guessed where it would be, mightn't they? Shall we stop pretending that we don't know who the real thief is? Though it isn't such a pleasant thought to some of us, is it, Talbot?'

'If you're implying that Talbot here had something to do with the theft,' said Gerry, 'you're quite wrong. I was with him all the time. In any case there is reason to believe that it was a lady.'

'Exactly,' agreed Mr Pratt. 'A lady

who specialises in theft! One night she employs other people to do it for her; the next day she may even do it for herself. A Lady Cheney, to be precise. And one of her associates is brazen enough to come here with you for the express purpose of making false accusations against Mrs Pratt. I suggest you call at the dower house in the village and collect your missing property from there, but my advice is that you dump your friend in the duck pond on the way. Now get out, the pair of you!'

He flung the door open and gestured them out with his foot to speed them off the premises. The American barely resisting the temptation to use his fists, they left the house and drove towards the village seething and dispirited.

'That man's an artful bastard,' said Talbot with grudging admiration. 'Ted Nicholls would say anything for money, but it's just possible that screwy old dame did snitch it. I'll wager she sends us back to the Pratts, but now we're here we might as well try her. Though I feel like death.'

He must have looked like it too, for when Lady Cheney opened the front door she sprang back as if at the sight of a ghost.

'And the gentleman from the press as well!' she exclaimed suspiciously. 'This is somewhat late for a social call. My housekeeper is already in bed, and I was about to turn in myself. However, I am eager to have your report about — about you know what I refer to. You were not successful?'

'No ma'am,' said Talbot, following her upstairs to the drawing room. 'What's more, I reckon there can't possibly be anything of value in that — '

She shut him up in mid-sentence by demanding imperiously: 'Is Mr Montague privy to my secret?'

'The night was so peculiarly eventful, answered Talbot unabashed, 'that as a mere foreigner I felt bound to seek advice from a friendly native.' He flopped onto the sofa beside Gerry.

'Were you injured then?' she enquired, looking him over without any sign of sympathy.

'Indeed I was. Attacked and shot at.'

'Dolt!'

'Pardon?' Talbot flushed with anger.

'Dolt, dolt, dolt,' repeated Lady Cheney, as though she were the injured party. 'Fighting in the gallery and playing at cowboys and Indians instead of doing what you undertook to do. It's most vexatious.'

'How did you know it was in the gallery I was attacked?'

She ignored the question. Dismissing him from her attention, she enquired pointedly, 'And what can I do for Mr Montague before I turn in?'

'You have been to London today, I believe, Lady Cheney?' Gerry asked by way of reply. After their rout by the Pratts the indirect approach seemed advisable.

'I have.' She looked at him challengingly. 'For luncheon with a friend and tea with my sister who lives in the palace at Hampton Court. Why do you ask?'

'Because the Featherstonehaugh manuscript disappeared from my flat this afternoon,' he ventured, throwing caution overboard.

Lady Cheney rose from her chair majestically. 'Do I understand you aright, young man? Are you accusing ME of stealing? Have you taken leave of your senses?'

'Mr Pratt suggested — ' Gerry began, but was cut short.

'What Mr Pratt suggests or does not suggest is of no concern to me. You will excuse my not showing you downstairs. Please be sure to close the front door securely behind you. There are such very undesirable people in the neighbourhood these days.' She turned her back on them and started annihilating the fire with a succession of fierce short-arm jabs with the poker.

13

Two-faced like janus, the Fanfare worked hard to reconcile respectability and naughtiness. Situated in an area which specialises in gaiety by night, it was something between a restaurant and a night club. Beneath an old-fashioned air of being morally and socially above reproach a counter-suggestion lurked. Exclusive by reputation, it in fact catered for anyone who happened to walk down the stairs and pay handsomely for food, dancing and a floor show. Hours: seven p.m. to three a.m.

Inside, on the evening after Gerry Montague's fruitless pursuit of his manuscript in Abbots Cheney, dinners were being served in such a subdued light that it was impossible to be sure whether the chicken was cat. On the small stage there was dancing to Tommie Thomson's Serenaders and (when Tommie flagged) to Carlo and his Caribbeans. Among the customers were quiet suburban husbands dragged out at pistol point to celebrate wedding anniversaries, rowdy successful punters, and bald businessmen with girls who weren't their daughters.

Dress was mixed. Dark suits and cocktail dresses predominated, but a few black ties and evening gowns exchanged pointed stares with a sprinkling of brazen sports jackets and jumpers. Carlo was playing exotic sambas while the sparkling moselle bubbled out of champagne bottles and Tommie (with the aid of a game of poker and a bottle of gin off stage) regained his verve for some more xylophone solos. The waiters were weaving hectically between the crowded tables in an effort to finish serving before 10.30, when the curtain was due to rise on The World's Most Amazing Floor Show. This was advertised as featuring a large number of Parisian Artistes.

'I said, what do you do with yourself all day on the stock exchange,' shouted Angel. Their table was sandwiched between a pillar and the band, and Carlo was deep in a soul-stirring cadenza played fortissimo on the saxophone.

'Persuade old ladies to sell their 2½% consols and buy equities instead,' Gavin Cheney shouted back. 'It's fiendishly boring and I'm not very good at it. By the time I've brought them to the point of agreeing, the yield on blue chips is so low that they lose most of their income and kick up hell.'

The music died away. 'Why do you do it then?' she asked softly.

The question was sympathetic and threw Gavin slightly off balance. Despite the milieu he had not invited her out for a romantic evening. This was to be a business session.

Her dress was made of green silk, with red dragons breathing gold fire all over it; the collar came high up under the chin in Chinese style. She wore no jewellery and looked inscrutably oriental. He felt ashamed of having brought her to such a place, distracted from the business in hand and certain of being out-manoeuvred if he embarked on it.

'What can a poor landless earl do if he's my age?' he asked in reply. 'I could afford to build a stylish villa in somewhere like Ibiza and lord it among the natives and remittance men, but where's the fun in that? Or I could draw director's fees from umpteen third-rate companies that wanted to use my name as a front for some malpractice or other. No, I'm afraid stockbroking is about the best I can manage, and it keeps my mother happy. She believes I'm going to restore the family fortunes by working in the City.'

As he finished speaking he put an elbow on the table and rested his cheek in the palm of his hand. Despite pink, boyish features and a faintly rakish air he could be tough, she sensed — both mentally and physically. Also, she suspected, he kept up a pretence of being more of a fool than he was.

'You've quite a bruise there,' she pointed out, noticing what he was covering up.

'Too true,' he admitted. 'It's jolly painful. Some ass opened a car door into my face just as I was bending down to open it myself.'

'I'm so sorry,' she said. 'I've never heard of that happening before.'

'Haven't you?' He sounded disappointed.

'And what's more,' she continued, abandoning sympathy and inscrutability, 'I don't believe it. You're a liar, Lord Cheney. And a poor one at that. It must come from years of 'noblesse oblige' and 'honi soit qui mal y pense'. The City hasn't assimilated you yet. You should watch Dad telling a whopper.'

Gavin flushed. 'I have,' he retaliated. 'Several times in one weekend.'

'Now, now.' She wagged a manicured finger at him. 'No side tracks. You broke into the tennis court on Monday, didn't you?'

'The floor show will be beginning any minute,' he said, refilling their glasses. 'Must we go into this High Cheney business now?'

'Look who's talking,' she laughed. 'Do I owe this invitation to love of my bright eyes after all? If so, I should have consulted my parents and they could have asked your intentions.'

'They don't know you're here, then?'

'Dear Gavin' — she patted his hand maternally — 'funnily enough, Cheneys are not exactly popular at High Cheney just now. In any case there are other plans for me — or were.' She looked at him quizzically.

'Do go on.' She had withdrawn her hand and he was plotting to re-establish contact.

Angel shrugged and sipped her wine. 'It's simply that Mummy thought Talbot B. Talbot was suitably rugged and affluent, and it so happens that he is temporarily wifeless, poor man. Dad is interested in a tie-up with the dried fruit industry for a chain of stores he controls; so what could be more convenient? The only snag is that Talbot has suddenly developed into Public Enemy No. I and we've all come to hate him like poison. If he wasn't so stinking rich we'd think he'd been bought by Cheney gold, if there was any.'

Gavin was saved from coping with this remark by the lights going out. The curtains rose on a bevy of Frenchified lovelies, more reminiscent of Camberwell

Green than the Left Bank. Some parts of their bodies were magnificently upholstered in fur and feathers, and others completely unadorned. Looking to Angel like half-plucked chickens, they danced and sang, simpered and posed, mindful of the old, old rule: if you can't smile, show your teeth.

'Poor wretched girls,' she whispered. 'Surely they can't enjoy it?'

'Would you?' asked Gavin.

'Once perhaps; but not twice nightly. What happens to them afterwards, do you think?'

'After the show or after they are too old for the back row?' Gavin allowed himself a faint leer.

'When they're too old for this sort of thing.' She ignored the leer.

'As soon as they reach retiring age, which is thirty, they go back to their father's vicarage and marry the curate.'

She put out the tiny end of a pink tongue at him: he had scored a point for the first time in the evening. She seemed to be enjoying herself, he thought, despite the unbelievable awfulness of the place.

The chorus was succeeded by a guitarist, the guitarist by comics, the comics by a tap-dancer, and the tap-dancer by a broad-beamed West Indian lady vocalist who evoked hoarse memories of crocodiles basking on Central American riverbanks. The show finished with a brisk, breathless can-can, the ladies of the chorus each twirling frantically round on one black-stockinged leg while holding the other straight up in the air. The curtains fell to ragged applause, and the subdued lighting was restored.

'No,' said Angel, 'Dad wouldn't approve of this. Quite apart from you, he's very strait-laced where I'm concerned. When you rang I told him it was an invitation to a party being given by a girl friend from art school. She lives in Knightsbridge and is lending me a bed for the night, so I'll be able to make up a convincing story. You and Dad are not the only liars. As a matter of fact, your call last night came soon after we'd had Talbot and Mr Montague down pretending we'd stolen that blessed manuscript again.'

'Your father stole it the first time,

didn't he?' Gavin couldn't stop himself asking.

'Borrowed is the word; but yes, I'm sorry to say he did. This time, though, he didn't, and they had the nerve to accuse Mummy of doing it for him. It wasn't you by any chance, was it?'

He looked her in the eye and shook his head vigorously.

'I believe you this time,' she said. 'And now what about this tennis-court escapade? Talbot didn't deny it when Dad said the other person was you.'

'If he knows, why ask me?' Gavin became morose and confiding at the same time. 'Mother's a great one for bees in the bonnet. We've even had to send her away to a rest home to calm down a bit when some mania or other gets a stranglehold on her. At present she's suffering from a chalice fixation, and it looks like being the worst outbreak of the lot.'

'So?'

'For goodness sake don't tell anyone, but she's convinced that some old family chalice is hidden in the tennis court, and nothing I say makes the slightest difference. The family solicitors assure me there's a chalice in the Vatican which is almost certainly the one. It's been there for a hundred and fifty years at least, but the ruby is missing and Mother insists on believing that it isn't the same one. On Monday she wanted me to search for it. She's always been suspicious of your father restoring the tennis court — it's on the site of the abbot's lodgings, you know — and Nicholls' death right on top of the disappearance of the manuscript set her off thinking that someone had made a discovery or found a clue or something.'

Gavin lit a cigarette and surveyed the motley crowd with well-bred superiority. He had made a terrible mistake: he should have gone the whole hog and taken her to Churchills or the Four Hundred. What could she be thinking of him? There were even American service men dancing with girls they had obviously picked up for the night.

'I refused, of course,' he went on, 'and then friend Talbot walks in and she talks him into it — without a word to me. All through dinner she fills me up with the familiar guff about my not taking the family heritage seriously enough; with the result that I feel a worm and decide to do it after all. And what happens? No one finds anything, and Talbot and I bash into each other like prize-fighters, each thinking that the other is one of your father's minions. And that's the truth, so help me.'

He looked so crestfallen that Angel stifled a laugh and patted his hand again. Poor Cheneys, she thought, no wonder they had gone under. The family's supply of luck had run out.

'Though I must say' — he brightened up, responding to sympathy — 'it was pretty exciting. When I came across the wire round the court I broke into a potting shed, pinched an old rake handle and used it for pole-vaulting over the fence. That was all right, but when it came to getting out again in a hurry I found I'd left the thing in the gallery during the scuffling. So I had to jump without it, got my foot caught and set the alarm off. Just like a P.O.W. escape film. It can't be legal for your father to touch up the wire with umpteen volts. They gave me the deuce of a shock.'

'It's on his own property,' Angel retorted, 'and you're a fine one to talk about legalities.'

She glanced at the dance floor and Gavin at once took the hint. Tommie Thomson's Serenaders were thumping out an old-fashioned waltz.

'I can't go more than one way round,' he warned, 'but when you're dizzy we can sway gently on one spot until you recover.'

'Certainly not,' she replied. 'I not only reverse; I insist on reversing.' And she swept him towards the throng.

Once on the floor they found small talk impossible, and the joint exercise induced camaraderie. Angel was as good as her word and together they survived the hazards of reversing. When the band changed into slow time they revolved in silence, treasuring the idiotic snatches of conversation which reached them from other couples.

As soon as they returned to the table she withdrew to the cloakroom and he scored a brisk victory over a waiter who tried to make him buy another bottle of wine or feel mean. That and the dancing cheered him up. Now he had to consider the right approach. So far Angel had extracted a chunk of information out of him and he had nothing to show in return except what he would have learned in due course anyway.

'Your father's some tycoon,' he said when she was sitting opposite him again. 'They hold their breath and look over their shoulder when his name is mentioned in the City. Do you keep up with all his business activities?'

'Keep up with them? They've always been a total mystery to me.' She sounded genuine, but he couldn't be sure.

'He must discuss them at home sometimes, surely?'

'Even if he did, neither of us would understand. Actually I don't believe anyone has the slightest clue to Dad's business ramifications except himself. His fellow-directors are all specialists in this or that and don't know about anything else. The Inland Revenue, I gather, is continually wailing that it can't follow what's going on. Why are you interested?'

'There are rumours.' His senior partner, knowing of the Cheney-Pratt connexion, had asked him to scavenge for information. When Gavin demurred he had insisted it was important. Hence the evening out — that and the need for information about Mr Pratt's domestic activities too. The more he warmed towards Angel the more of a cad he felt about it.

'Rumours?' she repeated.

'Yes, in the City. Rumours that your father has bitten off more than he can chew in his latest take-over and is short of ready cash. There've been rumours before and his credit's not as good as it was. He can borrow the money somehow, I dare say, but the terms may be too stiff. The insurance companies have invested in him in a big way, and they're said to be getting worried. If they pull out he's finished.'

'I see.' Angel stared meditatively past

his ear. 'This is news to me. Dad's always attracted gossip. I don't expect there's anything to it.'

He judged from her tone that at least she believed it might be true. She realised this immediately and added: 'You won't do anything to help spread these rumours, will you, Gavin?'

Blazes, he thought, first she outsmarts me in conversation and now she switches on the feminine appeal. What could he say?

'Of course not, Angel,' he assured her, using her name for the first time. One's duty to a lady came before one's duty to a senior partner, he supposed.

'You're sweet,' she said. 'Let's dance again, shall we?'

14

Earlier that same evening, in the autumn dusk, Talbot and Gerry had arrived back in Hampstead. After a night at the Cheney Arms they had attempted a second call at High Cheney and the dower house and been rebuffed both times. Mr Pratt's lodge gates were closed, and the lodge-keeper told them that no visitors were being received. At the dower house Lady Cheney was said by her retainer to be 'out', the tone of voice implying unmistakably 'out to you'.

As their car drew up outside Gerry's block of flats they were greeted by the sight of Mlle Deschamps emerging. She was wearing a fur coat with a cossack-style hat and appeared startled to see them. Gerry climbed out of the car and they shook hands.

'Ah, Mr Montague,' she smiled, 'I had been intending to call on you but they told me you were out. So I was leaving disappointed.'

'Please come up now,' he invited. 'It will be a pleasure to talk to you.'

She looked at her wrist-watch. 'Alas, it is a little late,' she said doubtfully. 'Evidently this is not a convenient time for you, and for my part I have another appointment. But I shall be in London for a few days more. I will telephone to you from my hotel tomorrow morning.'

While she was speaking Talbot had disappeared into the flats and the Frenchwoman watched him go. Gerry said it would be no trouble if she cared to come up for a few minutes now she was here. But she brushed the suggestion aside and hurried off.

No sooner had she gone than Talbot reappeared. He had run all the way up and down the stairs. 'The manuscript's back again,' he panted.

'Back?' repeated Gerry in disbelief. 'How do you know? The flat's not open, is it?'

'It's lying on the door-mat,' said Talbot. 'Where is she?'

They both looked round. She had slipped well away and was moving at speed downhill towards the High Street.

'Come on,' yelled Talbot over his shoulder. 'We've got to grab her.' He was already running. Instinctively Gerry joined in the chase, and the Frenchwoman, seeing them follow, broke into a run. The road was narrow, dark and deserted, but traffic and bright lights lay a short way ahead.

A burst of speed by Talbot brought him level with her threequarters of the way down. He seized her arm and dragged her to a standstill. She swung at him with her free fist, but he secured that as well. While they were struggling a car turned up the hill and the driver slowed down.

'It's all right,' Gerry assured him. 'Just a little domestic brawl.' Convinced by his manner and accent, the driver let in the clutch and moved slowly off. Heavens, thought Gerry, I hope none of the neighbours are around.

'You'd better free her,' he said to Talbot, 'and we'll all go to the police station together. It's the other side of the traffic lights. We can't take the law into our own hands in Hampstead.'

'Can't we!' grunted Talbot, twisting one of her arms behind her back and frogmarching her back up the hill. 'If she prefers the police all she has to do is yell.'

Her eyes were blazing and she staggered as obstructively as she could. But her lips remained tightly shut until Talbot placed his left hand on her shoulder to help propel her along. Then with a quick twist of the head and body she contrived to bite his thumb and struggled hard to free herself. He held her fast and jerked her arm up towards breaking point. Pain brought tears to her eyes and she went limp.

'No foxing,' Talbot threatened her. 'Either you walk or I'll drag you along by the ankles.'

Sulkily she walked and eventually, with Gerry following and throwing nervous glances around him, they reached his flat apparently unobserved. From the floor of the hallway outside his front door he scooped up a brown-paper parcel.

Once in the drawing room Talbot pushed his captive without ceremony onto the sofa, and she sat where she fell rubbing her arm and heaving like a rough sea. Gerry eagerly opened the parcel and started to work his way methodically through the pages of the manuscript, which lay neatly arranged inside. While he did this, the American, with a muttered drawl about the dangers of catching rabies from a mad bitch, went to the bathroom to put disinfectant on his thumb.

It was some time before Gerry finished going through the folios, although this time they were numbered and in their correct order. 'There are two pages missing,' he said at last: 'consecutive ones.' Both the men looked at the Frenchwoman, but she answered them with one of her mysterious smiles and a slight shrug of the shoulders.

'Quit playing around with us,' demanded Talbot. 'Where are they?'

'Why ask me? I know nothing of this,' she said emphatically. 'You find me here and your manuscript back, and you dash to conclusions. It could have been returned at any hour while you are away.'

'In that case what did you come here for?' asked Gerry.

'I shall not discuss that after what has occurred, particularly in the presence of this Yankee muscle man. You will forgive me for saying, Mr Montague, that I do not like the company you keep.' She glared at Talbot.

'Any abuse from you is a compliment to me,' he observed. 'Now what about telling us who informed you Mr Montague was away, and whether it was before or after you had been up here? Was it the porter — or a stranger we can't check with? Maybe you're going to tell us you never came up the stairs at all?'

'And maybe I do not have the intention of telling you one single damn thing, you ill-mannered ruffian,' she shouted, rising indignantly to her feet. 'You will regret this, my friend. I am now making my journey to the police to lay a charge of assault against you. If you attempt to stop me leaving I shall scream so loudly that all Mr Montague's friends will believe terrible things of him. And let me remind you that you do not have a shred of evidence connecting me with this miserable manuscript, so you need not think it any use making counter-accusations to the police. Au revoir.'

She swept out of the flat and Talbot instantly galvanised himself into action.

'I'll lay a grand to a dime she doesn't dare show that face of hers in a police station,' he declared, jumping up. 'She's got those two pages tucked away somewhere, and there's only one chance of recovering them. You stay here where I can be sure of reaching you by phone. I'm going to tail her.'

Gerry sat slumped in gloom. 'If you're right she will have burned them or posted them to France,' he protested. 'I suppose they're the ones Pratt wanted to hang on to too. We owe him an apology this time — not to mention Mrs Pratt and Lady C.'

'Buck up,' said Talbot, slapping him on the shoulder. 'You've had nearly all your precious bits of paper returned to you — all except the ones that really matter. Still, I've a hunch that Frenchwoman has more to hide than those two sheets; so if the strong-arm stuff fails we can fall back on something more refined, say blackmail. You'd better lend me your topcoat. Goodness knows where I'll be spending the night.'

Snatching up Gerry's coat from the hall, he ran out and down the flights of stairs, taking them three at a time. Outside he could see the Frenchwoman some way ahead as she crossed a pool of light under a street lamp. By the time she reached the traffic lights at the bottom he was fifty yards behind and not anxious to be nearer. She was hurrying but had not looked round.

Now she crossed the road and was clearly visible standing at the corner of Heath Street and the High Street. Gerry had said that the police station lay straight on down the High Street, but she was not going on. Instead she lingered on the kerb trying to hail a taxi. Her face sometimes turned in his direction, but he kept in a patch of shadow. How quickly would he be able to find a taxi to follow hers?

After several minutes she gave up and turned into the tube station. Immediately he rushed across the road, bought a ticket at random and caught the next lift down. At the bottom he made for the south-bound platform and was in the nick of time to board a train. He had not seen her on it, but she wasn't on the platform and was unlikely to be travelling away from central London.

At every station he looked cautiously out and scanned the alighting passengers. She could scarcely be missed in that fur coat. But when there was no sign of her at Tottenham Court Road he began to grow apprehensive. Could she have been expecting to be followed, taken a north-bound train for one station, and then come back on a later one?

But at Leicester Square there she was, stepping off the train and tripping briskly through the long tunnel to the Piccadilly Line. There were a lot of people around, but not too many: he could keep her well in view without being conspicuous. They boarded an Earls Court train together, and he chose the next compartment to hers, now satisfied that she was heading for Kensington.

He was so busy congratulating himself on his knowledge of London that she almost eluded him by getting off at Green Park. Glancing through the windows between the compartments, he noticed her disappearance just in time and managed to hold back the closing doors and scramble out onto the platform. This cost him nothing worse than a moment's delay and a rebuke from a West Indian porter. When he reached the foot of the escalator she was already gliding past the brassière and corset ads near the top.

The night air in Piccadilly was cold. His ticket had been accepted without a glance by the collector. Now where was she? Buses, cars and taxis filled the road; she couldn't have crossed. Yet a quick look either way along the pavement revealed no trace of her. He swung round perplexed and almost knocked her over. She was right behind him, engrossed in finding change to buy an evening paper from a street-seller. He turned sharply away and hid his face by pretending to light a cigarette in the shelter of the entrance to the underground. Seeming not to have noticed him, she waited for a gap in the traffic, crossed the road and vanished into the Ritz.

Putting his life in jeopardy, he dived across the road in pursuit. Why hadn't she used the subway? His parents had once brought him to stay at the Ritz as a boy, and he prayed that the geography of the place would come back to him. By tailing her in at the Piccadilly entrance he remembered that he would miss the reception desk, which stood beside the main door on to Arlington Street. This left only one porter to pass, and he reassured him with a quick affable grin. In front lay the Palm Court with its naked gilt nymph. A sprinkling of guests were sitting there over coffee and brandies; to left and right the corridor stretched out — empty.

After an effort of memory he turned briskly left and found the lift. 'I'm with

Mlle Deschamps,' he told the lift man. 'She's this minute gone up in the elevator, I believe.'

'The French lady, sir. Yes, sir. Fifth floor.'

'Paying a cab off takes a darned long time when you're not familiar with the currency,' he grumbled. 'Now I've even forgotten the number of the room.' They had reached the fifth floor and he stepped out of the lift.

'I will ask at reception, sir, and come straight up again and let you know.'

Deciding that this might arouse suspicion, he told the man not to worry. 'I expect she'll be waiting for me outside,' he said. 'If not, I can ask the maid.'

The corridor was as empty as the one below. He walked the length of it without picking up a clue. Not a sound reached him, even from his own footsteps. All the doors were shut. Three were marked 'service' and one 'bath'; the one he wanted might be any of the others.

He was half way along, walking back towards the lift and wondering what the next move was, when he heard the sound of someone opening a door behind him. Swiftly he side-stepped into the bathroom, leaving the door ajar so that he could see out. In a matter of seconds the figure of the Frenchwoman flashed across his line of vision. She had removed her coat and hat and had the appearance of going downstairs for dinner or a drink at the bar.

Talbot gave her time to reach the lift-shaft; then he sneaked along towards the end of the corridor she had come from. One of the doors stood open by a crack. He pushed it gently and slid through.

It led into a suite. The hallway inside was lit, and there on a peg hung the fur coat. All four doors leading off were closed, and he tried each in turn after listening for any indication of occupation: they were bathroom, lavatory, bedroom and sitting room. The sitting room was in a corner of the building, poised over Piccadilly on one side and Green Park on the other. The curtains were drawn back and he looked down in turn on the string of lights humming with traffic and the still, deserted avenues. The glare from outside enabled him to see that the room contained a sofa and four armchairs as well as various tables and writing desks.

Returning softly to the hall, it suddenly occurred to him that if she hadn't closed the door behind her it might be because she would be coming straight back. His best prospect was the bedroom, and he'd better hurry. He went in, switched on the light and began to open a suitcase lying on the luggage stool. At that moment his ear caught the sharp snick of the catch on the outer door. He crouched behind the bed, waiting. A door opened, but not the one into the bedroom. Desperately he looked round for a hiding place.

There seemed to be no cupboards, so he tried one of the pair of full-length mirrors. It came open, revealing a walk-in cubby-hole for trunks and hanging clothes. One could go in by one mirror, walk right through and out by the other. He secured both the keys to prevent anyone locking him in, switched off the light, tiptoed into the cupboard and drew the mirror into place behind him.

After a short while someone came into the room. Sounds of undressing reached him, to the accompaniment of running bath water from the next room. It was certainly his quarry; her brand of scent, wafting into the cupboard, identified her.

He waited until the bath was over and a creaking of springs indicated that she had climbed into bed. Then he stepped out with a flourish.

Mlle Deschamps, sitting upright in bed, looked up from the evening paper she was reading. Her eyes narrowed at the sight of him, but her face registered no surprise or panic.

'Pardon me,' he said. He had expected her to jump out of her silky skin and had prepared some soothing words, but her only sign of nervousness was to pull the bed-jacket more tightly round her throat with one hand. The other lay beneath the bed-clothes.

'Mr Montague sent me to pick up his property. There's nothing to be frightened of. Just give and I'll go.'

'Frightened!' she spat out. 'Of a bully

who twists the arms of ladies? Naturally I am not frightened. To tell the truth, I was expecting you, Mr Talbot. Do you imagine I am in the habit of leaving the door to my hotel room open?'

'You left it open for me?'

'For you certainly. Tailing people requires intelligence, and intelligence is not your strong suit, is it? I had a feeling that you might be pursuing me, so what do I do? I stop in Piccadilly to make certain. You are so clever that you nearly walk into me.' She laughed in derision.

'And why did you want me in your bedroom?'

'Not for any romantic reason, I assure you, my dear friend. We may have been expelled together, like Adam and Eve, from Mr Pratt's Garden of Eden, but you must not allow that to put ideas into your head. No; I wish to tell you in private to stop meddling in my affairs and go back to America. The papers you are looking for are not here, so I could have no objection to your searching my apartment. On the assumption, that is, that you are not a common thief.'

'You operate on pretty big scale, don't you, Mlle Deschamps?' he said, ignoring the provocation. He threw a petticoat off a chair and sat down.

'Indeed yes.' She was flattered. 'You have seen the view from my sitting room? I am an art dealer, as I have told you, and whenever I come to England I bring over a number of pieces for sale. This hotel is near Bond Street, and somehow the atmosphere of a room at the Ritz induces my customers to pay higher prices for what I offer them. You understand?'

'No trouble with the customs?' he enquired.

'Pictures are not easy,' she admitted. 'But, for example, if one wears gloves think how many rings one may carry unobserved by making use of every finger.'

He stood up. 'It's interesting to meet a real crook,' he said. 'I first had my suspicions when you tried to steal the manuscript at High Cheney with that phony act of spilling wine on your dress.

Just how long have you been doing this sort of thing?'

'As a young girl in Paris during the German occupation I — how would you call it? — picked up bad habits. We all did — we had to, to survive. You were comfortably in your pram in America at that time, I think.'

She had allowed the bed-jacket to fall open and now picked an imaginary thread off the lace edging of her night-dress.

'After the war,' she went on, 'I was in an antique shop here in London. Then I returned to Paris to join my father in his business. We love beautiful things. Also, we love to live well and my father is not rich like yours. So — ' she opened her eyes and shrugged a fleshy pair of shoulders expressively. 'My father has many friends. One of them is the President of our tennis organisation and when he told us what was happening at High Cheney I guessed that Mr Pratt was really hunting for the heirlooms. Among antique dealers they are a legend. It was a small matter to have the invitation

254

transferred to me.'

She was lying back boasting and provoking him, and he reacted brusquely: 'So now you think you've got a clue to them in the manuscript? Well, I don't believe you when you say the missing pages aren't here. No more stalling: you'd better give them to me now.' He moved towards her.

'That's enough,' she snapped, her sweet voice turning sour. There was a revolver in her hand.

'I hate you so much, Mr Talbot Bloody Talbot,' she went on, 'it would be a pleasure to kill you. Unhappily that might be too troublesome, but now you may have the true reason why I wanted you in my room. I am going to shoot you. You have broken in at night and I shall enjoy wounding you before ringing for assistance. The only question is where.' She pointed the gun up and down his body as though undecided. 'Nothing below the waist can be fatal, I think.' She gave another of her laughs — a gay tinkling one.

Talbot retreated and sat down again.

There seemed no doubt about it; she intended to shoot him! Cold fingers crept down his spine.

'How I detest you!' she continued gloatingly. 'You should be taught a lesson. Still, it's a pity you are not to be trusted; otherwise we might strike a bargain. Over this.' She fished in her bosom and produced two pieces of paper.

'A bargain?' he asked hoarsely. He was trying hard to appear relaxed, but his voice betrayed him.

'Yes. You were right about the manuscript sheets being here; I confess it. What intriguing handwriting that clergyman had!' She was talking comfortably, but keeping a steady grip on the gun and watching him for the smallest movement. 'The story advances one a little in our mystery, but it would be agreeable to me to have the co-operation of someone who knows tennis. It is imperative that you do not see what is written, but if I were to ask you one or two questions and you were to answer truthfully, then I might permit you to select where you would prefer to be shot. The final result, though, would be dependent on my aim, naturally.' She tinkled again.

'What is it you want to know? Let me see.' he put out a hand.

'Oh no,' she smirked. 'But certainly not. If you are so forward, I withdraw the offer. There is someone else who will help me, I think. I was merely playing a game with you before delivering the *coup de grâce*. They must be returned to safe custody.'

In the second when she looked down to stow them away he dropped out of the chair and flung himself on the floor. Protected by the side of the bed, he rose, grasped the eider-down and holding it in front of him like a screen bundled it over the Frenchwoman's head. As he did so, he visualised her firing. The bullet would whip through the eider-down, shatter the double window-pane and be lost over Mayfair — if he didn't stop it on the way.

But before she squeezed the trigger he had wrenched the revolver out of her hand. Hastily he broke it open. Idiot!

She had been bluffing, as he should have guessed. The chambers were all empty!

With the other hand she was holding fast to the bell-pull; outside in the corridor an alarm was pealing hysterically for aid. With a grim, cold gesture and no regard for the proprieties he ripped open the front of her night-dress and extracted the crumpled papers from between her breasts. As he did so he gave her a quick, insulting look, intended to convey that he had seen better elsewhere and the papers were all he wanted from her, thank you very much. As if the bell were not enough she began screaming 'Assassin, assassin' at the top of her voice.

Deciding not to risk explanations, he ran for the door. It was locked. Already he could hear an urgent knocking on the outer one. Crossing the floor at a stride, he snatched open the window. It was full length and gave onto a narrow balcony overlooking the street. So far as he could see, the balcony ran all along the front of the buildings, but a series of spiked iron railings divided it between the rooms.

He glanced back. The Frenchwoman

had opened both doors and was shrilly pointing him out. Perilously he clambered onto the stone parapet: the noise of the traffic below was deafening. Balancing with his hands stretched out like a tight-rope walker, he kept his eyes fixed on the roof-tops ahead and placed one foot hesitantly in front of the other. One false step and he would be a sprawling corpse in the middle of Piccadilly.

15

With his long body jutting into mid-air Talbot grasped the iron spikes and swung himself round them. Angry voices were raised behind him, and he dared not even now drop down to the safety of the balcony. He would be captured for certain in the next-door suite.

Instead he continued resolutely along the balustrade. The coolness of the night had cleared his head, and he felt in such control of every nerve and muscle that he allowed himself a downward glance at the red tops of the buses and the tiny pedestrians on the sidewalk. At once a wave of vertigo overcame him. He swayed and, feeling himself fall, hurled the whole weight of his body towards the building. By a fraction of a second he made it. Instead of tumbling into space he found himself lying on his back on the balcony.

Picking himself up, he clambered back

onto the parapet, teeth gritted. Keeping his eyes fixed level and straight ahead, he edged one by one round three more rows of spikes. The section of the balcony where he now stood was shared by two windows. Unlike the ones he had passed they were uncurtained. One he could see was a sitting room and the other a bedroom: both seemed unoccupied. He leapt down and smashed one of the windows near the catch with his fist. Then he put his hand inside to open it and stepped warily into the room.

It was full of furniture — massive Edwardian furniture. He flopped onto a gilt settee and wiped the sweat off his face. He was still wearing Gerry's overcoat, which was far too short for him and had impeded his acrobatics. From a looking-glass surmounted by a trumpeting angel he learned what a wreck he looked. Without a wash and brush-up he couldn't possibly try to pass himself off as a guest. For the moment he must concentrate on finding somewhere safer to hide; the search party would be working its way along.

He went through the hall and opened the outer door stealthily. Sounds of disturbance reached him from back down the corridor. He ventured a peep. The backs of two or three men were disappearing into one of the rooms. Instantly he edged out, closing the door behind him, and with the coast momentarily clear made a dash up the corridor, across it and into the refuge of the bathroom. He locked the door and sat down on a stool, panting with relief.

If there was a fire escape it would be on this side of the hotel. He opened the window and looked out, but there was a sheer drop and no sign of a ladder. Suddenly he remembered another inside staircase at the opposite end of the building to the main one which ran up alongside the elevator.

Talbot decided that when the excitement had blown over this secondary staircase would be his best hope. In the meantime he could do nothing but remain alert and wait. He returned to the stool and sat staring at a notice above the bidet which read: 'Ritz Hotel. COIFFEURS. Ladies' and gentlemen's salons on the first floor.' How many visitors to the Ritz used the bidet, he wondered.

His preoccupation was shattered by a discreet knock on the door.

'Yes,' he barked, assuming a pukka-sahib, Poona-colonel voice. 'Who's theah?'

'I beg your pardon, sir,' came an obsequious voice from outside, and he heard the next door-handle being gently turned.

An hour later he slid back the bolt and peered out. A uniformed porter was sitting at the end of the corridor with the whole length of it in full view. Talbot withdrew his head hastily. It would be impossible to move out without being seen: the corridor was perfectly straight and the lighting full on.

'Never pass up a chance of relaxing' was one of his father's maxims — and that (or something else) had kept the old boy free of ulcers in spite of a life-time of pressures in the money-making race. When nothing more attractive presented itself Talbot was always ready to go along with this. With the mat as a pillow he stretched out in the bath, his legs hanging over the edge, and composed himself for sleep.

The night passed uncomfortably but uneventfully. His clothes provided poor insulation against porcelain, but he managed to doze in short spells. At six o'clock he checked on the watching figure; it was still there. The same at seven. But at eight it had gone.

He washed and tidied himself, took off the overcoat to carry on his arm, and crossed to the mirror. His sports jacket and trousers were casual but expensive and might pass. He was unshaven but his beard was light. Was it worth risking a visit to the gentlemen's salon on the first floor? No, he decided regretfully; it certainly wasn't.

Humming a gay pom-pom-pom tune of his own composition, he walked out, turned away from the main staircase and reached the secondary one without meeting anybody. At the bottom a closed door barred the way. Fortunately the catch was on his side: there was no porter, and the door was evidently intended to stop unauthorised entry. The prevention of an unauthorised exit had not been catered for.

He found himself emerging into the main ground-floor corridor beside the entrance to the restaurant and face to face with a prowling official who might have been a house detective or even a plain-clothes policeman. The man stared suspiciously at Talbot, who asked himself how frank la Deschamps was likely to have been about the whole affair. His guess was that she would have suppressed a lot, but would that have included his description? Once he had escaped from her room, would she really want him caught? Emotionally she might, but as a hardened racketeer couldn't she be relied on to concentrate strictly on self-interest and the main chance? A scandal wouldn't do her much good, and she would have to reckon with his accusing her of theft and splitting on her smuggling activities.

'Good morning, sir,' said the man. 'Can I help you at all?'

'No, thank you,' he replied, and as he spoke a glimpse of the ornate room in front of him struck a providential chord in his memory. 'Breakfast in the Marie Antoinette room as usual, I presume?'

The other's suspicions faded visibly. 'Yes, sir,' he smiled. 'Breakfast is now being served.'

'Good,' said Talbot. 'I'll dump my coat in the cloakroom and be right back.'

A moment later he was outside in the arcade. He turned quickly into Green Park, put a hundred yards or so between himself and the hotel, wrapped the coat round his shoulders and sat down on a bench with a long-drawn-out sigh of relief. Behind him the traffic, as always, was bustling along Piccadilly; in front between the grass and the yellowing leaves on the trees stretched the railings and wall of the palace. He'd made it!

In the bathroom he had run his eye briefly over the manuscript pages before secreting them inside one of his socks under the sole of his foot. Now, even before looking for food and drink, he was going to read them through. Under the interested scrutiny of a tramp on the next bench he took off his shoe and sock and extracted the wad of paper. It was in poor shape but still legible. The Reverend Mr Featherstonehaugh's calligraphic flourishes were nothing if not distinct.

During the play of a game of tennis with Sir Edmund Cheney one day (he read) *the King chanced to put down a fine chase, which fell better than a yard. When the two players crossed at the net preparatory to playing off the chase, the King, who had for some time coveted a hunting dog, the property of Sir Edmund, challenged his opponent with these words:*

'I wager you, Sir Edmund, any mortal or other thing you care to name against your bitch, Grey Bess, that you will not gain this point.'

Now in days gone by, regrettable to relate, betting was a common practice in the tennis court, and large sums of money, not to mention valuable estates and chattels, were won and lost in this lamentable manner on the outcome of a single chase. Yet the wagers were more commonly offered and accepted among spectators in the galleries than between the players, and the King's laying of a wager after he had made a good chase was an exercise of the royal prerogative hardly in conformity with the precepts of good sportsmanship. For by the etiquette prevailing at court Sir Edmund was bound to accept the challenge.

This he did with a good grace, pointing to a curious picture which hung in the dedans. This painting was said to have been executed by that consumate artist, Hans Holbein the younger, at the King's express command, and was reputedly of an obscene nature, depicting in an indelicate manner the person of the King himself with the two great loves of his life: Women and Tennis. The full-length figure of His Majesty is shown in his accoutrements of state, but in place of the customary orb and sceptre he is holding a tennis racket in one hand, while the other is exploring the person of a female companion of unknown identity. There are other details too gross to mention, and it is a sad commentary on the morals of ancient times that an artist of Holbein's sublime stature should have been compelled — doubtless a refusal would have imperilled his head — to prostitute his art in the perpetration of an indecency of such enormity.

The King frowned at Sir Edmund's choice, for the picture was a treasured favourite. Confident, however, of a successful outcome (Sir Edmund being a player of moderate ability), he made ready for play by ordering his page to deliver the service on his behalf, himself standing planted four-square for the defence of the dedans. Alas! His Majesty had overlooked a matter of some consequence. I refer to the bisque. Then as now, this was the most generally accepted form of handicap in tennis. The player to whom it is awarded may exercise his right to it on one occasion only during each set, but at any time that he so determines. By the simple and sole expedient of pronouncing the word 'bisque' he makes the next point his own.

Now Sir Edmund, as the weaker

performer of the two, was in the invariable habit of receiving a bisque from the King and had not yet expended it during the present set. Accordingly he held up his hand to bid the King's man desist from serving, stepped forward to the net, bowed low and said: 'Bisque, my liege.'

We are given to understand that the ensuing explosion of His Majesty's wrath was terrible to witness.

'A bisque is not a better chase, Sir Edmund,' he thundered. 'I challenged you to beat my chase, which you cannot do except on the floor or in the dedans.'

'Your Majesty,' declared Sir Edmund unabashed, 'will pardon his humble servant, but the ladies and gentlemen in the galleries will bear me witness that the challenge was not to beat the royal chase but to win the next point. Your humble servant submits that he has fairly won the point and waits upon the marker, who will no doubt be pleased to confirm his submission.'

The court marker was one, Anthony Ansley by name, who had held the same office under King Henry's father, and he, although in some agitation, resolutely supported Sir Edmund's contention. The King strode from the court, and Sir Edmund the same day prudently retired to his country estate to allow his sovereign's wrath to cool and to await his pleasure.

A week after his arrival there, a posse of men in the King's uniform rode up to the door, and Sir Edmund's family resigned themselves to his death and their disgrace. The bold knight is reported to have received them with Grey Bess seated at his side, her head resting on her master's lap. But instead of demanding the dog and removing Sir Edmund to the Tower, the royal servants handed over the King's picture, which they had brought with them, remounted their horses and returned along the road to London whence they came.

Since that day the painting, which is known to connoisseurs as the Cheney Holbein, has been enveloped in mystery and never exhibited to the public view. The author has good reason to believe, *however, that it still remains in the possession of the family*.

(*Note: This passage omitted at the express and urgent request of the Lord Cheney*.)

So!

Talbot stuffed the papers into his pocket and went in search of fried eggs and coffee.

Afterwards he strolled back to Bond Street and entered the gallery of a firm of art dealers. One of their windows displayed a skating scene by a seventeenth-century Dutchman and the other was devoted to a primitive Madonna and Child, painted predominantly in gold. The firm's interests seemed catholic enough for his purpose.

The gallery was barely open at that hour and no one took any notice of him until he called 'hey!' to an assistant's back. The man turned round. He was young and well-groomed and took unkindly to being 'heyed'.

'Do you want anything?' he asked in an aggrieved voice.

'Yes; I want to buy a picture,' said Talbot.

The assistant reluctantly put down the feather duster with which he had been flicking the tops of the picture-frames. 'Any particular subject or artist?' he enquired.

'Yes; a Holbein.' Talbot spoke as though he were ordering four ounces of Cheddar cheese.

'A Holbein!' The young man was taken aback and gave Talbot a quick appraisal, indicating that in his opinion prospective buyers of Holbeins might be expected to wear overcoats which fitted.

'H-O-L-B-E-I-N,' Talbot spelt out: 'Hans the Younger. Have you any? I imagined you dealt in all the Old Masters.'

'Our stock is exceptionally large, sir,' said the assistant reprovingly, 'but I really couldn't say whether there are any Holbeins on the market at the present time. Will you excuse me? The manager may be able to help you.'

When he came, the manager eyed Talbot shrewdly and announced that they had no Holbeins in stock, nor did he know of any for sale. Would something else of the German School, perhaps of a rather later period, be of interest? The price would be more reasonable.

This gave Talbot his opening for enquiring what a Holbein would cost.

'What indeed!' exclaimed the manager. 'With Renoirs and Cézannes and Picassos sometimes fetching a hundred thousand pounds! Not that anyone can tell nowadays until a picture is actually put up for sale, you understand. So much depends on its condition, subject matter, size and so on. Above all, on the prevailing fashion. Today millionaires are installing El Grecos in the bathrooms of their yachts; tomorrow they may want Holbeins for the kitchens of their country cottages. Who knows? At the moment Impressionists are being bought for investment; in a few years it may be Pre-Raphaelites. However, if you've set your heart on owning a Holbein you would need to be pretty wealthy.'

'I *am* pretty wealthy,' said Talbot

evenly, 'wealthy enough to buy up this joint anyhow, I reckon. Let's take one example. What would the Cheney Holbein cost me?'

The manager opened his eyes wide for the first time that morning. 'Has that turned up?' he asked.

'I've no reason to think so,' Talbot answered. 'It simply came into my head as one example of a Holbein not already in a public gallery.'

'It's listed in the reference books as missing,' said the manager. Talbot could sense that his interest was enormous. 'I believe it contained a full-length portrait of Henry VIII, as well as some rather special features which — er — might enhance the value. Benedetto Gennari painted a very hot picture for Charles II which is still in existence, you know, and Rowlandson did the same thing for George IV. But this would be in a different class. Only an idiot would hazard a guess at what it would fetch at today's prices.'

'Be an idiot then,' urged Talbot. 'Just for once.'

The manager allowed himself a smile and pronounced judgment: 'Let us say, shall we, that you would be most unlikely to receive any change from a quarter of a million pounds. Possibly half a million.'

'Pounds, mind you, not dollars, sir,' he added, getting his own back a little as he bowed Talbot out of the gallery.

16

'You are chairman of a property company on the Kent coast.'

Mr Pratt's remark lay half way between a statement and a question. It was Thursday, the day of Talbot's escape from the Ritz and his foray into Bond Street, and Mr Pratt and Major Winterton were enjoying an expense-account lunch at an eastern outpost of the West End — the Waldorf Grill.

The major, who thought he had been invited in order to talk tennis, came smartly to the alert. Feigning deafness, he pretended not to have heard and continued dissecting a sole bonne femme with his customary precision.

Mr Pratt was not a man to be deterred. 'Not doing very well down there, are you?' he pressed.

'Eh? Oh, I beg your pardon.' The major recognised reluctantly that this was to be a topic for discussion, not an opening conversational gambit. He cleared the bones to one side of his plate with the air of a general bringing his campaign to a successful conclusion before turning to other matters. 'That company of mine, you mean? It has given us one or two nasty turns over the past few years, I don't deny it, but we are round the corner now, I'm glad to say. Not that there has ever been any big money involved. It's a modest little show.'

'You lost £20,000 in your last financial year,' Mr Pratt observed.

Such bluntness pained the major, who was a blunt man himself. 'That was exceptional — just a temporary setback,' he protested. 'We are doing very much better now. Things have not been at all easy in that area since the war. It was evacuated and went to seed and hasn't come back into favour yet. Too far from London for comfortable commuting; precious little local industry; and in the front line again for the next war. I grew to like it when I was stationed at Shorncliffe a long time ago and decided to make my headquarters there when I came out of the army. It's a grand, healthy spot with decent people living there and a great future. Mark my words!'

'Your interest in the company is 17%,' said Mr Pratt, spearing a segment of fried scampi and rotating it methodically in a pool of tartare sauce. 'You sank all your pension rights in it, I dare say.'

By now the major was thoroughly alarmed. 'I don't think it's quite as much as 17%,' he said. 'But where is this leading, may I ask?'

'Unless you've sold part of your holding since the last report was filed at the Board of Trade, it's 17¼% precisely,' declared Mr Pratt, laying on the table a sheet of paper containing a list of names and figures. 'The largest single shareholding. For half a crown at Bush House I've also had a chap studying the annual balance sheets. At your present rate of progress you should be in Carey Street inside three years.'

The major gulped and thumped the table angrily. 'That is defamatory, sir,' he declared, raising his voice. 'I must ask you to withdraw that remark and apologise.'

'I lunch at the Waldorf,' replied Mr Pratt, 'because the tables are so far apart. Unless you choose to shout, we can't be overheard. So the question of defamation doesn't arise, and why should I withdraw a plain statement of fact?'

'I did not accept your hospitality in order to be insulted,' glared the major.

'My offer isn't insulting,' said Mr Pratt. 'On the contrary, it's outrageously flattering. I'll buy your shares at twice what you paid for them, and you can stay on as chairman at double your present remuneration, with a five-year contract.'

The major, who had risen to his feet and was about to fling his napkin onto the table, subsided into his chair and spread the napkin neatly over his knees again. Not a quick thinker, he was exploring his mind frantically for the snags. His dearest wish was to be bought out of this ailing company and he'd have been content simply to see his money back.

'The conditions?' he asked.

'That you use your influence with the other shareholders to induce them to sell. I shall need it as a wholly-owned subsidiary.'

'It would have to be on the same terms as mine.'

'I'll agree to that provided they accept the offer by a certain date. After that they'll be lucky to get anything at all. It'll be expensive, but your company has certain attractions for me, surprising though it may seem.'

'It is a first-class concern,' said the major, with more loyalty than truth.

'If viewed from a rather special angle,' agreed Mr Pratt. 'You're in the right line of business for me, in an area where I'm not already operating, and your losses are splendid tax assets — I congratulate you. But there's another condition: no haggling. I know the property market; you won't get a higher offer from anyone else and I'm not going to improve mine. You don't want to fall between two stools looking a gift-horse in the mouth, do you? Is that understood?'

'It is and, speaking for myself, I shall probably agree. Never did like the bazaar way of doing business — ungentlemanly. Is that all?' Under a thin cloak of wariness the major was now bursting with excitement. For months he had been devising means of getting out of the company.

'Yes, there's one more thing: your help over this affair which blew up last weekend.'

'Poor Nicholls,' sighed the major. 'I can't get over it. You don't think there was anything about the way he died that hasn't come out? I mean — '

'Certainly not. I'm pleased to say the inquest went off very quietly yesterday afternoon. Young Ted and I were the only two required to give evidence, and there was nothing but the barest mention of how much he'd had to drink. Accidental death and no scandal. Of course I had a few words with the coroner beforehand.' Mr Pratt treated the major to one of his power-behind-the-scenes looks.

'Here,' he went on. 'You'd better read this.' He took from his pocket a typescript copy of the pages Talbot had seized from Mlle Deschamps the previous night, and passed them across the table.

'By Jove!' exclaimed the major when he had finished. 'By Jove! I suppose the story is authentic. I've never heard it before and Featherstonehaugh wouldn't have been above making it up if half what they say is true. As for the picture, there have been odd rumours about it, but never that it still exists.'

'I'm satisfied about the authenticity,' said Mr Pratt. They had moved on to the cheese course, and he broke off. 'Have a port with your Stilton. Waiter! Two large ports — Croft's '35 and no nonsense, mind. The matter that concerns me' — he turned back to the major — 'is the whereabouts of the picture.'

'Can't the Cheneys help? It would still belong to them, I presume.'

'You presume wrong,' Mr Pratt corrected him sharply. 'It belongs to me.' He explained that he had bought everything on the estate and the terms of the contract included the ownership of items such as this.

The major's eyebrows rose to the middle of his forehead. 'Do you mean that you knew about this before you purchased the property?' he demanded.

'You're at liberty not to believe me,' declared Mr Pratt handsomely, 'but it so happens that I didn't. This has only come into my hands since the weekend. But, funnily enough, I had my suspicions that there might be something else hidden at High Cheney. One day while the negotiations for the sale were still going on I was searching in the library for information about the family, when this fell out of an old family Bible.' He handed over another piece of paper and took a generous gulp of port, eyeing his guest beadily over the top of the glass.

At the head of the single sheet of writing paper stood a coronet, die-stamped in deepest blue. There was no address, and the untidily scrawled message, beginning 'To the Head of the Family,' bore no date. 'Keep the tennis court in good repair' (it ran). 'This is my special wish. Tennis was the foundation of our fortune. Should we fall on ill times, look there again. There is that which will mend matters at H.C. in the tennis court. Do not show this to yr. wife & daughters.' The signature was the single letter 'C'.

The two men looked at each other across the table. 'You've shown this to Gavin?' the major enquired.

'Not yet,' replied Mr Pratt blandly. 'He hasn't been around much at High Cheney and the message specifically forbids me to show it to Lady Cheney. Anyway, I'm head of the family there now, and I've put the court back into good repair, which is more than the rest of them did. According to my calculations, this was written by the eighth earl, who was the last tennis-player in the family: his wife nagged him into giving it up, they say. I've shown it to no one else, and the chances are that you and I are the only people to have seen it since it was written. There were several Bibles, and the one it was in must have gone out of use.'

'You should have shown it to Gavin.'

Mr Pratt nodded. 'But first,' he said, 'I wanted to find out what it was about. I made some fairly extensive enquiries and learned about a gold chalice, which Lady Cheney believes is still lying in some secret hiding-place on the premises.'

'So you kept quiet, simulated an interest in tennis and had the court restored on that pretext?' The major's tone indicated that in his opinion a man could hardly sink lower.

'I'm too old to play myself, but I hoped Angel would take the game up — I'm sure she will if Ted stays,' replied Mr Pratt. 'But I won't pretend that I didn't hope the chalice would come to light. The abbot's lodgings stood on the site and Lady Cheney was obviously on the trail. When nothing turned up I was stuck; then someone told me about Montague's manuscript and it occurred to me there might be a clue there. The copy of the *Annals* in the library at High Cheney is inscribed to the eighth earl from the author 'in deep gratitude for his never-failing generosity.' The inscription ends with two exclamation marks, so I suspected the manuscript might contain something interesting. I'd found out about Rev.

Featherstonehaugh's blackmailing tricks.'

'Kept a mistress in St John's Wood, too, you know,' grunted the major. 'Nice and handy from Lord's. Quite a chap for a padre!' He leaned back. Two whisky sours, half a bottle of Durkheimer Spielberg and a large port were beginning to take their toll. Long service in India had accustomed him to a siesta after tiffin, and he was torn between somnolence and contempt for this upstart who was using the royal and noble game of tennis as a means for money-grubbing ends. His mind was also awhirl with speculation about the exact nature of the obscenity depicted in the painting.

'I'm now told that Lady Cheney is even further round the bend than I'd thought and that the chalice is in Rome,' continued Mr Pratt. 'Also, the bit about not showing one's wife and daughters makes sense if the writer is referring to this picture. Featherstonehaugh stayed at High Cheney and played tennis there quite often. It looks to me as if he actually had a sight of it. Then he threatened to publish this passage and collected handsomely for holding it out. The earl's wife was a pious old thing and might have insisted on the picture being destroyed. So, to guard against future trouble, the earl hid it somewhere in the court — in the walls or under the floor — and left this note behind. To judge from the writing, he was pretty gaga at the time — probably scared stiff of his wife, poor man.'

'What would it be worth, an old painting like that?'

'A thousand or so, possibly. It's not the money that interests me — heaven knows, I've enough of that.' Mr Pratt's face exuded frankness from every pore. 'You can't imagine what pleasure it would give a rough diamond like me to own a historic painting like that. I'd loan it to the National Gallery if they would exhibit it. And after I'm gone it could stay there with a gold label on the frame saying 'The Alfred Pratt Bequest'. They might even call it the Pratt Holbein.'

'There's glory for you,' commented the major. 'Alice in Wonderland, you know.

Damn fine book — complete mystery to foreigners.' Two more large ports had put in an appearance and the major was growing fuddled.

Mr Pratt, on the other hand, although expansive, remained purposefully clear-headed. This was business. Off duty he could become merry on far less; on duty alcohol was a weapon. 'Foreigners!' He took up the word. 'We must look out there; they're after it. Make no mistake about that. I need an ally, Winterton.'

'After what?' The major leaned forward. He was in danger of losing the thread.

'Our Holbein,' said Mr Pratt. 'Our Bluff King Hal.'

'I don't know about 'our',' the major protested. 'If you ask me it belongs to the Cheneys. A fine fellow, young Gavin. Chip off the old block. Mustn't do him down.'

Mr Pratt's patience was reaching exhaustion point. But he restrained himself and adopted an injured tone.

'As soon as the picture is found the legal ownership can be decided — in the courts, if necessary. But I assure you no one would dream of doing the Cheney family out of its rights, least of all me. I've already done them one good turn by paying a lot more for their house than anyone else would have done — just as I'm going to do with your company. The important thing now is to act together; otherwise the Americans or the French will steal the picture from us.'

His attempt to rouse the major's xenophobia was only partially successful. 'Mustn't allow that, of course,' he responded. 'But if you're referring to Talbot Talbot and Mlle Deschamps, I must insist that Talbot is above suspicion. He's all set to be the finest amateur player since Jay Gould. The Frenchwoman I can't answer for. She holds herself well, but probably she's no better than she ought to be.'

Mr Pratt related how the two of them had been discovered together in suspicious circumstances beside the court on Monday morning; how his telephone enquiries to Paris had shown the woman to be a complete fraud — and would the major take up the matter with the

French tennis association; how Talbot had actually broken into the court at night and even returned, the following day, and shamelessly accused Mrs Pratt of stealing Montague's manuscript. They were a pair of international crooks who would stick at nothing.

The major protested again that this could not be true of a man like Talbot. As for the French hussy, he was now inclined to believe that he had been maligning Nicholls and that she had been responsible for the first disappearance of the manuscript. His alarm at hearing that it was lost again jolted him into mental activity and he wanted to know how Mr Pratt came by his copy of the story about Henry VIII and Sir Edmund.

Mr Pratt declared with literal truth that he had obtained the relevant pages from Gerry and returned them to him before the second loss. 'Don't you realise,' he asked the major in a lowered voice, 'that as well as being foreigners these two are both Roman Catholics? They might have been sent on a mission by the Vatican. I've been reading up some history. The

Popes have never forgiven Henry VIII for dissolving the monasteries, it seems. A portrait like this is just what they need to discredit him.'

Although robustly Anglican (as Mr Pratt's private dossier on him had reported), the major was still sufficiently alert to regard this as far-fetched. They were smoking Coronas now, and his main interest was to bring matters to a speedy conclusion and find somewhere for a quiet lie-down. An hour of the old shut-eye — studying for the Staff College, they used to call it — and he would be as right as rain again.

'What do you want me to do?' he asked.

'Help me find the picture. I'm not a mean man and if it's found you won't regret it. The little matter of your company is to be strictly between ourselves. You can be sounding out your fellow-directors and shareholders on behalf of an unknown bidder, and you and Mrs Winterton can both come down to High Cheney tomorrow. Pretend it's for another tennis weekend. Bring your things and have a game with Ted. We must get off the mark quickly and beat the other side to it.'

The major, aware for some time where the conversation had been leading, accepted without demur: 'On the understanding that this is all above board and not detrimental to the Cheneys, I agree. But I'm not at all clear how I can help.' He waved away some cigar smoke as though to clear his thoughts.

'Take this for example.' Mr Pratt rapped the typescript sheets with his knuckles. 'There's too much mumbo-jumbo here for me; I'm out of my depth. So far as I'm concerned, a bisque is a soup; it took me long enough to learn that and I'm not starting again at my age. I need someone who knows all about tennis to advise me and examine that court by the square inch. You run tennis in this country, don't you, and you were a sapper, I'm told?'

The major nodded.

'There you are then. We'll spend the weekend on it, and you can check all the measurements for secret cubby-holes.

You must know all the likely hiding-places in a tennis court, and I'll have some workmen available in case you want an excavation or demolition squad.'

'That won't be necessary, I'm positive,' protested the major. The fellow was now threatening to have the court pulled down unless the picture were found! 'If the eighth earl was a lover of the game, as he undoubtedly was, he wouldn't have secreted it where the court would have to be damaged to retrieve it.'

'You're right,' agreed Mr Pratt, sealing their compact by rising and putting his arm round his guest's shoulders. 'That's the sort of point I would never have thought of. We're both military men, we saved the Old Country from Hitler, and now we're going to rescue a bit of the national heritage before it's smuggled abroad.'

'A real feelthy peecture,' mused the major with a discreet snigger. 'I wonder what the royal old reprobate is shown as doing. Hotting up that wench, I'll be bound. Died of V.D., didn't he?'

They moved heavily up the stairs out

of the restaurant, and among the aperitif tables at the top the major spied a sofa. He took out his watch. 'I've an appointment not far from here in a few minutes,' he announced. 'I'll wait here.'

Before parting they arranged details for the next day, and by the time ex-sergeant Pratt had collected his fur-collared coat from the cloakroom, a gentle, rhythmic wheezing had already broken out from the direction of the sofa.

17

Mrs Winterton was a memsahib. Brought up in a country rectory, she had been shipped out to India at the age of seventeen in what was unkindly known as the Calcutta fishing fleet. Her sister had married into jute and she was expected to do the same. Instead she had married Lieutenant Winterton and followed him from cantonment to cantonment, accompanied by a string of servants and polo ponies. After this splendour life in England since 1947 had provided an anti-climax of insolent but irreplaceable servants and long bleak winters. She had even had to learn to cook.

Perpetually discontented and unsure of herself, she was anxious, above all, about the major, who spent most of his life in clubs and dabbled in business. She couldn't understand what he was up to with his property company and didn't believe that he could either.

Since his retirement from the army they had lived in two small flats: one near Regent's Park and the other (belonging to the major's company) on the Leas at Folkestone overlooking the Channel. On Fridays their established routine was to leave London and spend the weekend on the coast, but the previous evening the major had peremptorily announced a second visit to High Cheney. She wanted to know why they were going again and had been told 'tennis', only to find on arrival that there were no other guests and young Nicholls, the professional, was away at his father's funeral. From his air of suppressed excitement she was convinced that her husband was being lured by Mr Pratt into some nefarious activity and would end up in prison.

She was sitting by herself in the morning room at High Cheney, day-dreaming at the french window and re-living the happier parts of her life. Outside on the left the drive sloped down towards the village; on the right stood the tennis-court building, where the major had been mysteriously occupied for the past four hours. What could he be doing there all that time, she wanted to know; first with Mr Pratt and now with Angel, neither of whom played the game.

She shivered. Another almost sunless summer had slipped away and it would soon be dark. In the old days she would have been making the annual descent from the hills — from Darjeeling or Mussoorie; from the lakeside at Naini Tal; or dear Simla with those evening walks along the Mall while the sun set on the snow peaks of the Himalaya. The monsoon would be laying the dust in the plains and the married quarters coming to life again for another winter of balls and gymkhanas. Dare she risk the major's anger by going down to the court to see what was happening?

It was as well she didn't. In the court the major was in a state of seething frustration. He had laboriously tapped the entire surface of the walls and floor, probed into and behind the grille, explored the gutter at the bottom of the net, tested and dug a knife into the woodwork surrounding all the galleries and been over the dedans and ante-room inch by inch. With the aid of the ladder he had even clambered into the rafters and over the roof. During the whole of this meticulous search his host had been of no practical assistance: he had merely stood around smoking a cigar and making pertinent but impractical suggestions. When he had returned to the house, Angel had taken his place, ostensibly to hold the foot of the ladder. At least she was easy on the eye, but she didn't pretend to believe in the picture's existence and watched him with a smile which the major found tiresome.

In the remaining daylight he was checking the measurements of the court against the plans in order to find out whether any false walls or fronts had been built. The discovery that while the width of the penthouse over the side galleries and the grille ran to seven feet the dedans penthouse measured eight roused him, until he found that this was specified by the architect and recalled that this discrepancy had been a feature of the old court at Lord's. It was when he was engaged in measuring the angle of the tambour that the posse of uninvited guests entered the court.

Now that they knew what they were looking for, Talbot and Gerry had decided on one more, immediate frontal attack on the Pratt domain. Gavin had disappointed them by being unable to come, but Timothy had left his sick-bed to join the party and the three of them had motored down to High Cheney in his car for a show-down. Surprised at finding the wire fortifications removed, they had stopped the car half-way up the drive and walked across to the court.

'Ha! Hullo there!' Caught, as it were, in the act of aiding and abetting the enemy, the major greeted them a trifle sheepishly.

'How do you do, sir,' said Timothy. 'Are you secretly preparing a rival work to Featherstonehaugh and Gerry? Winterton on The Tambour or something like that?'

'I'd start at Tuxedo if I were,' replied the major, 'there's a fiendish angle for you! No, no; I'm just putting in time

300

before having a game with young Ted. What have you chaps come for? Pratt didn't tell me he'd invited you.'

Gerry and Talbot had been exchanging frigid courtesies with Angel. The atmosphere was strained, and no one answered.

'The same thing as you came for, I reckon,' replied Talbot after a pause. 'But uninvited.'

'You don't mean the Featherstone-haugh manuscript?' enquired the major.

'That has been recovered, I'm glad to say,' Gerry answered. 'Talbot and I are here to present our apologies to Mrs Pratt and the whole family for making a most inexcusable mistake about who took it. The culprit turned out to be Mlle Deschamps.' He bowed to Angel, who accepted the apology with a smile.

'I'm most relieved,' said the major, 'and not at all surprised. Never did trust that woman. A foreigner, you know, and bogus.'

Nettled by this reference to foreigners, Talbot looked pointedly at the ladder, the plans, a tape measure and the rest of the major's surveying paraphernalia. 'Which brings us to the missing Holbein, which is presumably the object of this exercise of yours.'

'If you know there's no point in denying it,' declared the major, assuming his most charming smile and surrendering gracefully. 'I was on my word of honour to Mr Pratt not to reveal it, but since you know let's not beat about the bush. Miss Pratt will be gracious enough, I'm sure, to satisfy her father that I did not give away his secret. Let me make it quite clear, however, that my task here is solely to unearth the picture. It's my contention that, if found, it will belong to the Cheney family, and I have told Mr Pratt so. I don't imagine any of you gentlemen will dissent from that?'

'Not at all,' said Gerry. 'So far as the picture is concerned, we are here as Gavin's representatives.'

'None of the gentlemen may dissent,' put in Angel, 'but I do. It belongs to my father, not the Cheneys. All the family effects were sold with the estate.'

'If that is so — and I'm not for one moment doubting your word, dear girl — then the lawyers can sort it out afterwards. It's no concern of ours.' The major was anxious to avert another split.

'Except for this,' Angel persisted. 'The relevant clause in the agreement, as I think Mr Talbot knows, applies only if the picture is discovered on the estate.'

'It's hardly likely to be found anywhere else,' said the major.

'Unless it's first removed from here.'

'Come, come! No one is going to do that,' the major assured her.

'Aren't they?' Angel turned and looked enquiringly at Talbot.

'Not if it's against the law, they aren't,' he replied.

'Well, it is,' she said emphatically. 'And if there are any more attempts someone may get hurt. So please don't try.'

'Okay, okay.' The American waved her threats aside. 'But now we're here we should have a word with your old man and get one or two things straight. And don't you think that since there are four of us here he might let us have a game?'

Angel shrugged her shoulders. 'One of you had better ask him,' she said. 'He's up at the house, and I'll be courtmartialled for dereliction of duty if I leave my post.'

'Jolly good idea!' exclaimed the major. 'Timothy can nip up. Where is he?'

They looked round. Timothy had disappeared, and at that moment the smell of burning reached them, followed by the sight of coils of smoke billowing through the curtains at the back of the dedans.

'Fire! Quick!' yelled the major.

They ran out of the court and met Timothy in the passage.

'What's the matter?' he asked. 'There's a smell of burning, and I've just seen old Lady Cheney haring away from the building as if she were running an Olympic hundred yards.'

'The ante-room, man,' the major shouted, pushing him to one side.

When they flung open the door flames were already licking up towards the ceiling from a pile of newspapers stacked on the floor in the middle of the room.

The carpet was alight and the oval oak table was beginning to crackle. Regardless of the danger, the major dashed forward to rescue a collection of old tennis books and records from the table. Gerry rushed up behind him with a bucket of water from the dressing room and threw it over the blaze. After a sharp, hectic engagement the five of them, aided by a ready supply of water, stamped out the flames and dragged the smouldering carpet and charred table out into the open air. The damage was minimal.

'Can't afford to lose a tennis court, by Jove,' panted the major. 'Too few of them left as it is. What a terrible act of vandalism!'

'Which way did she go?' Talbot asked Timothy.

'Down the drive,' said Timothy. 'She'll be past the gates by this time. I'll follow her in the car.'

He made to leave, but the major stopped him.

'We'd better all go to the house and report to Mr Pratt,' he said. 'It's his property and he must decide what's to

305

be done. Rather a delicate matter all things considered, but one can't very well overlook arson.'

Mrs Winterton rose in alarm, like a ruffled hen, when they trooped into the morning room. An illustrated weekly with bright glossy photographs of debutantes slid off her lap onto the floor.

'What's the matter?' she asked. 'Has there been another accident?'

'Of course not, my dear,' snapped the major. 'Keep calm, or go upstairs and have a lie-down if you prefer.'

Disobeying this command, she stayed and made polite conversation to Gerry Montague. The task of informing Mr Pratt of the latest developments had been delegated to Angel, and the men awaited his entry uneasily. From her husband's furrowed brow Mrs Winterton deduced that the others had caught him red-handed in some crime, and when she heard the word 'arson' spoken by Talbot her knees gave way and she sat down again abruptly.

Mr Pratt took them doubly by surprise. He padded into the room unobtrusively and mounted a fine display of bonhomie. All smiles, he readily accepted the apologies about the manuscript and invited them to make free use of the court for a game as soon as they had finished discussing the unfortunate affair of the fire. Afterwards the three new arrivals must have dinner and stay the night. He even exchanged a warm handshake with Talbot.

'Very handsome of you, I'm sure,' murmured the major, with the others adding their assent. He then gave Mr Pratt a graphic account of the fire and its extinction, ending with a plea for mercy for Lady Cheney — 'an elderly lady of the best family and unimpeachable character, if somewhat eccentric ways.'

'But, major,' interrupted Mrs Winterton in agitation once or twice towards the end of his speech — she always called him major in public. Each time he shushed her angrily and continued.

'I don't understand,' Talbot commented, 'why Lady Cheney should wish to burn down the court when she believes that it houses a valuable heirloom in the shape

307

of a medieval chalice. Unless she was pulling my leg, of course. And if all the rest of us are agreed that the object of this treasure hunt is really a Holbein, and we have no secrets from each other and are prepared to leave the question of ownership to attorneys, will someone kindly tell me what evidence there is that it's hidden in the court?'

'That's a fair enough request for cards on the table: I respect frank speaking.' Mr Pratt stood in front of the hearth with his thumbs in his waistcoat pockets. His pose was that of master of all he surveyed, including the present situation. 'To be frank myself,' he went on, 'that old girl is bonkers.'

'How could you, Daddy?' protested Angel. 'She's as sane as any of us.'

'It's a tribute to your charitable nature if you think so' — Mr Pratt spoke with affection — 'particularly after the trouble we've already had with her. But she wasn't leg-pulling. She's obsessed with this holy grail or whatever it is, and when her raiding party on Monday night failed she must have decided that if she can't have it no one shall.'

'Why didn't she pull the place apart brick by brick while the Cheneys still owned it?' asked Gerry.

'My information is that the old earl kept her in hand,' answered Mr Pratt. 'He wouldn't have any of her nonsense. Then the trustees stopped her and she was shut up in a home. She shouldn't ever have been let out. It's sad, but that's what must happen again, I suppose.' He sighed unconvincingly.

'You're not to!' exclaimed Angel indignantly. 'There must be a mistake. She's perfectly harmless.'

'Except for a small matter of setting fire to a tennis court,' Timothy insisted.

Angel favoured him with a frown but said nothing more, and Talbot pressed his point about how the picture was known to be in the court. He was seconded by Timothy.

'Shall we let them into the secret, major?' enquired Mr Pratt in a tone of the friendliest co-operation. His inflection also served to let everyone know that he and the major were in alliance and who

309

the senior partner was.

'By all means,' the major approved heartily. 'These young fellows are all tennis-players. What better guarantee of their integrity could there be than that? Eh?'

'I'll take your word for it,' replied Mr Pratt, eyeing the American as he spoke. 'Here you are then. You can all read it.'

He produced the sheet of paper from the family Bible and handed it over avuncularly. Timothy read it through quickly and turned away to study the view of the park through the window. Gerry and Talbot took it more slowly, as did Angel, who asked the same question as the major had:

'Have you shown this to Gavin? It's from his great-grandfather, isn't it?'

'Yes, I think so. He hasn't seen it yet, but he shall have it next time we meet.' Mr Pratt was still affability personified, but the strain was telling and a different note crept into his voice as he picked up the telephone.

'You're not going to ring for the

police,' pleaded Angel.

'It goes against the grain,' her father assured her, 'but if her ladyship develops a taste for setting fire to places it may be this house next or the church or the whole village. It's our duty, I'm afraid, not to leave her in circulation.'

'I'm positive she's all right,' Angel persisted. 'I'll go and see her.'

'You'll do no such thing, Angie,' her father commanded.

'Stop me then.' Angel turned defiantly to leave the room. Mr Pratt caught her by the wrist, and an undignified family struggle took place.

'All right,' conceded Mr Pratt at last, running out of breath and coming second in determination. 'You know this sort of thing is bad for my heart. What do you want me to do? If we don't report it we shall become accessories after the fact and land ourselves in a fine old mess when she burns something else down. The insurance company might even have a claim against me. And how can I tell the police I wanted to but my daughter wouldn't let me? Be sensible, Angie.'

'Arson is a serious crime,' said Timothy, stepping towards the telephone. 'I'm a lawyer and I won't be party to a conspiracy of silence. Let me do it if she won't allow you to.'

But Angel anticipated him and snatched the receiver from the cradle herself. 'At any rate,' she begged her father, 'let me ring Lady Cheney first and see what she says.'

'That's most improper. This is a matter for the police, and we have no discretion to consult what may be the guilty party first.' Timothy prepared to pick her up bodily and carry her away like a naughty child.

At once Mr Pratt closed the family ranks. 'Leave the girl alone,' he snarled, 'and let her speak to the old dame first if she wants to.' With a furious mutter of protest Timothy recoiled towards the french window.

'Hullo,' called Angel into the mouthpiece. 'May I speak to Lady Cheney please? It's Miss Pratt.' A hostile crackle reached them from the other end. 'Even so, will you please tell her that I would like to speak to her.' Another sharp crackle. 'It's urgent and very important.' This produced nothing more than a third, even briefer crackle, followed by a click.

'Well?' Mr Pratt demanded.

'It was the housekeeper,' said Angel. 'She kept saying that Lady Cheney was out and then hung up on me; she had her high-falutin voice on. It doesn't take all this time to get from the court to the village. Lady Cheney must have given instructions to refuse any calls from us. Or else something has happened to her on the way home.'

'Perhaps I can help,' began Mrs Winterton, but the major silenced her with a gesture and took over the telephone.

'Let me try, my dear girl,' he said. 'You're quite right to want to give her an opportunity of speaking before the police are notified. No one wants a scandal if it can be avoided; just think what the Sunday papers will make of it. She may have acted on an impulse and be deeply regretting it already.'

As soon as the housekeeper answered

he bellowed into the telephone in his curtest orderly-room manner: 'Major Winterton speaking. Be so kind as to inform Lady Cheney that I wish to speak to her on a matter of the greatest urgency.'

The crackling was no less sharp than before. 'Out?' he repeated as if rebuking a recalcitrant sepoy. 'Do you mean she won't speak to me?' The crackling became even fiercer. 'In London?' he said in astonishment. 'Are you positive?'

'What an extraordinary thing!' he exclaimed, putting the telephone down. 'That woman swears Lady Cheney's in London. Gone up to spend the weekend with Lord Cheney, she says.'

'That tallies with what Gavin said,' Gerry put in. 'I remember now; the reason he couldn't come down with us was that he was expecting his mother.'

'Then she must have cried off without telling the housekeeper,' said the major. 'But where the deuce can she be now?'

'Does anyone have Gavin's telephone number?' asked Angel. Gerry looked it up in his diary and she put through a call to London at once. It was Gavin who answered, and Angel asked whether she could speak to his mother.

After a brief wait what was unmistakably Lady Cheney's voice came rasping querulously through the receiver. Angel said that owing to some rumours which were circulating she wished to satisfy herself that her ladyship was in good health. The reply appeared to be emphatic, and there was a rider which brought a blush to Angel's cheek. She said, no; she didn't want to speak to Gavin just at that moment and rang off in some confusion, putting the receiver down with a triumphant clatter.

'It doesn't in the least surprise me,' said Mrs Winterton plaintively. 'I keep trying to tell you I would have seen Lady Cheney from where I was sitting if she had approached the court. But no one will listen to me.' She looked at the major accusingly.

'You were reading a magazine,' he countered.

Mrs Winterton denied the charge. 'It was on my knees, but I was thinking and didn't look at it once. I was keeping a special eye on the court, knowing you were there.'

'Day-dreaming. You must have dropped off.' The major seemed determined to be unkind.

'In that case, ma'am,' Talbot intervened, 'now that we know that the culprit could not have been Lady Cheney, would you oblige by telling us who it was?'

'I don't know,' replied Mrs Winterton. 'That's the puzzling part. I can't help you.'

'Really, my dear!' exploded the major. 'Either you were watching the court or you weren't!'

'I have already made it clear that I was.'

'Then who was it, my dear lady?' pressed Mr Pratt. 'Don't spare any of us. Nothing but the truth, please.'

'Really, Mr Pratt, I'm not in the habit of speaking anything else,' she replied. 'There was no one.'

'No one?' Several incredulous echoes rose to the ceiling.

'No one at all went near the court.

There is no possibility of my being mistaken.'

'Now, come,' began the major and 'In that case . . . ' said Mr Pratt simultaneously. Talbot, a step ahead of the others, strode across the room.

The french window stood ajar and a car was disappearing from view. Timothy Forsyth had left unnoticed for the second time that afternoon.

18

The sky next morning was overcast. Leaving his hotel by car, Talbot drove through the Saturday shoppers in Knightsbridge, high above the heads of those in Hammersmith, and out at last into the open stretch of the Chertsey Road. Clouds were massing over the church spire on Richmond Hill as he crossed Chiswick Bridge, and the water of the river ran black between mud banks. It was time to get back to America, he decided. Even the East River looked better than that.

Avoiding Richmond, he returned to Middlesex via Twickenham Bridge and again cut across a loop of the river, heading for Hampton. A member of the Royal Tennis Court, he made a point of playing one game at Hampton Court whenever he came to England. The pace of the ball off the walls was different from what he was accustomed to in New York and at the Tuxedo Club, and not caring much for Henry VIII and Charles II and all that history business he would have torn up the Tudor floor and put down a decent composition surface. Altogether it was far from being his favourite court and he never played his best in it. But as the tennis-player's Mecca it had his respect and patronage.

At the lion-and-unicorn gates of the palace he waved one of his rackets at the official on duty and drove up towards the main gate-house. Parking the car at the end of Tennis Court Lane, he made his way to the dressing room deep in thought.

Timothy's sudden departure from High Cheney had struck the rest of the company literally dumb. It made clear to them all that he had been lying about Lady Cheney and must have started the fire himself. All the old suspicions about his behaviour on the night of Nicholls' death were revived; but no one ventured much comment. The major even left the room without a single word, purple with rage that the honour of tennis should have been blemished by its reigning amateur champion. It was as though the adjutant had put a match to the regimental colours.

Talbot had returned to London by train with Gerry Montague. When he reached his hotel he suddenly realised that it was Timothy who was due to be his opponent at Hampton Court the following morning. Several telephone calls to Timothy's number produced no answer and Talbot had little expectation of his showing up. But he decided to make the journey nevertheless, since the professional was always available for a game.

The dressing room stood open but empty. In the middle of changing he became conscious that the clothes on the peg next to his must be Timothy's. Someone at any rate had changed for play, and it would hardly be the professional, who had his own quarters above. As he tied up his laces, Talbot grew apprehensive. Did he really want to meet Timothy again after all? Everything was growing infernally murky and he half-wished he had driven to London Airport instead and taken a plane for the clear skies of California.

The court also stood empty. This was about all he could see: what with the black walls and the grey sky outside it was in little more than half-light. If Timothy had changed where could he be? Talbot decided to loosen up with some practice services: the noise should attract attention. He reached for the ball basket, and at that moment Timothy emerged from the gloom of the dedans.

'There you are!' he called to Talbot. 'I thought you might be going to stand me up. Dykes is having a cup of coffee. He'll be down by the time we've finished knocking up.' He was in a curiously buoyant mood.

'The thought was mutual then,' Talbot replied. 'After your dramatic exit yesterday I reckoned you'd be in Rio or Tangier. One or two people at High Cheney are keen to have a word with you.'

'The keenness is also mutual, if you mean friend Pratt.' Timothy was unashamed. 'To coin a phrase, I can explain everything. Rough or smooth?'

'Smooth. Do you mean you've found the picture?'

Timothy spun one of his rackets deftly and the rough stringing fell uppermost. 'My lucky day!' he commented. 'Yes, I've discovered the picture as well.' His eyes were bright and the corners of his mouth turned up in triumph, but Talbot could sense the nervous tension underneath. He recalled that Timothy was a gambler.

'Where is it?' he asked. 'And when and how did you find it? Was it when we were talking to the major in the court yesterday?'

'Possibly,' smiled Timothy. 'Now let me ask a question: what's the information worth?'

'Are you serious? If you've found the hiding place someone else will too. Maybe they have already.'

'I can assure you on the best authority that they haven't,' said Timothy. 'And when they do, perhaps the picture won't be there. Certainly I'm serious — deadly serious. I'm in a financial hole.'

'An attorney going in for blackmail,'

said Talbot. 'Have you gone crazy?'

'Not the first anyhow. My knowledge of law is good enough to be certain of that. As for the second, 'We are merely the stars' tennis-balls struck and bandied Which way please them.' Webster.' He picked up a ball and struck it to illustrate the point. Talbot returned it and they began a desultory knock-up.

Baffled, Talbot changed tack. 'Ted Nicholls came to see me last evening,' he called out, cutting an elegant forehand onto the side wall below the last gallery. The ball curled into Timothy's backhand corner and died there. 'He'd just buried his father.'

'Oh yes.' Timothy was at pains to show no interest. He turned his back and scooped some more balls out of the box.

Talbot moved up to the net to collect some on his side. 'Yes, he was on his way back to High Cheney from the funeral,' he said. 'The coroner played ball with Mr Pratt, it seems, and the inquest went off without any awkward questions. Accidental death. But I'd offered Ted money for information about what really happened that night, and he came to take up the offer.'

'And told you that I murdered the old man because I'd had the pleasure of beating him and got drunk afterwards?'

'Not in so many words. But he implied that you tipped him off the ladder for a lark.'

'So I'm not a murderer; just a humble manslaughterer!' Timothy boasted a ball into the grille with a vicious thud. 'And you believed him?'

Talbot stopped playing and leaned against the grille wall. 'Nope,' he said, 'I didn't. He was telling me what he thought I wanted to hear in order to relieve me of some hard currency. The prospect of repeating anything in a court of law made him mighty vague. In the end he pretty well admitted that he believed your story. Old Nick had knocked himself about in his cups before.'

'Thank you for the acquittal.' Timothy made a mock bow as though to a judge. 'Now, if you contrived to keep Ted's grasping hands off your dollars, what about venturing some of them on the hazards of tennis?'

'Very well,' Talbot agreed. 'Best of three sets. No handicaps. And five pounds on the match.'

'Five pounds!' repeated Timothy with an air of disdainful astonishment.

'What are you sneering at?' demanded Talbot. 'For a guy in a financial hole you're being let down lightly. Make it a hundred if you'd rather, but don't start howling that you're embarrassed afterwards.'

'Since I intend to win, the question won't arise. But I don't want you to feel unhappy about the possibility of causing me embarrassment. What about this? If I win you pay me a thousand pounds; if you win I tell you where the picture is and you can do what you like with it.'

Talbot hesitated. To set against a ridiculously large sum of money was the tantalising thought of bringing the whole affair to a quick conclusion and getting back to California for some sunshine. 'What use is that to me?' he asked. 'I don't want to steal the thing.'

'You've been taking a great deal of interest in it, and I've no doubt the rightful owner will refund you the money. What's a thousand pounds to your Dried Prunes Corporation? I'm taking by far the greater risk. I intend to auction my knowledge of the picture's whereabouts to the highest bidder. Believe me, it'll fetch a good deal more than a thousand pounds. The odds are very sporting, in my opinion.'

As the top amateur players in their respective countries, they were well matched. Talbot was rated the better player, but playing at Hampton Court without practice put him at a considerable disadvantage. Also, the week's adventures at High Cheney and the Ritz hadn't helped his physical fitness. Balancing this was Timothy's nervous tautness: under pressure he might snap like a violin string.

'It's the hell of a lot of money,' said Talbot, 'but it's on. May the better man win!' And with the lights now on and Dykes in the marker's box the game began in earnest.

Timothy's tactics were straightforwardly aggressive: to go all out for winning strokes and batter his way through to a lightning victory before Talbot had grown accustomed to the court.

Talbot, on the other hand, reconciled himself in advance to losing the first set, but determined to drag it out for as long as possible. He would then have played himself in sufficiently to move over to the attack in the second set, and with superior stamina and his eye well in he should romp home in the third. His opening policy was to play on the floor, slowing down the game with cut and spin. He would vary the pace and undermine Timothy's confidence by breaking up the rhythm of his game.

The very first service set the pattern of play. Designed as a shock assault, it was a railroad which sprang off the penthouse, took the grille wall high and shot back up court like a rocket. Watching it gravely, Talbot made no attempt at a stroke, and the second bounce fell well outside the winning area. A hazard chase of worse than two: the point remained in abeyance.

Similar in style, the second service came with more twist and less power behind it. This time the ball hit the floor before the grille wall and reared sharply up level with Talbot's nose. Caught out of position, he contented himself with a hard, high forehand boast which found the battery wall well above the net and ricocheted back across the court into the second gallery before Timothy could reach it. Another chase. The score was still love-all, but Talbot had gained the service end.

They crossed in silence, Talbot wasting time by daubing the handle of his racket with rosin to prevent it from slipping. So far so good; but he now had to defend two uncomfortably long chases. Good-length shots by Timothy would win both points unless they could be cut off, and the first service must be kept against the gallery wall; otherwise it could easily be put away into one of the side galleries up court.

He served and Timothy volleyed crisply

across the court. Talbot took it on his forehand and instinctively made a fullblooded drive for the winning gallery. The ball flew low over the middle of the net and found the netting separating the second and winning galleries. He had missed the target by the narrowest margin and paid for it by losing the point. Censuring himself for a departure from plan, he took a vow not to indulge in any more flashy stuff until the second set. Fifteen-love against him.

The next service Timothy returned with casual accuracy into the last gallery and followed this up by laying down a short chase. His next return was a straight force which whistled past Talbot's head into the extreme edge of the dedans. Forty-love against the American, and a short chase to beat if the game was to be saved.

'Chase better than two,' called the marker after they had changed ends again.

A rapid interchange of shots followed, each of Talbot's forces being returned on the volley by Timothy, until Talbot

329

found his length and won the chase on the floor. Fifteen-forty.

The next rest was interminable, both players retrieving a succession of apparent winners. After Talbot had scraped up two low shots off the tambour Timothy was at last forced into an error, a backhand boast off the main wall barely failing to clear the net-cord at its highest point. Thirty-forty. Cautiously Talbot returned the next service short and laid down a chase better than five.

They crossed again, and this time Timothy's return of service sped full-pitch onto the wall below the dedans. Talbot left it alone, confident of winning the chase, but the ball fell short of the five-yard line and the marker called 'chase off'. The score remained at thirty-forty with Timothy leading.

To take his opponent by surprise, Talbot served a severely cut ball hard onto the wall above the penthouse. It flicked the roof on the way down, and Timothy, misjudging the pace, abandoned the volley which he had been preparing. On meeting the grille

330

wall the ball skewed off abruptly towards the other side of the court, and as soon as it hit the floor leapt into the air as if made of india rubber. In a flash Timothy, who had been following it round like a panther on the trail, made a second change of plan. Switching from the forehand he had been shaping for he swung round on his toes with his back to the net and, perfectly balanced and controlled, caught the rising ball with a stinging backhand. The arc he was describing became a complete circle, and the ball hummed back across the net to Talbot's backhand.

Only a player with Talbot's power of anticipation would have been there to receive it, let alone return it effectively. As it was, he had the head of his racket poised high and swept the ball back with a classic force across the court to the grille. Timothy was too late for the volley, but the ball missed its target by inches and rebounded up the court. It was still travelling too fast for an effective stroke, and he let it fall — a fraction outside the winning area. Another hazard chase!

They changed ends for the third time, and Timothy's service hugged the side wall in the approved manner. But Talbot crouched and stroked the ball with his racket, underneath to one side, making its flight just sufficient of a parabola to take it curving over the net and into chase the door.

'Won it!' cried the marker, and the score was deuce.

In all they crossed four more times, with advantages ebbing and flowing, before Timothy clinched the first game after twenty minutes of concentrated play. Talbot's eye was almost in already.

Nevertheless, Timothy won the next game as well and held onto his lead to secure the first set at 6-4. By that time, quite apart from the physical strain, they were both suffering from mental fatigue. It was like running a marathon and competing in a chess tournament at the same time.

'How long can we have the court for, Dykes?' Timothy asked. They had taken their full hour on the one set.

'For another hour if you wish, sir,'

he replied. 'Mr Montague has booked it after that.'

In the next set Talbot let loose his whole artillery, pounding relentlessly away at the openings and setting out to annihilate Timothy's finely judged craftsmanship with a ferocious barrage. He peppered the grille and tambour from the service end and the dedans from the hazard side. It was a devastating exhibition of the power game, over-shadowing Timothy's efforts in the first set and winning Talbot this one in under fifteen minutes without the loss of a single game. Not for a long time had anyone treated Timothy's play with such contempt.

The American's winning streak continued into the final set. With the first four games in the bag, he was virtually home; but suddenly the strain of his steamrolling tactics began to tell. He felt limp and totally exhausted. Timothy, on the other hand, had not allowed himself to become rattled and still had reserves of energy. Far from cracking, he was playing with icy determination, tenaciously keeping his head and his length until the storm passed. In the fifth game this happened: as he tired Talbot began to miss the openings, hitting high and giving his opponent easy returns off the penthouse. With one of those sudden reversals of fortune common in tennis Timothy burst into the ascendant and, with Talbot floundering to regain mastery, won five breathless games in a row.

The next one took nearly as long as the very first. Both players were drawing desperately on all the skill and cunning they could muster. Steadily one moved ahead and the other pulled him back: fifteen-all, thirty-all, deuce. Tension was at breaking point as Timothy won the advantage six times — six match points, and each time Talbot coolly saved the day with all the assurance of a real champion.

Then Talbot held and lost the advantage himself, and Timothy regained it for the seventh time. But by now it looked as though he would never clinch it.

Timothy served and Talbot's return was a lob, almost to the roof but right on target for the dedans when it dropped — an impudent stroke in any circumstances and a superb one then. Having no choice but to make an overhead volley of a ball falling behind him, Timothy knew that a defensive shot would be useless. Even if successful it would be inviting murder from Talbot's next return. The ball was falling practically vertically, but he took a deep back swing and thumped it out of the mouth of the dedans towards the grille. Talbot was there defending, but the ball flew high and he left it for a simple kill off the rebound. It struck the angle of the penthouse roof and sprang upwards to touch the wire netting high in the corner. Talbot caught it in his hand as it fell and walked across to receive the next service.

Silence settled over the court, and he looked up, puzzled. 'Excuse me, sir,' said the marker in a broken voice, 'but that netting is in play.'

'What?'

'I thought you knew' — Dykes sounded on the point of tears — 'I usually warn visitors. It's a peculiarity of the court. As you can see, the play-line runs above the netting.'

The silence settled again as Talbot stared at the line of painted green wood which marked the limits of play: above was out of court; below, in play. 'Well?' he demanded, swinging round on Timothy. 'Aren't you going to say anything?'

'Yes,' said Timothy, 'I'm sorry the game should finish in this way. If it was a friendly I would suggest playing a let, but one can hardly do that in a match. Rules are rules, after all. Thanks very much for the game,' he added, 'and thank you, Dykes, for marking.' He put on his sweater and walked off the court.

'You goddam bastard!' Talbot swore at his back. 'Three thousand dollars for a mean trick like that!' Unable to face Timothy again until his temper had cooled, he collected some balls and hit them savagely across the net until Dykes came to tell him that the changing room was empty.

He had barely sat down in the bath when Gerry came in and demanded to know what had been happening. 'I passed Timothy at the gates,' he said. 'He was in such high spirits that he took both hands off the steering wheel and gave me the vulgarest sort of V sign. When I signalled to him to stop he accelerated like mad.'

Talbot lay back in the bath and told him the whole story.

When he had finished Gerry excitedly brushed aside the lament about Timothy's bad sportsmanship. 'Don't you see?' he exclaimed, his moustache bristling triumphantly. 'You say he already looked pleased with himself when he arrived here. Now' — he dug into a pocket — 'let me read you a bit of the old Earl's message. I took a copy for Gavin. 'There is that which will mend matters at H.C. in the tennis court.' If he meant 'High Cheney' it wouldn't have been necessary to put in 'at H.C.' at all, would it?'

'I don't get it,' said Talbot, towelling his long back systematically from the neck downwards. 'Yes, I do though!' he cried, as he reached the back of his legs. 'By all the saints and martyrs! H.C. — Hampton Court!'

19

The telephone rang with infuriating insistence — on and on. Reluctantly Gavin Cheney decided he had better answer it. After one of his rare Saturday mornings at the office he was in the throes of preparing himself a quick lunch before going out to meet his mother and aunt.

'Yes,' he said into the mouthpiece, with bare politeness. 'Oh, it's you, Timothy. No, it isn't actually. You caught me in the middle of an omelette. No, not eating it; cooking it. Of course I can. Never mind; it's past hope now.'

'I'm sorry.' Timothy's voice sounded genuinely apologetic. 'But I wanted to talk to you about higher things than omelettes. What would you say if I told you I'd found the Cheney Holbein?'

'What!'

'What would you say if I told you I'd found the Cheney Holbein?'

There was silence while Gavin reflected.

Timothy had a reputation for behaving oddly; could this be one of his jokes? 'I would ask where it was,' he replied cautiously.

'You mean whether it was on the estate at High Cheney or somewhere else?'

'That might be important, yes. But don't keep me in suspense, you ass. Where on earth is it?'

Timothy ignored the plea. 'My problem,' he said, 'is that I'm pressed for time. Otherwise I wouldn't have dreamed of discussing something like this over the telephone. The fact of the matter is, Gavin old boy, I'm desperately short of cash.'

'Oh!' Gavin went all cold at the realisation that someone who had been at the same school was behaving like a bounder. The great athlete Timothy Forsyth was scrounging for money, perhaps even hovering on the edge of blackmail. Holbein or no Holbein, Gavin nearly cut him off in sheer disgust.

'Don't sound so frigid.' Timothy spoke sharply: if Cheney had been a year younger he might have been Timothy's fag. 'I'm in a spot. My uncle has delivered his judgment and passed sentence all at once: he intends to ship me out to the Antipodes like a transported felon. An anonymous letter arrived saying that I'd got drunk, hauled Nicholls off that ladder and broken his neck for him. It was that so-and-so Frenchwoman being malicious. Uncle made some enquiries pretty fast, smelt a grade A scandal and fairly hit the ceiling. By a bit of bad luck a frightful bloomer I'd made over some geyser's estate came to light the same afternoon. So Uncle pulled a few strings in Leadenhall Street and booked me a passage for Monday.'

'I don't see what's so awful about going to Australia,' said Gavin. 'You'll probably like it.' He for one liked the thought of Timothy in Australia.

'It's not Australia; it's New Zealand. No tennis courts; no first-class cricket; no history. Anyway, I'm in no position to leave the country. The gee-gees haven't been running as predicted, and my bookie has turned finally nasty after a minor catastrophe at Kempton Park this week.

You know I haven't a bean of my own, and if Uncle gets to hear about this I shall never be allowed to lay my hands on any of the family cash: he's the trustee and has absolute discretion. What I need at once is a few thousand quid to pay off my debts and get myself a partnership in some other firm. Do you remember Sandy Beaumont? He's a solicitor in Warwick and I might be able to buy my way in there. With Leamington and Moreton Morrell both on the doorstep it would be almost as good as London so far as tennis goes.'

'Are you suggesting I should pay you for information about my own picture?'

'Ten per cent of the value. That's a fair perk, surely. It's what finders of lost property usually get from grateful owners.'

'But this may be worth half a million — and I might not want to sell it.'

'The actual financial arrangements are a detail. They can be discussed later, so long as we agree on the principle now.'

'I must say, Timothy,' Gavin declared, 'I dislike your attitude very much. I would be delighted to give you a present for helping me recover a family heirloom, but I won't have a pistol put to my head.'

'Boxes of chocolates don't interest me, old boy, thank you. Look! Someone else will tag on any minute now, and then you'll have only yourself to thank if the picture is smuggled out of the country to Paris or San Francisco or somewhere. It might even be taken back to High Cheney. You wouldn't want to lose it through being stuffy, would you?'

'You mean it isn't at High Cheney now?'

'I didn't say so. All I'm suggesting is that if by any chance it happens not to be there then it might be taken back surreptitiously for an official re-discovery. Do I make myself plain?'

'Perfectly. If it were already at High Cheney it wouldn't belong to me and you wouldn't be trying this on. Are you threatening me that if I don't pay up you'll move it to High Cheney and take a cut from Pratt? Isn't this what the law calls 'demanding money with menaces'

342

or something like that?'

'That's a very unpleasant way of putting it.' Timothy sounded quite hurt.

'I'm never pleasant to people when they do unpleasant things.' Gavin had lost his temper.

'All right,' said Timothy, turning to open threats. 'Don't say I didn't let you have first chance. If I'd known you'd pass up an opportunity like this I'd have put it to a proper businessman right away. No wonder the Cheneys are in the dog-house!'

'I've nothing more to say,' Gavin replied icily. 'Goodbye!'

'Back to your omelette then, Cheney,' jeered Timothy, and ten minutes later the telephone rang at Mr Pratt's office. A voice asked whether it could speak to the chairman.

Alfred Pratt had the City to himself that afternoon. Of all the offices and banks crowded into the money-making square mile Mr Pratt's private room in Mr Pratt's private palace was the only one humming with mercenary purpose. Wrapped in the weekend hush, he sat

343

in his shirt sleeves at an enormous desk littered with telephones, files, account books, smoked salmon sandwiches and a bottle of Scotch. In the next room his secretary was attacking her typewriter with controlled fury, her plans for Saturday afternoon wrecked.

'A Mr Forsyth on the telephone, Mr Pratt. He says it's important.'

'Well, well, well,' he purred into the receiver after she had put the call through. 'If it isn't the flaming incendiary himself! Where are you speaking from, if it isn't a secret?'

'My apologies for disturbing you, but I rang High Cheney and they told me you would be here. My apologies also for burning your carpet and table. I'm ringing from my flat and want to explain how it happened.' Timothy was at his suavest. 'It was a blind, as I dare say you realised. You see, it suddenly dawned on me on the way down yesterday that that elusive picture wasn't at High Cheney after all. When we arrived and saw that the major had been over the court with a tooth-comb without finding anything I felt certain it couldn't be. But I needed time to confirm that the picture was where I thought it was. So it occurred to me on the spur of the moment that it would be a good idea to keep attention focussed on your tennis court. Rather silly, really!'

'Not to mention criminal,' put in Mr Pratt.

'My intention not being to damage any of your property, that's arguable. But the point is that it worked.'

'So you've found the picture.' For all his practice of masking his thoughts, Mr Pratt couldn't keep the excitement out of his voice.

'That's what I'm ringing to tell you. You sound interested.'

'You know I'm interested. Where is it?'

'I haven't told anyone yet, because from your point of view it would be a pity if it weren't found at High Cheney. That's right, isn't it?'

'Let's meet that one later, shall we? Meanwhile I'll promise you this: if there's money in it for me there'll be money in it for you.'

'I was hoping you'd say that. It's a relief to have a businessman to deal with. Would fifty-fifty strike you as fair?'

'Before committing myself I'd need to know where the picture is.'

'On the other hand, I would need you to commit yourself before I told you where it is. What about my drafting a simple agreement and bringing it right over?'

'Fine.' Mr Pratt spoke as though the deal were clinched, adding in the same breath: 'but shall we say your share is to be limited to five thousand pounds?'

The other end of the line went dead. 'Hello, hello!' cried Mr Pratt in alarm. 'Are you there?'

'Just about,' said Timothy. 'Aren't you undervaluing Holbein a wee bit? Half a million has been mentioned to me, and half of that works out at more than five thousand, I believe.'

'My dear fellow, you can't be serious about fifty per cent — or about its being worth that amount of money.'

'I'll tell you what,' said Timothy. 'My interest is in ready cash now. I'll sacrifice

346

my share for fifty thousand on the nail. If you agree I can come round at once, collect the money and give you the information.'

'Just a moment! There are three snags to that. One is, suppose the picture turns out not to belong to me. The second is, suppose for some reason it turns out not to be where you say it is. Thirdly, by some oversight I don't happen to have fifty thousand pounds in cash on the premises; you'd have to be content with a cheque. But by all means come round and discuss it. Negotiations by telephone are never satisfactory.'

'I'm not coming without a clear undertaking from you.' Timothy sounded adamant. 'Surely the risk is worth taking. You stand to gain a clear four hundred and fifty thousand pounds, and I can assure you the picture's there all right and no one else is in the secret. You'll have a clean start. As for the money, I won't take a cheque, but securities will do. You must have some valuable bits of paper — bearer bonds or something — at the heart of that financial empire of yours.'

'Let me have your number,' Mr Pratt replied. 'I want to think about this for a few minutes. I'll ring you back inside half an hour.'

'Not later please,' Timothy urged, giving him the number. 'There are other fish in the sea, you know.'

Mr Pratt's mind was already racing over the possibilities. Had he been a fool not to close with Timothy, leaving himself a loophole? The proposition smelt fishy, but Timothy wasn't the only person in desperate need of ready money. The rumours which Gavin had reported to Angel were the exposed fraction of the iceberg; no one but Mr Pratt himself knew about the submerged portion. His proliferating empire extended so far and so deviously that even he himself had not been absolutely certain how serious things had become. After five hours at his desk on a quiet Saturday he now had the situation sized up. It was bad — very bad; but he could see the glimmerings of a water-tight solution.

It would involve the liquidation of three companies, the creation of six new shells and several shares exchanges between companies with completely different activities inside the group. The articles of association of all his companies had been carefully framed or re-drafted to permit them to switch without legal complications from asbestos manufacture to biscuit-making or from repairing umbrellas to wholesaling Bibles. The salvage scheme was a masterpiece — and within the law by a whisker. It hinged on one contingency, however: his ability to lay hands quietly on half a million pounds or thereabouts in cash by Monday morning. This would enable him to paper over the cracks and maintain confidence while the reconstruction plan was put into effect.

After various recent inroads on his credit the problem of arranging infusions of capital of this size had bedevilled him for some time. This had started him on the High Cheney treasure hunt originally; now, as he had feared, the crisis had come to a head. He had nothing acceptable to offer by way of security — bankers were too wary of his interlocking finances; and if it became known that he was trying to raise such a sum the whole thing would blow up in his hands.

Staking fifty thousand on the picture was the devil of a gamble, but what alternative was there? On the assumption that Timothy wasn't kidding the picture had been discovered, but not at High Cheney. The implication was that he would have to whip it quietly off there in order to claim it as his own. If he did this successfully he might be able to raise the best part of half a million on it on Monday provided its condition was reasonably good. This would lay him open to blackmail by Timothy for ever more, and there might be some nasty questions asked later if his ownership came to be questioned. Should it be made public that he had in effect stolen Cheney property and used it as security to raise a loan it would be the end of the line for Alf Pratt.

From his own point of view the risk would be worth it. If the worst came to the worst he would have plenty salted away for when he came out. His wife was tough enough to take it and anyway he'd become indifferent to her; she could look after herself. But Angel couldn't. The effect on her would be disastrous. Enclosed in the carapace which Mr Pratt had grown against the world was a soft centre now reserved exclusively for Angel. He looked out of the window at a Wren spire, while his thoughts travelled back across the river to his boyhood in a Deptford tenement. It was only three or four miles away, but he'd come the hell of a long way since then. He could smell the squalor of it still, and thanked heaven Angel would never know anything like it.

The diversion cleared his mind. No alternative was in sight. He must have that picture in his possession — permanent or temporary — when the banks opened on Monday. Timothy could have apparently irrevocable securities which could in fact be revoked if the plan went awry. Moreover, he must be made to sign something which would establish his complicity and could be used as a counter-weight in the event of his attempting blackmail.

'Get that Park number,' he yelled through the door.

The buzzer on his desk burped, and he pressed the switch. 'Will you take an incoming call first?' his secretary's voice enquired. 'A Major Winterton.'

Mr Pratt glanced at his watch. He still had a quarter of an hour. 'Put him through,' he said.

The major's voice was deafening. They hadn't had many telephones in India, where it was considered anti-social by the white raj not to employ some of the surplus millions to run from house to house carrying messages. Coming to the instrument late in life, he could never be cured of an early misapprehension that it was essential to shout.

'That you, Pratt? Oh, good! Had the devil of a job tracing you. It's about young Forsyth. He's taken leave of his senses. I haven't managed to speak to him yet — when I do he'll get a piece of my mind, and no mistake. Don't know what his poor father would have said.'

Mr Pratt picked up the receiver, which he had laid on the desk at a safe distance from his ear. 'Come to the point, will you?' he said. 'What about Forsyth?'

'Gerry has just phoned — Gerry Montague, you know. Timothy has taken a thousand quid off Talbot and — '

'What for?' Mr Pratt bent down and interrupted sharply.

'They bet on a game. If what Gerry says is true — and I don't doubt it — Timothy behaved in a downright unsporting manner. I've insisted that Talbot should send his cheque to me so that I can investigate the matter. As President of the Association, you understand. But something else arose out of the game, and that's what I have to tell you. Timothy has found the picture.'

'What picture? And where?' Mr Pratt sounded irritable and uninterested.

'Oh, come! The Holbein, of course. Timothy worked out where it was and told Talbot he knew. Then Gerry guessed.'

So it wasn't a secret any more! Mr

Pratt was furious. 'Well, come on, man,' he barked. 'Where is it?'

'At Hampton Court. I'm going down there this evening. Lady Cheney's sister has a grace-and-favour apartment, so I've arranged to have dinner there with them and Gavin. I don't quite know what your position is in this, but in view of our lunch and so on I thought it only right to tell you about it at once.'

'You know flaming well what my position is,' Mr Pratt shouted, in a counterblast against the major's eardrum. 'If that picture is at Hampton Court I don't get a look-in and your miserable property company goes up the spout. I hired you to help me with this picture, not to hand it over to someone else. Why didn't you ring me before the Cheneys?'

'Steady, old boy!' said the major soothingly. 'I'm trying to do my best for you, but it's an unfortunate development from your point of view, I agree. Still, you can't expect me to behave in an underhand way towards young Gavin.'

Mr Pratt swallowed hard. 'Where exactly is it hanging?' he asked. 'And how certain are you that this really is the Holbein?'

'You're not thinking of doing anything — well, I mean, doing anything about it?' enquired the major uneasily.

'I'm not thinking of anything. I'm simply giving you a chance to salvage your company if it turns out that any information you pass me is valuable. This one may be a copy, for instance; and if the original is still at High Cheney this might provide a clue to its whereabouts.'

The major cleared his throat while settling his conscience. 'All right,' he agreed. 'Half a dozen of us know already, so I don't see why you shouldn't. There's a painting of the eighth Earl of Cheney in the dedans at Hampton Court. He presented it himself in the year he gave up tennis. At the same time he set up a trust fund to provide a hundred pounds a year for the professional at the court, subject to the picture remaining continually in the dedans. What no one was aware of until I looked up the original deed a few moments ago is that the picture is only on loan to the Royal

Tennis Court and must be returned to the Cheneys any time the head of the family requests it. So if, as I anticipate, Gavin asks for it at dinner tonight, I am legally bound to take it off the nail and hand it over to him.'

'The assumption being that the Holbein is underneath?'

'It certainly looks like it. In fact, the more I think about it the more probable it seems. To judge from that suppressed bit of the Annals, Featherstonehaugh had actually seen the picture; and no one has since. His blackmail of the Earl was based on the assumption that if the story were made public the countess, who was a puritan and ruled the roost, would insist on the painting being destroyed. This would be rather an ingenious way of putting it out of her reach surreptitiously but not actually parting with it.'

'I suppose it's just about possible.' Mr Pratt remained studiously doubtful. 'No one has checked yet, I presume, on whether there is in fact a second painting underneath the Earl's portrait?'

'No. I've phoned Dykes and told him

to lock the dedans and not allow anyone in until I get down there. But there's little doubt about it to my mind. You remember the story of how it came into the family's possession. As soon as we read it Gerry or I should have put two and two together. That was the very dedans where Henry VIII kept the picture.'

'How do you know?' Mr Pratt asked. 'The court's not mentioned in the story, is it?'

'That's true,' admitted the major. 'It could have been one of the other royal courts — Windsor or Westminster or Sheen — but Hampton Court was his favourite palace, you know.'

'Well, I'm not convinced,' declared Mr Pratt. 'By no means! But thank you for letting me know. I must press on with other things now. There'll be unemployment on Tyneside unless I can iron out one or two problems between now and Monday morning.' Ship-building was one of the industries with which Mr Pratt's enterprises were not concerned, but he'd always found it advantageous to strew his path with red herrings. He also wanted to indicate to the major that he was far too busy with important affairs to bother about old paintings.

In fact there was only one thought in his mind: to get at that painting first and make sure that no Holbein would be discovered when the Earl's portrait was dismantled. It would be dark around seven o'clock. This would leave him about two hours before the Cheney dinner party had finished its coffee.

He depressed the intercom. switch. 'I want the car here at five,' he ordered. 'Miss Angel is in Town. Ring the flat and tell her I'll pick her up at 5.15. I'm taking her out to dinner, but she's not to wear anything too posh. Then book a table for two at the Casino Hotel on Tagg's Island. For 8.30. But before you do anything else get me that Park number.'

By now the half hour had elapsed, but Mr Pratt was confident that Timothy would be waiting: no one abandons the possibility of fifty thousand pounds lightly. It was essential to pretend to string along with this unpleasant young man and prevent him hawking his offer elsewhere.

The voice that answered was male, but strange. It stated that Mr Forsyth had gone out.

'Out?' repeated Mr Pratt unbelievingly. 'Who am I speaking to? And where can I reach him? It's most urgent.'

'I don't know, I'm sure,' said the voice, unimpressed. 'I just share the flat with him, I'm not his keeper. He phoned the Ritz and then went out in a hurry.'

20

'There's glory for you!' The major spoke his favourite phrase.

They stood in the passage behind the side galleries, staring through the netting into the vast well of the court. The rain had passed and moonlight slanted from a clear sky through the high windows, illuminating it in a ghostly half-light.

'This is the real England,' he breathed. 'The hallmark of civilisation. An art for real men, with its roots in history. 'To spring from one end to another of a Tennis Court; to judge the bound of a ball which is still in mid-air; to return it with a strong and certain hand; such games become a man; they tend to form him.' Who do you think wrote that, eh?'

'No idea,' replied Gavin, wondering how much gin the old boy had stowed away in the brief interval between sundown and his arrival at the palace. Erect between them, Lady Cheney gave no sign of having heard the question.

'A chap called Rousseau,' declared the major triumphantly. 'Even the intellectual johnnies have had to admit what tennis does for a man. Doesn't this stir you, Gavin my boy? Think of all those kings and ancestors of yours playing here and the ladies and gallants of the court watching from the dedans there and these very galleries where we're standing now. What scenes must have taken place on this very spot if we only knew about them!'

'Yes, indeed,' Gavin agreed. 'By scenes you mean quarrels, I take it.'

If this was a gentle tease the major failed to notice it. 'Quarrels!' he exclaimed. 'I wasn't thinking of them. But by jingo there have been some! Tennis can bring out the worst in a man as well as the best — we've seen that in young Timothy Forsyth. Yes, the Duke of Norfolk threatened the Earl of Leicester here one day with the first Queen Elizabeth sitting right there in the dedans. He objected to the Earl using the

Queen's handkerchief to mop his face. The Queen was furious — with the Duke, of course. And then there was an even worse bit of nonsense a few years later involving the heir to the throne.'

'I can see it happening in front of us now,' he went on. 'They are standing there beside the net, and Henry — that's James I's eldest son — is annoyed at losing a chase he should have won. The chase was long and his temper short, eh? He's playing the Earl of Essex and in the pique of the moment reminds him that his father was a traitor. Which he was — got his head taken off by Queen Elizabeth, you remember. They are both hot-tempered boys in their teens, and Essex in a tantrum leans across the net and smashes his racket down onto the prince's head. Blood spurts out onto the floor — royal Stuart blood. Can't you see him sinking to the floor there and the consternation among the spectators?'

'Good gracious!' exclaimed Lady Cheney, startled into interest. 'And did the young Earl lose his head like his father?'

'Unfortunately not,' the major answered. 'James I had rather an inflated opinion of his own wisdom, you know. He ticked them both off and told Henry that in the years to come the boy who had spilt his blood would spill the blood of his enemies.'

'And did he?'

'As it turned out, he didn't. Henry died soon afterwards — poisoned, some people say; and Essex became the leading Parliamentarian general. So you see, if it hadn't been for tennis we might not have had Cromwell. That's something the game has to answer for.' He lapsed into a brown study, and a suspicion of a tear ran down his cheek.

Mother and son exchanged glances. 'Is there anything wrong, Major Winterton?' enquired Lady Cheney.

The major sighed deeply. 'I'm a sentimental old fool,' he said. 'Our reigning amateur champion is bringing disgrace to the game; this business tonight is going to cost me a pretty penny; nothing is what it used to be. But there we are.' He blew his nose violently. 'Let's find the picture. I apologise for getting maudlin on an occasion for rejoicing. We mustn't keep dinner waiting, but I assure you there was a good reason for my insisting that we should collect it now instead of afterwards. No point in delay where something valuable is concerned. This place is far from burglar-proof, and there's no knowing what might happen if anyone — '

'I hope it isn't going to be a wild goose chase,' interrupted Gavin as the major took out the key he had borrowed from the professional and they moved towards the dedans. 'It all seems devilish improbable.'

'Look!' he added, pointing to the last gallery.

A square had been neatly cut from the netting, and a similar hole gaped at them from the dedans beyond. Unable to open the door, someone had hacked his way through from the passage to the court and from the court into the dedans.

Fumbling with haste, the major unlocked the door and dashed to the far end of the narrow gallery. He had not bothered to switch on the court lights, but the moonlight revealed clearly enough that the picture was no longer there.

He purged his feelings against Mr Pratt with a terrible oath in Hindustani, starting with 'son of a sow' and working steadily downwards. The knowledge that his own conscience was not entirely clear accentuated his rage. The accumulation of several large tots of gin and the unhappy transition from the strife and glory of the past to the realities of the present overwhelmed him. He sank onto one of the benches with his head between his hands.

'Major!' A clarion call roused him. 'There he goes! Look! There he goes!' Lady Cheney might have been in the hunting field.

She had stayed in the corridor and out of the corner of her eye noticed Mr Pratt emerging from a side door at the far end and attempting to tiptoe out of the building unnoticed.

Like a good soldier at the sound of an alarm, the major shrugged off his cares and sprang into action. 'Pratt, eh?' he bellowed. 'Hiding in the lavatory till the coast's clear! Come on, Gavin. After him, man.'

Together they tore down the passage, lugging open the doors of the long corridor and letting them fall back behind with a series of heavy thuds. Despite his age and intake of alcohol the major held his own, and they were abreast as they turned into the chilly open air of Tennis Court Lane. There all was serene. On the left the palace buildings stretched away out of a bright pool of lamp-light into dim shadow. On the other side of the lane cars stood parked at the foot of a high brick wall.

'He can't be far,' panted the major. 'A fellow in his condition!' They listened and his sharp ear caught a faint sound. 'Got you!' he cried, pouncing behind a black Rover and producing a crumpled Mr Pratt like a conjuror with a rabbit.

'Take your hands off me,' demanded Mr Pratt. He was stooping and had one hand over his heart. 'Leave me alone. I'm too old for these childish capers.'

'Too old!' expostulated the major.

'Why, I could give you fifteen years. You're not fit; that's your trouble. Where's the picture?'

'I haven't got it.'

'Come off it,' said Gavin. 'You're not going to tell us you just popped in to use the lavatory? Eh?'

'You keep a civil tongue in your head, young man,' Mr Pratt retorted, mustering his dignity. 'I came along out of curiosity after the major telephoned the good news, and because I was afraid that Forsyth fellow might be up to some trickery. I reached the court a few minutes before you and noticed that the netting was torn and the picture appeared to be missing. Then I heard someone coming and hid in the lavatory.'

'Mr Pratt *may* be speaking the truth,' declared Lady Cheney, who had joined them. 'For once, that is,' she added. 'I have looked in the lavatory. There is nowhere he could have secreted the picture there.'

'Thank you,' replied Mr Pratt with a glare. 'You'd be much better advised searching for Forsyth. He can't have gone far.'

'In that case you are coming with us,' ordered the major.

They wound their way through Chapel Court, past the door to the Chapel Royal and round the Fountain Court cloisters. The iron gates leading into the gardens beyond stood open. They peered out onto the formal lawns and flower beds, bounded by the dark expanse of the Home Park running up to the skyline. Under the cover of one of the near-by umbrella yews two figures were crouching.

'Who's there?' the major challenged.

'Quiet!' hissed one of the figures.

The major led his party over. 'It's Gerry Montague and the American,' Gavin announced to his mother as they crossed the path.

'Be quiet, you idiot!' whispered Gerry. 'And come under cover. He's given us the slip once. We've been on guard round the other side of the court since it became dark, but he must have climbed over the wall from here. He came out our way and we followed him, but he's disappeared. The Frenchwoman is here too.'

'The devil she is!' exploded the major.

While Talbot B. Talbot and the eleventh Earl of Cheney were exchanging informal whispered apologies for a painful misunderstanding in the upper gallery of the tennis court at High Cheney, Lady Cheney (who never apologised on principle) was occupied in muttering about the iniquity of the Ministry of Works in not employing security guards in the grounds at night. 'Me sister will be murdered in her bed one of these nights,' she prophesied to herself, apparently with some relish.

A breeze swept lightly through the trees and across the lawns. The pediment of Wren's apartments for Queen Mary rose majestically above them. To the south the gate to the Privy Gardens was closed, and the wall of the Broad Walk vanished towards the river. To the north the buildings straggled on as far as the tennis court with its distinctive upper wall of glass: beyond, the gate to the Wilderness stood ajar. Round the Great

Fountain itself the ducks were settling down for the night, and a swan in flight flapped noisily down the length of the Long Water in the park. The sight-seers had departed, and the grace-and-favour inhabitants occupied other parts of the palace. There was no sign of human life.

'Let's fan out and search behind every tree,' suggested the major. 'There are enough of us. He can't have got out into the park at this hour, can he? They lock the gates at five or six.'

Isolated in the middle of a section of lawn stood the statue of a naked, bearded he-man kneeling on a lion and wrenching the poor beast's lower jaw off. While Gavin was speculating whether he represented Samson or Hercules and before anyone had time to answer the major, the lithe figure of Timothy shot out from behind the plinth. Unmistakable in the moonlight, he ran like a stag for the gate to the Wilderness. Under his right arm he was clutching a bulky rectangular object.

'He's got it there,' shouted the major.

'Follow him, lads! Don't let him reach the road.'

They started in pursuit, Gerry — despite his age — taking the lead with Talbot; Gavin and the major forming the second wave; and Lady Cheney and Mr Pratt, with glances of mutual suspicion, bringing up the rear at a walking pace.

Once inside the Wilderness Timothy chose the path which led diagonally across to the Lion Gate. Ahead of him the traffic could be heard speeding towards Kingston Bridge or turning into Bushy Park for the dark cut through the chestnut avenue to Twickenham and Richmond. Gerry realised that if Timothy had a car parked beside the gate he would be away and lost in the arteries of Greater London in no time.

He put on a spurt, which in turn spurred Talbot into showing his paces as the fittest and fastest man among them. The distance between pursuers and pursued closed perceptibly, but Timothy was a good performer over a short distance and had a useful start. If he had not been hampered by what he was carrying they might not have gained on him at all.

Even as it was, the gain looked like being insufficient. The quarry would be through the gate first, and everything would then depend on how quickly he could start his car. Gerry's was the best part of quarter a mile away, parked in the fore-court of the Mitre opposite the main gates.

At that moment Talbot, who had overhauled Gerry, let out a whoop of triumph. The gates were locked, and Timothy, after fruitlessly rattling a handle, looked over his shoulder, hesitated for a second and then fled away along a shadowy path between the maze and the back of the King's Arms.

'He'll have to go through the Tiltyard to the main gates.' yelled Gerry. 'We'll follow. You two cut him off.'

Obediently Gavin and the major swung off across the long grass, weaving between the trees and bushes as straight as they could go for the entrance to the Tiltyard and Moat Lane.

Timothy at once wheeled and, keeping

round the outer edge of the maze until he came to the entrance, flung the picture over the turnstile and hurled himself after it. Recovering it on the other side, he disappeared at speed down a narrow path into the depths.

'Gone to earth,' called Gerry, and the pack gradually assembled. They circumambulated the maze, inspecting it meticulously for an alternative exit. The hedge was mongrel and moth-eaten in places, a blending of privet, holly and yew, but closely planted with the object of preventing people from crawling through. In the thin spots there were spiked railings.

'Right,' said the major, assuming charge of the operations. 'If Lady Cheney and Mr Pratt would stand at these two points and Gerry near the entrance we shall keep the whole of the outside under observation and have one fit man ready for pursuit in case he breaks out. Gavin and Talbot are our shock troops. They can go in, and I'll climb the attendant's ladder and see whether I can spot him over the hedges.'

Apart from two initial fleeting glimpses by Gerry they had had no indication of Timothy's position. Nothing could be heard above the hum of traffic, and the major spotted no movement from his look-out post on top of the wooden steps. The shock troops clambered over the gate beside the turnstile, and the murk of the maze quickly swallowed them up.

'Timothy,' called out the major commandingly. 'Come out at once. Show a little respect for your family if you've none left for yourself. Have you lost all sense of honour, man?'

The words fell into the night unanswered — except by Lady Cheney, who loosed off the tart comment that if, as she understood, the young man was a solicitor he had no sense of honour to lose.

Two heads came into the major's area of vision as Talbot and Gavin plunged deeper along the twisted paths between the hedges. They ran hot-foot into cul-de-sacs, then they separated only to meet face to face two minutes later, all the time making no apparent progress towards the centre. Timothy remained as if already transported to New Zealand, and the major confused them by shouting out misleading directions.

At last Talbot found himself on an outer path with only one layer of hedge separating him from Lady Cheney, whom he could see through the foliage standing erect with her umbrella at the ready.

'It's no good,' he called to the major. 'I'm coming out and we'll start again.' As he spoke he rounded two sharp corners and reached the middle.

It was an oblong clearing with a small tree and a bench at either end. On one of the benches, sheltered from the major's view, sat Timothy with a mocking smile on his face.

'What a shocking time it took you!' he said. 'I suppose you don't have mazes in America.' Then he stood up and greeted the major blandly: 'Did you want me, major? I'm just coming out.'

Picking up the picture at his feet, he dodged past Talbot and began to run back through the maze. Talbot turned in pursuit, drew close and kept grimly on his heels, chasing him down the labyrinthine ways like the hound of heaven. Before long they met an infuriated Lord Cheney. He tagged on behind, and after five tortuous minutes of hard going they were all back in the middle.

Timothy sat down again, panting and laughing. The other two stood blocking the path while they regained their breath. The major bustled down from his eyrie and rattled the gate which provided a short cut from the centre to the exit. The hedge grew above it and there was no space for climbing over.

'Here,' he ordered. 'Slide the picture through and then bring him out between you at your own pace.'

Timothy made no show of resistance, and after five minutes the whole party was clustered round the picture, which was loosely wrapped in a sheet of brown paper. Timothy's arms were tightly held, but his expression of cheerful insouciance had not altered. 'This Theseus and Ariadne stuff takes it out of you, doesn't it, Cheney?' he remarked to Gavin, who was panting like a thirsty hart.

A deep hush settled on the party as the major reverently slipped off the single strand of string and with a flourish held the picture up to the moonlight. Then a gasp of surprise broke out. They were looking at a photograph of the Hon. Alfred Lyttelton lounging against the opening of a dedans.

The major turned it over and then back again. 'It's the wrong picture,' he snapped accusingly at Timothy.

'I don't know what you're talking about,' Timothy snapped back, his good humour banished. 'I borrowed it from the court to show to a friend and you all start chasing me as though I were a criminal. An action for defamation might lie.'

'So might you!' retorted Lady Cheney. 'Don't you try your legal jiggery-pokery on me, young man.'

'He's changed it somewhere,' suggested the major, bewildered.

'No, he hasn't,' said Gerry. 'I think I can guess what's going on. He's acting as a decoy while that Frenchwoman makes off with the Holbein.'

21

Gerry Montague's suggestion had a nasty ring of truth about it.

'You must be wrong,' Gavin objected, but without much conviction. 'It was Mlle Deschamps who wrote to Timothy's uncle and threatened a scandal. If it weren't for her . . . '

'Of course it's true,' interrupted Mr Pratt roughly. 'He went to the highest bidder. Look at his face.'

Timothy had been released and was standing a few paces apart staring attentively in the direction of the palace, where the hammer-beam roof of the Great Hall rose high above the clustered silhouettes of the lesser buildings. In a fit of fury the major marched up to him and shook a hairy fist in his face.

'You young rogue!' he fumed, 'you traitor! Here; take this.'

Timothy recoiled from the expected punch on the nose, but found that instead the major was brandishing a cheque at him in the other hand. It was for a thousand pounds and signed Talbot B. Talbot. He took it with a smile of triumph, only to have it instantly snatched back by the major, who tore it into small pieces and scattered them on the ground. A fierce snorting and clearing of the throat gave notice of a Grand Military Dressing-down.

Before the major could start, however, Gerry put his finger to his lips and pointed down the path. Someone was running towards them through the Wilderness, and it sounded like a woman.

They withdrew expectantly into the shadows, dragging Timothy with them. The runner rounded the bend into their midst. 'Stop! It's Angel!' exclaimed Mr Pratt, just as the younger men were on the point of pouncing.

'Oh, there you all are!' she gasped. 'Quick! I was looking for Dad and came face to face with the Frenchwoman. She ran away and dodged up a staircase into the palace. Unless she got out by another way she's still up there.'

The young contingent — Gavin and Talbot, with Gerry just qualifying — moved off for another chase. Angel led the way between high walls back into Tennis Court Lane, then across it and through some passageways, past the old Tudor kitchens and out into Wolsey's Base Court, low-flanked and open to the stars.

'This way,' she whispered, beckoning them through Ann Boleyn's gateway and straight across the next courtyard, where the stone of the Wren colonnade glistened white. The place was deserted at this hour — even by the Ministry of Works custodians — and, lightly as they ran, the patter of their steps echoed round the enclosing walls.

'Sh,' warned Angel, and they tiptoed through the next archway and tore breathlessly up a staircase. The balustrade was elaborately ornamented, and brightly coloured frescoes of allegorical scenes covered the entire area of walls and ceiling.

'Jeez!' muttered Talbot unappreciatively. 'She can't have got anywhere from here,' said Gavin. 'It leads to the state apartments. They're locked up at nights.'

'But she did!' Angel insisted. 'I saw her go up and she didn't come down. I waited.'

At the top a double door stood open. Its lock projected and some wood was splintered — it had been kicked open. Inside, a panelled gallery stretched away into the distance, the moonlight slanting through the windows onto a row of ladies of easy promise in low-cut Restoration dress. Plump and smug, their well-bred faces hinted at favours bestowed. Some of them rather resembled Mlle Deschamps, Gavin was thinking, when with a start he looked up and saw her in the flesh standing motionless in the shadows at the far end of the gallery. As their eyes met, she turned and was gone.

'She's here,' he called, and broke into a run.

The next room was the Cartoon Gallery, hung with mock-Raphael tapestries, and he was just in time to see her disappear from the far end. With the others at his heels he followed her through a series of small chambers and closets — room after intercommunicating room; then round the corner of the building into another series — the full stretch of the corridor running the length of the Queen's apartments. Each room was hung with pictures or tapestries and dotted with period chairs and other furniture, but not with anything that one could hide behind. She had vanished from sight.

They hurried on round another corner, and before them, straight as an arrow, ran the corridor through the King's apartments. This section of the palace had been built for William and Mary — equal monarchs with separate and equal accommodation. Here in the King's quarters it was darker. On one side of them were windows overlooking the Privy Garden and the river; on the other a series of rooms similar to the Queen's: dressing room, state bedrooms, drawing room and a chain of audience and presence chambers. Eventually they came to a full stop in the Guard Room, whose other two doors were locked.

'This is uncanny,' whispered Gavin.

'Where can she be?'

'The whole place gives me the creeps,' said Angel, looking up at the medieval weapons on the walls and drawing towards him with a shudder. 'Fancy even having effigies on the beds!'

'Do they?' asked Gerry in surprise. 'I've never noticed it before.' They looked at each other uncertainly.

'It's her then,' hissed Talbot.

They doubled back the way they had come. In the King's Bedchamber the effigy had vanished from the velvet coverlet under the vast four-posted canopy, leaving the impress of a body behind it.

'She lay doggo there and slipped back as soon as we went through,' said Talbot with a curse.

He took the lead on the return run and at the bottom of the Queen's staircase instinctively turned towards the main entrance. The idea of her escaping was unbearable, and he increased speed, stimulated by the open air of the courtyards. As he passed through the Great Gateway and across the moat he was rewarded with a sight of her.

She was already the other side of the Outer Green, passing out of the Trophy Gates into the outside world. Her arms enfolded a picture, which was hugged to her chest and made her ample body waggle suggestively as she ran. She was not built for this sort of thing and stumbled with exhaustion.

Talbot sped on confidently, when to his dismay he saw a car crawling along the road. At the wheel was Timothy coming to pick her up!

'Stop her!' he shouted despairingly, and immediately, as if in answer, the major shot out from behind a parked car on the other side of the road. He had evidently been keeping an eye on Timothy and hidden himself there to spy. Now he dashed over to the driver's window and engaged in a desperate tussle. It appeared to end when the major was propelled backwards flat onto the road. But instead of ushering his accomplice aboard and driving off Timothy flung open the door and fell savagely on the major. They were rolling interlocked in the gutter when the American arrived to the rescue.

He hauled Timothy off, gathered his coat-front in one hand and delivered a succession of staccato jabs to the face with the other. Then, letting go of the coat and pushing him backwards at the same time, he gave himself space to swing a full-powered upper cut to the point of the jaw. The crack reverberated through the night, and Timothy went down like a felled ox. Talbot sucked his knuckles and turned to help the major, who was sitting on the grating of a drain triumphantly holding up Timothy's ignition key.

Their triumph was brief. Blowing his whistle shrilly for reinforcements, an outraged policeman was moving swiftly across the road to take them in charge.

'Brawling in the public highway,' he intoned. 'You'll have to come to the station. All of you,' he added sternly to Talbot, who was showing signs of making off.

'It's quite all right, officer,' said the major, rising to his feet and brushing himself down.

'Would you say that again, sir?' demanded the policeman, and when the major obliged he sniffed and gave a nod of suspicion confirmed. 'As I thought. Drink! I can smell it from here.'

Taking advantage of his intervention, Mlle Deschamps had disappeared down an unlit path sloping towards the river, and under cover of the major's indignation Talbot gestured to Gerry, Gavin and Angel, who had now caught up, to sidestep the law and follow her.

They found her on the deserted towpath standing defiantly over the picture, her chest heaving. 'Perhaps you would hand over that painting,' said Gavin. 'It belongs to me, I believe.'

By way of reply she snatched it up, clutching it to her and burying its face in her bosom. 'Don't come near me,' she threatened. 'If you try to take it I throw it into the river.' She backed towards the edge of the water.

'Be sensible,' Angle begged. 'The police are here. Mr Forsyth — '

'Mr Forsyth!' The Frenchwoman took up the name scornfully. 'I agreed to let him have a half share and he believed me. He is a foolish young man, don't you think?'

'I wouldn't know,' said Gavin. 'But you have my word for it that if you give me the picture now we'll forget the whole matter.'

'The word of Milord Cheney!' she sneered. 'With no security. And what is the whole matter?'

The question hung for a second before Angel grasped the implication. Her mind flashed back to that lurking figure in the shrubbery exactly a week ago. 'So it was you who killed Mr Nicholls.'

'Yes, I killed him! I kept watch that night after your father stole the manuscript before I could get it. I came to High Cheney to search for this mysterious Holbein and the ruby missing from the Boniface chalice, and I believed the manuscript contained a clue. I followed Nicholls to the court. He was climbing down the ladder with something in his hand, and I threatened him with my revolver. He could not know it had no bullets but he just grinned at me like a chimpanzee. He was still half-drunk and

387

when I demanded what he was holding he insulted me. I lost my temper. If I could, I would have shot him. Instead I swung him off the ladder and broke his neck for him — and all he had in his hand were two of those stupid tennis balls.'

The Frenchwoman spoke softly, with slow venom, careful that only Angel should hear. She was playing for time: for a respite to recover her breath and think out her next move.

But now Mr Pratt came hurrying down the slope with Lady Cheney. 'Now then, Emilienne my girl, give me the picture and give yourself up,' he urged. 'No nonsense! The game's over.'

For an answer she shrank back. 'Keep away,' she warned, 'if you ever want to see the picture again.'

Ignoring the threat, Mr Pratt dived forward. She lunged at him with the picture, cutting open his forehead with the corner of the frame; then retreated upstream back towards the bridge. Undeterred, Mr Pratt drew on a hidden reserve of agility and outflanked her by nipping across the towpath and cutting her off from the river. Gavin and Angel closed in from the other side with Gerry.

Seeing herself becoming trapped, she advanced threateningly on Angel, who instinctively drew back. In an instant she had rushed past up to the pavement leading to the bridge. Lady Cheney caught her a glancing body-blow with her umbrella, but otherwise she escaped unscathed.

Gavin and Gerry were after her at once. She turned across the bridge, which was wide and empty except for passing traffic. They were bound to catch her before she reached the other bank, and sensing this she suddenly clambered onto the stone parapet half way across. With her face jaundiced in the glare of the sodium lights, poised between sky and water, Middlesex and Surrey, she held the picture out over the middle of the stream.

'Come a yard nearer, and I drop it,' she threatened.

The two men halted in their tracks. 'A fat lot of good that will do you,' reasoned

Mr Pratt, lumbering up behind them. 'Come down or you'll fall in yourself.'

'Stay where you are,' she warned them, lowering the picture but remaining on the parapet ready to execute her threat. 'I have the idea that someone may wish to offer me a share in the picture as an inducement not to let it fall.'

'Aren't you an art-lover,' Angel appealed to her. 'Surely you wouldn't damage a historic painting like this?'

The Frenchwoman favoured her with a peculiar, inscrutable look. 'I am waiting for Milord Cheney to speak,' she said. 'But I cannot wait long.' As if to emphasise the point she held the picture out into space again, this time even more perilously, with only one hand.

'Oh, I say,' protested Gavin, aghast. 'What on earth can a fellow say?'

'He can say,' his mother prompted him, 'that gentlemen do not bargain with murderers and thieves.'

'So!' enunciated Mlle Deschamps with an awful monosyllabic explosion. 'Blame yourself, you stuck-up son-of-a-bitch,' she shrieked at Gavin. Bringing the picture down with a crash against the Lutyens balustrade, she started battering it against the stonework and tearing the frame and canvas to pieces. The others swooped on her in horror to stop the devastation, but like Medea disposing of her children she was already scattering the fragments. One by one they fell through the moonlight into the depths of the river.

Lady Cheney spitting 'Call my boy the son of a bitch, would you?' was in the first wave of attackers. She hooked her umbrella handle round the Frenchwoman's ankle and tugged at it like a dervish. Either this or the general hustling or her own leaning caused Mlle Deschamps to overbalance. With an ear-splitting scream of terror she toppled off the bridge and fell plummeting down to join the submerged fragments in the Thames.

Gavin at once stripped off his coat and mounted the parapet in preparation for a rescue jump. But nothing disturbed the surface of the water as it hurried towards the sea. The Roman invaders had crossed not far from here. Saxon fishing villages had dotted the banks round the great metropolis of Kingston when Middlesex was still an impenetrable forest. The river had been fouled by man since Spenser's day, but still ran the same course. What was one human body to ruffle its composure?

They ran round to the bank, found a life-belt and threw it in at random. The current was drawing the water at speed round the bend where Tijou's iron screen marks the end of the Privy Garden. They moved raggedly along the towpath towards it, passing under the windows of the Royal Banqueting House. She might be carried downstream for a mile or more under water.

They had almost given up hope when Gerry saw her. Osiers stood by the riverside, the water swirling round their roots and lower branches, and caught by the foot in one of these a bedraggled body was bobbing face downwards. They pulled her out, laid her on dry land and tried artificial respiration. Not a flicker of life rewarded their efforts, and they stood in a solemn, helpless circle trying to muster some charitable thoughts. Mr Pratt and Lady Cheney did not try too hard, but Angel, after retailing the Frenchwoman's confession, was weeping softly. A few unhypocritical words were called for, but no one seemed able to rise to them.

At last it was Gerry who obliged, recalling a sentence from a seventeenth-century sermon which he had come across during the researches for his book. Turning in the direction of the tennis court, he recited it.

'Thus like a tennis ball is poor man racketed from one temptation to another, till at last he hazard eternal ruin.'

'Amen,' responded Lady Cheney.

22

In the age-old setting of river and palace a single death seemed trivial. As the moonbeams ran over the forest of chimneys and the gargoyles cast their shadows on the mellowed brick, one could imagine that, inside, a Venetian embassy was still awaiting Lord Chancellor Wolsey's pleasure; or that the Virgin Queen was still sitting in her pearl-encrusted Paradise Room, both of them the wonder of Europe.

The ambulance had come and gone; so had the police. Names and addresses were taken, and Gerry had left for the police station to find out whether the major and Talbot were in need of bailing out. The tragedy had drawn them all together, and Lady Cheney had even taken Mr Pratt to her sister's apartments to bathe his forehead. Emilienne Deschamps was already little more than an unpleasant memory and a bundle of flesh and bone on a mortuary slab. No one had wept for her but Angel.

'What a shame about your picture, Gavin,' she commiserated, drying her eyes. They were walking along the deserted towpath eyeing the river for debris.

'Can't be helped, can it,' he replied. 'The pundits say we have to deserve success, and I didn't believe in the bally thing's existing even. It's your father I'm sorry for.' He ventured an arm round her shoulder. She was wearing a grey cape-stole over her cocktail dress, and he burrowed his fingers into the silky fur.

'It didn't belong to him, as things turned out,' she said.

'But he needed it, you know — if it was of any real value. The rumours I told you about at the Fanfare are hotting up. It's still very hush-hush, but it seems he's way down a big financial hole and falling fast.'

'Are you sure?' she asked in alarm. 'Poor Dad! But what about you? Couldn't you have done with it?'

'As a matter of fact I could,' he

admitted. 'But don't ask me why.' He slid his hand down onto her arm. 'You're cold. We should go in.'

She looked at him for a moment, her chameleon eyes stole-grey. 'Come on then,' she said and changed into a brisk stride.

'Whoa!' he called, swinging round. 'Stop a moment! Isn't this a bit of my property?' He knelt on the bank and fished a sodden piece of flotsam out of the water. The fragment of canvas portrayed half a neck and the edge of a lace collar.

Wryly they took it with them — the last of the Cheney inheritance. Angel was silent and Gavin wondered whether this was a passive objection to his holding her arm. As they were crossing the moat she broke away and stood gazing over the edge onto the trim grass surface below.

'Gavin!' she cried, turning abruptly. 'I've got an idea!'

'Go on,' he urged. 'If it concerns me.'

'Of course it does, you idiot.'

'Then let me say it first,' he begged.

'Really!' she exclaimed. 'Do stop being romantically suggestive and be serious. Did your great-grandfather wear lace collars?'

He laughed in surprise. 'I haven't a clue. It wouldn't be likely, would it? But if you're referring to the Last of the Cheney Holbein I'm reserving the right to assume that this is a piece of Henry VIII, not Great-grandfather. Its more interesting that way. Don't you agree?' He held the fragment up to the moonlight in mock reverence.

Angel wrinkled her nose, and Gavin noted that she looked particularly attractive in a state of slight disarray. After all that running around, the debs he knew would have made straight for the ladies' to repair the damage to their make-up before daring to expose themselves to male scrutiny. That Angel should be unselfconscious about a shiny nose seemed the guarantee of a genuine article.

'I'm sure Victorian men didn't wear lace collars,' she said. 'And from my studies at the Slade — such as they were — I reckon Holbein painted on wood, not canvas.'

'You mean the picture underneath wasn't the Holbein after all?'

'I don't mean that at all. Didn't you notice the funny look that woman gave me when I said she was too much of an art-lover to destroy a Holbein? And don't you think she would have been the one to put Timothy up to that decoy lark?'

'Sorry, old girl,' said Gavin. 'I don't follow.'

'Well, follow now,' she retorted, leading him into the palace and up the Queen's staircase again.

Again they entered the gallery hung with Lely's buxom beauties — Lady Denham, Mrs Middleton, the Countess of Northumberland and all. Gavin viewed them unimpressed. Immediately to the right of the door they had come in by was another leading to part of Wolsey's original palace. This was open, and with a sudden exclamation Angel, who had been prowling round as if trying to pick up a scent, slammed it to with a flourish. As she did so the moonlight fell full on a crookedly hung picture which had been hidden in darkness behind it.

It was the portrait of a man, and a wave of recognition swept over Gavin. The head was as bald as a bandicoot above and heavily bearded below, but the face between was the image of his own. His great-grandfather stood before him, artificially posed with a tennis racket in one hand and two balls in the other. Apparently about to knock the cover off a third, invisible ball with a fierce forehand stroke, he was nevertheless standing bolt upright with his back to the net, gazing out of the canvas with an expression of calm dignity. The tag underneath read simply: 'The Eighth Earl of Cheney, Tennis-Player.'

'Bless my soul!' Gavin exclaimed in amazement. 'What's the ugly old devil doing here?'

'Don't you see?' Angel was impatient with him. 'When we were chasing her out of here she knew she would never get away, so she grabbed a picture off the hook beside the last door and shoved the eighth earl in its place. It was probably a portrait of Sir Peter, who painted all these unblushing brides. She planned to make everyone believe that the Holbein was lost and gone for ever, sneak back here later and smuggle it off to France. There might not have been too much fuss about the missing picture — it can't have been much good or it wouldn't have been hung behind the door. Perhaps no one would have connected it with the Holbein, and anyway there would have been no proof that the Holbein ever existed.'

'The trouble with you, Angel,' said Gavin admiringly, 'is that you are clever as well as being pretty and an heiress. You're extremely lucky to have found a man foolhardy enough to take you on.' Acting on impulse was a Cheney characteristic, and Gavin's version of the family's Latin motto was: Why muck about? When he started speaking he hardly knew he loved the girl; by the time he'd finished he was positive he did.

They exchanged smiles. 'That must be the meanest proposal in the whole history of man's ill-treatment of woman,' she observed. 'But, for the benefit of these ladies, you may kiss me once while your application's being considered.'

The kiss was followed by an impromptu gallop down the length of the gallery and back, during which Gavin decided he had definitely done the right thing. Then they took the picture downstairs and crossed Fountain Court to his aunt's. There the atmosphere in the drawing room was heavy with despondency. All the unsuccessful hunters had assembled for a post mortem.

'Ah, there you are, Angel,' said Mr Pratt, jumping up as soon as she appeared. 'We must be going.' He had barely thirty-six hours left before the City resumed business and the Pratt cat would be out of the bag.

'In a moment, Daddy.' She pointed to the picture Gavin was carrying, and Mr Pratt sat down again open-eyed.

The others gathered round and began loosening nails at the back to remove the frame. 'Would the ladies not prefer to stay near the fire and keep warm?' suggested the major, growing anxious about the suitability of the subject for feminine eyes.

While Gavin and Gerry carefully prised the stretcher of the canvas off a wooden panel, Angel obediently retired to the sofa to sit between Lady Cheney and her sister and be tantalised a moment later by a gasp of wonder from the men.

'Is this going to be reserved exclusively for male goggling,' enquired Lady Cheney, 'like the ridiculous room in that villa at Pompeii the guide wouldn't let me into?'

'No, Mother,' Gavin assured her. 'There's been some rather special bowdlerising. You may look.' With a gesture of triumph he propped the painted panel on the back of an armchair where the ladies could view it.

Undimmed by the varnish and years of concealment from the light, the colours were radiant. The king was dressed in the brightest red from head to foot — cap, doublet, hose and pointed shoes. A white ostrich feather curled regally from his cap, and his shoes were adorned with delicate white pompons. His beard was a light gingery brown, and he stood with his feet planted apart, arrogant wilfulness smouldering in his eyes.

Beside him stood a lady looking coyly down. She wore a green brocaded skirt, but was bare from the waist upwards, exhibiting an expanse of white flesh covered only by an emerald necklace. The royal hand was dallying woodenly with her pale circular breasts.

In his other hand the King held a tennis racket and two balls. Underneath, balancing the lady, was a pyramid of tennis balls arranged like cannonballs. Behind stretched a net cord, and above gaped the opening of a lune, round the curve of which ran the legend, Defensor Fedei, in minute gold gothic letters. In the middle of the royal person a curious act of vandalism had been perpetrated just below the waist. Here a hole had been cut, presumably by puritan hands, and a large reddish stone was embedded in the wood.

'The colours! Oh, the colours,' said Angel, overcome by their brilliance; while Lady Cheney leaned forward and jabbed a bony finger at the stone. 'The ruby!' she exclaimed. 'The ruby from the Boniface chalice!'

Mr Pratt took out his handkerchief, flicked off the dust and gently polished the surface of the stone. It developed a sultry gleam. 'That's a ruby, all right,' he declared.

'But it's enormous!' gasped Angel.

'Congratulations, Gavin!' said Talbot laconically.

Gavin thanked him. 'I take it you are referring to this,' he added, 'and without your help goodness knows what would have happened. But there's something else you may care to congratulate me on. Angel has agreed to marry me — I think.'

'What!' Mr Pratt, looking to Lady Cheney for support, responded with an emphatic 'Oh no she don't!'

Lady Cheney favoured him with one of her most powerful glares. 'Quite the best thing that has happened to the Cheneys since I married his father,' she pronounced. 'A very sensible, spirited gel!' She turned and pecked Angel on the cheek, while Mr Pratt looked on flabbergasted and the others offered Gavin their congratulations.

'I don't know what your Ma will say,' he muttered.

'Mr Pratt,' Gavin addressed him, holding up the picture. 'Would you like this, sir?'

'On what terms?' enquired Mr Pratt suspiciously.

'Your consent to my marrying Angel now instead of when she is twenty-one. And High Cheney.'

'Gavin!' exclaimed Lady Cheney, overcome in turn.

'I'm not pretending I like the place, Mother,' he said. 'But I suppose it ought to stay in the family. If Mr Pratt would lend us the picture we can use it to lure the public in at half-a-crown a nob and build ourselves a cosy flat in the tennis court.'

'Very well,' agreed Mr Pratt quickly, 'if — '

Angel interrupted him even more hastily. 'Don't be an ass, Gavin. The picture and that ruby are worth far more than High Cheney. You know they are, Daddy. You're to let him have High Cheney back for what you paid for it. That's fair.'

'Whose side are you on?' Mr Pratt demanded. 'You've made up your mind to marry him, it seems.'

Angel nodded.

Silence fell while her father wrestled with what was left of his conscience. 'All right,' he said at last, 'in that case he can have the place back anyway; we can fix the terms later. What I need at once is an interest-free, unsecured loan of half a million for six months. It could be raised on that.' He pointed at the picture.

'Here you are then.' Gavin handed it to him.

'And this is for you in exchange.' Mr Pratt, suddenly scenting an end to his troubles, burst out into playfulness and pushed Angel across the room to him. 'Gavin, my lad, you've saved the day for Pratt Holdings, and about forty of my companies could do with an earl on the board. I'll see you get good value for this.'

'The forty whose shareholders are most in need of hood-winking,' Angel put in. 'You be careful, darling.'

'Well, if he won't you'll have to instead,' Mr Pratt warned her. 'A countess might do the trick just as well.'

The major took advantage of the general laughter to change the subject and enquire whether Gavin's sacrilegious remark about using the tennis court as a flat was seriously intended.

'You should keep Ted Nicholls on,' urged Gerry. 'Let him teach you both the game and form a local club to keep him busy. The last hundred years should serve as a warning to all present and future Cheneys not to neglect tennis.'

'But it's such an odd game,' protested Lady Cheney. 'Hazard worse than the door and that sort of nonsense. I asked last weekend what a hazard chase is and I still have not the least idea.'

'That's because one has been going on ever since,' said the major jovially. 'It's difficult for the layman to grasp, but now the excitement's over let me explain . . . '

But Lady Cheney had already turned to her son to urge that he must now concentrate on finding the rest of the chalice. Talbot had borrowed the telephone to arrange a flight home. Angel was talking to Lady Cheney's sister about weddings. Gerry was engaged in an examination of the details of Henry VIII's tennis racket.

'Give me a ring tomorrow afternoon, major,' said Mr Pratt on his way to the door. 'No hard feelings. We'll fix up that deal, eh?' He took the picture from Gerry and with a call of 'Come on, Angie', and 'Good night, all' vanished into the night.

Angel caught him up in the cloisters. 'Wotcher, countess!' he greeted her, giving her as affectionate a squeeze as half a million pounds' worth of Holbein would permit.

The sound of voices raised in alarm and the belated blowing of custodians' whistles reached them from the state apartments. They quickened their pace and passed unobtrusively through the main gates. Someone else could do all the explaining.

Tennis and the Chase

Tennis is the game from which lawn tennis was devised. Often called real tennis, royal tennis or (in America) court tennis, it is played in an indoor court. There is a net across the centre of the court, and as in lawn tennis the ball is hit backwards and forwards across it with a racket, either full toss or first bounce. The method of scoring is the one used in lawn tennis.

The walls of the court, unlike those of a squash or rackets court, are not plain, flat surfaces. Three of them are broken by sloping penthouses just above head-high (these roofs as well as the walls above and below are in play), and all four contain hazards. The hazards are: 1 the galleries (openings with netting at the back to stop the balls and protect spectators): these are below the penthouse roofs and consist of the side galleries along one side and the dedans at one end; 2 the grille *(a square opening with a wooden back); and 3 the tambour (a projection of the wall which causes the ball to fly off at an angle).*

Service is always from the same end of the court and does not alternate with each game, a change of service being brought about only by the laying of a chase. This is done by the striker returning the ball over the net in such a way that his opponent misses it: a chase is then laid at the point where the ball hits the floor on its second bounce.

The floor of the court at the service end is marked in yards from the back wall, and if the second bounce falls on the four-yard line 'chase four' is called by the marker. The point is not won by the striker, but held in abeyance until either of the players reaches forty or until two chases have been made. They then change ends, and the player who was serving before and is now receiving service has to return the ball so that the second bounce falls less than four yards from the back wall. If he succeeds (or if his opponent hits the ball but fails

410

to return it over the net) he wins the chase and with it the point. If the second bounce falls further than four yards from the back wall (or if he fails to return the ball at all) he loses it.

At more than six yards from the back wall the chases are named after the side galleries — last gallery, second gallery, the door and first gallery. These being a long way from the back wall are bad chases. Even worse are chases which fall on the other side of the net. To distinguish it from the service end this is known as the hazard side, and when the second bounce of a shot from the player on the service side falls in the half of the hazard side nearer to the net a hazard chase is laid. The other, or back, half of the hazard side is 'the winning area', and here — as in the dedans, the grille and the winning gallery — a point is won outright.

Although points are won and lost as in lawn tennis when players hit the ball into the net or out of play, the distinctive features of tennis are the hazards and the chases, both of which have been

411

lost in the development of lawn tennis. To lay a good chase — the best is 'better than half a yard' — requires great control of length, speed and cut, and the combination of hazards and chases offers an enormous variety of possible situations and possible strokes for each situation. Moreover, the ball, which is like a lawn-tennis ball but solid, may be chopped, cut, twisted or topped by the (asymmetrical) racket so that it behaves in weird and widely differing ways after contact with a wall. The best tennis players literally stroke the ball rather than hit it.

Tennis is so old that the origins of the game — and the word — were already lost in antiquity when an Italian wrote a treatise on it in 1555. Many references to it occur in the history and literature of western Europe. Perhaps the most famous is the occasion when the Dauphin of France made a present of some tennis balls to Henry V of England. Both men were players and the best balls were made in France, so this might have been reckoned a friendly gesture. But the *young King was sensitive about being thought a play-boy and chose to take offence.*

The incident has been described by Shakespeare in a well-known scene at the beginning of Henry V, *when the King thanks the French ambassador for the gift in these ungracious words*:

'We are glad the Dauphin is so
    pleasant with us;
His present and your pains we thank
    you for.
When we have matched our racquets
    to these balls,
We will in France, by God's grace,
    play a set
Shall strike his father's crown into
    the hazard.
Tell him he hath made a match with
    such a wrangler
That all the courts of France will be
    disturbed
With chases.'

Other titles in the Linford Mystery Library

A LANCE FOR THE DEVIL
Robert Charles

The funeral service of Pope Paul VI was to be held in the great plaza before St. Peter's Cathedral in Rome, and was to be the scene of the most monstrous mass assassination of political leaders the world had ever known. Only Counter-Terror could prevent it.

IN THAT RICH EARTH
Alan Sewart

How long does it take for a human body to decay until only the bones remain? When Detective Sergeant Harry Chamberlane received news of a body, he raised exactly that question. But whose was the body? Who was to blame for the death and in what circumstances?

MURDER AS USUAL
Hugh Pentecost

A psychotic girl shot and killed Mac Crenshaw, who had come to the New England town with the advance party for Senator Farraday. Private detective David Cotter agreed that the girl was probably just a pawn in a complex game — but who had sent her on the assignment?

THE MARGIN
Ian Stuart

It is rumoured that Walkers Brewery has been selling arms to the South African army, and Graham Lorimer is asked to investigate. He meets the beautiful Shelley van Rynveld, who is dedicated to ending apartheid. When a Walkers employee is killed in a hit-and-run accident, his wife tells Graham that he's been seeing Shelly van Rynveld . . .

TOO LATE FOR THE FUNERAL
Roger Ormerod

Carol Turner, seventeen, and a mystery, is very close to a murder, and she has in her possession a weapon that could prove a number of things. But it is Elsa Mallin who suffers most before the truth of Carol Turner releases her.

NIGHT OF THE FAIR
Jay Baker

The gun was the last of the things for which Harry Judd had fought and now it was in the hands of his worst enemy, aimed at the boy he had tried to help. This was the night in which the past had to be faced again and finally understood.

PAY-OFF IN SWITZERLAND
Bill Knox
'Hot' British currency was being smuggled to Switzerland to be laundered, hidden in a safari-style convoy heading across Europe. Jonathan Gaunt, external auditor for the Queen's and Lord Treasurer's Remembrancer, went along with the safari, posing as a tourist, to get any lead he could. But sudden death trailed the convoy every kilometer to Lake Geneva.

SALVAGE JOB
Bill Knox
A storm has left the oil tanker S. S. *Craig Michael* stranded and almost blocking the only channel to the bay at Cabo Esco. Sent to investigate, marine insurance inspector Laird discovers that the Portuguese bay is hiding a powder keg of international proportions.

BOMB SCARE — FLIGHT 147
Peter Chambers

Smog delayed Flight 147, and so prevented a bomb exploding in mid-air. Walter Keane found that during the crisis he had been robbed of his jewel bag, and Mark Preston was hired to locate it without involving the police. When a murder was committed, Preston knew the stake had grown.

STAMBOUL INTRIGUE
Robert Charles

Greece and Turkey were on the brink of war, and the conflict could spell the beginning of the end for the Western defence pact of N.A.T.O. When the rumour of a plot to speed this possibility reached Counter-espionage in Whitehall, Simon Larren and Adrian Cleyton were despatched to Turkey . . .

CRACK IN THE SIDEWALK
Basil Copper

After brilliant scientist Professor Hopcroft is knocked down and killed by a car, L.A. private investigator Mike Faraday discovers that his death was murder and that differing groups are engaged in a power struggle for The Zetland Method. As Mike tries to discover what The Zetland Method is, corpses and hair-breadth escapes come thick and fast . . .

DEATH OF A MARINE
Charles Leader

When Mike M'Call found the mutilated corpse of a marine in an alleyway in Singapore, a thousand-strong marine battalion was hell-bent on revenge for their murdered comrade — and the next target for the tong gang of paid killers appeared to be M'Call himself . . .

ANYONE CAN MURDER
Freda Bream
Hubert Carson, the editorial Manager of the Herald Newspaper in Auckland, is found dead in his office. Carson's fellow employees knew that the unpopular chief reporter, Clive Yarwood, wanted Carson's job — but did he want it badly enough to kill for it?

CART BEFORE THE HEARSE
Roger Ormerod
Sometimes a case comes up backwards. When Ernest Connelly said 'I have killed . . . ', he did not name the victim. So Dave Mallin and George Coe find themselves attempting to discover a body to fit the crime.

SALESMAN OF DEATH
Charles Leader
For Mike M'Call, selling guns in Detroit proves a dangerous business — from the moment of his arrival in the middle of a racial riot, to the final clash of arms between two rival groups of militant extremists.

THE FOURTH SHADOW
Robert Charles

Simon Larren merely had to ensure that the visiting President of Maraquilla remained alive during a goodwill tour of the British Crown Colony of San Quito. But there were complications. Finally, there was a Communist-inspired bid for illegal independence from British rule, backed by the evil of voodoo.

SCAVENGERS AT WAR
Charles Leader

Colonel Piet Van Velsen needed an experienced officer for his mercenary commando, and Mike M'Call became a reluctant soldier. The Latin American Republic was torn apart by revolutionary guerrilla groups — but why were the ruthless Congo veterans unleashed on a province where no guerrilla threat existed?

MENACES, MENACES
Michael Underwood

Herbert Sipson, professional black-mailer, was charged with demanding money from a bingo company. Then, a demand from the Swallow Sugar Corporation also bore all the hallmarks of a Sipson scheme. But it arrived on the opening day of Herbert's Old Bailey trial — so how could he have been responsible?

MURDER WITH MALICE
Nicholas Blake

At the Wonderland holiday camp, someone calling himself The Mad Hatter is carrying out strange practical jokes that are turning increasingly malicious. Private Investigator Nigel Strangeways follows the Mad Hatter's trail and finally manages to make sense of the mayhem.